The Cornish

Amand

Also by Amanda James

Another Mother

The Calico Cat

Rip Current

For Carrie, who has supported my books and writing from day one. Thanks, it is very much appreciated!

Chapter One

It's raining on the ocean. A mass of bruised clouds spread across the horizon and a fresh salt wind whips dark curls across my eyes, as if it's trying to dry my tears. It can't though. I bow my head, wrest my hair free and let them come. My shoulders shake, my body trembles and there's an angry heat in the pit of my chest. I swallow hard but still there are more tears. Waiting. Building. Pushing for release. The waves swirl around my wellingtons and the tears fall too fast, too heavy, too full of despair. Somewhere in my mind, a voice says it might be nice to just let the waves come, like my tears. Let them come, rise up, take me away, end this pitiful existence. This empty life of mine that used to be so full.

A dog barks, and freezing cold water trickling down inside my boots makes my head snap up and away from the mesmerising raindrops pelting the water. Behind me, cannoning along the wide expanse of Mawgan Porth beach, a black Labrador ignores the commands of its mistress. 'Hattie! Hattie! Here now!' Hattie runs on, then stops, turns her head on one side, pink tongue lolling from the corner of her mouth, and cocks her ears. The woman, round and slow moving, puffs her cheeks and tries a whistle. The wind snatches it, and the woman shakes her head, shouting to the dog once more.

I look at the waves now at my knees and something makes me pull my feet out of the sucking sand and towards the shore. A shaft of sunlight spears the dunes. There's just me, the dog and the woman on a windswept rain-soaked beach in March. The scene speaks to me – it feels like it's the start of a story, not the end. What had I been thinking? I hadn't been, had I? Just wallowing in self-pity. Again.

Almost free of the water, except for that in my wellies, a black shape hurls itself at my legs and then wet paws on my chest complete a soaking. 'Hattie! Hat-eee! Bad Hattie, bad dog. Come here!'

Hattie doesn't want to go there; she seems far more intent on licking my face. Ordinarily, I wouldn't have appreciated wet dogs barrelling into me, totally out of control, even though many dog owners seem to think it's a privilege bestowed upon me; but today, the laughing face of the dog, the thumping tail in the waves and the mischievous gleam in Hattie's eyes draws a bubble of laughter from my throat. It encourages the dog and she licks and paws some more.

'Okay, okay. That's enough, Hattie,' I say, pushing the dog away and squelching a few steps up the beach. The dog stops her antics and trots alongside as if she belongs. It's nice to imagine for a few seconds that the dog is mine. Belonging is a comfort, natural, a safety blanket that I've always been lucky enough to have wrapped around me. As a child I belonged to my parents, then I grew up, fell in love, had my own family – they belonged to me, and I to them. Now, though, I've lost the blanket and the chill stabs at my skin like ice needles... both children are grown and gone and my husband... my husband...

'So sorry, dear. Hattie is being so naughty today. She's not usually this unruly...'

I look down at the small round woman standing in front of me. The roses in her cheeks have probably been put there by a mixture of embarrassment and exertion, but I imagine it's mostly embarrassment, so to put her mind at rest, I say, 'It's honestly not a problem. Hattie seems like a very friendly dog. You're lucky to have her.'

The roses pale a little. 'Thanks, I am. She's been such a comfort to me. We've been inseparable since my Peter died five years ago. God knows what I would have become without her.'

The woman looks a little too closely at my eyes, which feel like they are ready for yet more tear shedding, and before Hattie's owner can ask if I'm okay, I mutter some nonsense about dogs and loyalty and hurry away up the beach.

Through the kitchen window, the ocean looks indistinguishable from the grey charcoal horizon that underlines the sky. On afternoons like these it's as if the elements have morphed into each other presenting a uniform wall of moisture – beach to water, water to sky. Thick. Deep. Impenetrable. Everything feels grey, dismal and cold. I think about Hattie's owner who's been without her husband for five years and wonder if it looks less grey to her. Perhaps colours are seeping back to her edges, warming away her longing and loneliness… Hattie would help too, no doubt. Perhaps I should get a dog.

On the balcony, tea in hand, wrapped in a blanket, I inhale the damp salt air. A dog would be more trouble than it would be worth, I decide. They are tying, need walking, and jump all over the furniture with half the ocean dripping from their fur… and how much would a dog really help? When I'm lying awake at 2am in the bed that's too big, it's Adam's arms I want around me, not a dog across my feet. It's early days. He's only been gone six months. Give it time, everyone says. People seem to know about time and healing. I'll be buggered if I know how. Even people, who as far as I know, have never lost anyone, all seem to be authorities on grief and "moving forward", as they say. Moving forward to where and to what? I don't want to move forward. I wanted to move back to the day my husband's car came off a country road and into a tree. Wanted to warn him. Rise up like an apparition from the white line and shriek at him, wave my arms, make him stop before it's too late.

Adam had apparently been going too fast round a bend, obviously not expecting a herd of escaped cows in the road. The times I'd told him about driving too fast on those little Cornish lanes… I swallow a mouthful of tea and hold the warm mug to my chest. What's the point in going over it all again? I do this most days and it's getting old. Ancient. Standing out here looking at the wall of grey in the damp won't help either. I ought to get on with the new novel really. I'd been three chapters in when Adam was killed… I'm still three chapters in. Each day I resolve to pick up where I left off and each day I fail. *Come on, Sam, at least open up the document and look at the words… even if you don't write anything, it beats what you've done so far today.*

But my attention is diverted, and my God, Abi Harper hasn't changed one bit! Still with the little furrow in her brow, even when she's smiling, leaving her with a permanently puzzled expression. Mind you, on closer scrutiny of her new Facebook profile photo, I see she has actually changed quite a bit. There are deepish lines under her make-up if you look closely and strands of grey in her chestnut hair. She's not aged as well as she might have, but brave of her to update the old profile photo that she's had for ages. And anyway, thinking about it, she's forty-five like me, what do I expect? Sometimes I disregard the passage of time – in my head I'm still eighteen. A glance in the living room mirror tells me I still look like I'm in my late thirties, despite the harrowing past six months. There isn't much grey in my dark hair and my lines… okay, so there might be a few more than there were before Adam died. I sigh. This is not getting on with the novel, is it? No. I'd fully intended to go straight to documents and bypass Facebook, but lately I've turned procrastination to a fine art.

Just as my finger hovers over the minimise symbol at the top of the screen, Abi posts again. It's a reminder invite about a reunion at her old school in a few weeks' time. I didn't see the original post, for some reason, so scan the information. It's for anyone whose last year at Hind Grange was 1990 and 1991. Twenty-seven or twenty-eight years… how is that actually possible? Further down the page is the original posting along with who is going, who can't make it and who the maybes are. Two names stand out from the list of those going. Penny and Dan Thomas. Still together then? Funny, I wouldn't have given them more than a few years. Perhaps that was just sour grapes though. Even after… I do the calculation, twenty-nine years, the sting of rejection and betrayal niggles away when I think of how my best friend and first love went behind my back. It's faded and normally forgotten, but shreds of it are still there, hidden, sulking, waiting for recognition at moments like this. They say the first cut is the deepest, don't they? What I did in revenge is still lurking too – though I wish it wasn't.

I click on Dan's profile photo and my breath is taken by the familiar twinkle in his dark eyes and the sexy lopsided smile that used to make my heart skip a beat. Yes, the eyes are sitting on a good few crinkles but, somehow, he's grown more handsome. Men tend to do that. Bastards. Because we aren't Facebook friends, I can't access his timeline, so switch to have a closer look at Penny Thomas-was-Kershaw's photo. A tickle of glee capers in my tummy as I see the years have not been nearly as kind to her as they have to her husband. The jade eyes have faded to blades of winter grass and under them, the crinkles are pronounced and very noticeable. The red hair is still lustrous but has had considerable help from a colourist. Then I tell myself off. What's the point in thinking mean thoughts? Mean thoughts make a mean person. Yes, Penny betrayed me in the worst way when we were sixteen, but 1989 was a long, long time ago. Another lifetime. Time to forget. But a vindictive little voice that I try to keep silent whispers in my ear – *Yeah, and the bitch paid for it at the time.*

The document is opened at last and I type *Chapter Four*, and then read back over the last three chapters of the suspense novel – just as I have done every few days for the last month. Okay, now time to move the story on. This is the chapter where the baddie is introduced. He, of course, can't be seen to be the bad guy at first, that would give too much away. There will be a second bad guy too with different motives, and he must appear as the one that has the solution to all the heroine's problems, the knight in shining armour. Near the end, the readers will see them in all their terrible glory. But which one is the killer? They will have to wait until the last few pages when the final twist is revealed.

I watch my fingers hover over the keys, type a sentence and then delete it. Type and delete. Try as I might, I can't get Dan and Penny out of my mind. How come they are still together, have each other, are candidates for the happy ever after, while I'm misery personified? Their foundations were built on lies and deceit. Mine and Adam's were built on honesty and trust; yet, he has been taken. He has been ripped from my side, my heart – lost forever. They are together. I am alone.

The cursor flashes on and off, on and off, as if taunting me. I need to either knuckle down to write, or go for a walk or… something. Anything but this reopening of old wounds and re-examining new ones left by Adam's death. Perhaps I should send friend requests to both Penny and Dan, start afresh, put the past behind me. I don't want to be a bitter and twisted lonely old cow, but if I keep this up, I soon will be. Maybe they won't accept me, Penny especially, but at least I'll have tried to move forward.

Cold, shaky and a bit foolish is how I feel after sending the two friend requests. Perhaps I've been a bit impetuous. What good will it do anyway? It isn't as if I'd ever see them again.

The kitchen clock says it's almost wine o'clock, and who am I to argue? The day has flown, and I've done absolutely nothing with it. Tomorrow is another day, however, a Saturday, and after I've seen my daughter and grandson for breakfast, I'll make a start on chapter four if it kills me.

Sipping the wine, I draw the curtains on the dark and switch on all the lights. Would I ever get used to living alone? I heave a sigh and plop down on the sofa in front of the TV. A takeaway and Netflix will help me feel better, along with a few more glasses of wine. As I retrieve the remote for the TV from under the cushion, my arm nudges the laptop and the screen lights up. It's still on my Facebook page, and there are two little red icons on the screen. Clicking on them, I discover that both Penny and Dan have accepted the friend requests. This makes me ridiculously pleased. For goodness' sake, we aren't schoolkids any more. About to shut down the laptop, I stop when I see I'm tagged in a post.

Sam! How the devil are you? So pleased that you got in touch. Tell me I'll see you at the reunion in a couple of weeks! xxx

Dan's three kisses throw me a little. Even though kisses have become part of everyday punctuation over the last few years, isn't that a bit over the top? And go to the reunion – not in a million bloody years! I can think of nothing more cringeworthy. I can't say no though just like that, can I? It would look a bit rude. Perhaps I'll shut down Facebook and pretend that I've not seen the message until tomorrow. By then I'll have thought of the perfect excuse as to why I can't attend. Yes, that's what I'll do.

Later on, full of takeaway, wine and a feel-good movie, I wish that my thoughts would stop wandering to where a perfect excuse might be hiding. If I wasn't so lonely I'd never even consider going. Cornwall is a long way from Sheffield after all. In fact, that's the perfect excuse right there – no need to look any further. I also wish my thoughts would stop wandering to those three little kisses at the end of Dan's message.

Chapter Two

'Mum, come and see what Adam's doing!'

I hurry from the kitchen just in time to watch my five-month-old grandson attempting to crawl across the rug. Upon seeing me, he collapses in a heap, his chubby legs waving in the air and chortles in that way that makes his grandma's heart melt. I pick him up, inhale that fantastic baby smell and look into his grey-blue eyes, so like his namesake's. 'Is that the first time he's done that, Helena?' I look across the room at my daughter's beaming smile.

'More or less. He tried it yesterday but only for a second or two.'

'It's early to be crawling.' I boost Adam in the air and smile at him. 'We have a genius on our hands, don't we? Oh, we do. Yes, we do.'

'To be fair, Mum, he wasn't really crawling, just trying.' Helena tilts her head, gives a wry smile.

'Nonsense! He was crawling, so make sure you put that in your progress book thingy you keep.'

'Yes, Mum.' Helena grins and hurries into the kitchen to retrieve the pancakes we can smell burning.

I follow her in and place Adam in his highchair. 'Do you want me to take over now?'

'No, I've rescued it. Do you have maple syrup?'

'In the cupboard.' I put a selection of toys on the highchair tray to keep Adam occupied until his pancake is cool enough and think about how much I treasure times like this. It's so nice to have other people in the house on the cliff again. Though I adore the place, it's massive, and even when my husband was alive it did feel a bit too big for just the two of us, but it was left to us in Adam's parents' will. They had bought it not long before they got ill. Two years later they were sadly gone.

Even though their home was too big, Adam used to talk about plans to extend it and make it into a small guest house for when he retired from his job as an architect, because he would be so bored doing nothing. I smile at thoughts of me and Adam in our sixties running a guest house, it was a ridiculous idea at the time and I always told him so, but now I'd give anything to do that with him. I'd work from dawn until dusk if I could have him back. No point in wishing for things that will never happen, is there? I shelve the thoughts and help my daughter put the breakfast things on the table.

'Did I tell you that Carl is up for promotion?' Helena shoves a forkful of food into her mouth. It's like I'm looking into a mirror. Well, a mirror set back to when I was twenty-four.

'No. So, he could get head chef?'

'Yep. Though it would mean longer hours and he's already working so hard.' Helena furrows her brow and helps little Adam with his breakfast, most of which is all over his face.

My heart goes out to my daughter. It must be so difficult for her and her Carl. He's trying so hard to get ahead, make a success at the stylish bistro just off Fistral Beach in Newquay, but it's killing him. He hardly has time to spend with Helena and Adam either. But that's the nature of the game and I just hope he has the determination and strength to see it through. Also, that my daughter can cope with raising her son practically alone. I'm always there to help, of course, and do so at least twice a week, but I'm careful never to force myself forward. It's a tricky balancing act.

'Mum, you with us?'

'Oh sorry, love. Yes, he's working so hard already. It will be a great opportunity for him though… you know that I'm always here to help, you just have to say.'

'I know… I just don't like asking you to do more. You have your own life…' There's an awkward silence as both of us realise that actually isn't true. 'And your writing to get on with.'

'Hmm. Not been doing much of that lately.' I push my plate to one side and pick up my coffee cup.

'Writer's block?'

'Kind of… yes, I suppose it is. My head won't stop living in the past, thinking about your dad and all the plans we–' The look on Helena's face and a knot of emotion in my chest stop my words.

'Oh, Mum. That's only natural. I think about him loads too… wish that he'd lived to see his grandson and…' Helena's big blue eyes well up and I wish I'd just kept my misery bottled up inside where it always lives. Before I can rescue the situation, my phone beeps and the screen lights up with a Facebook message. I read it and shake my head.

'Who was that?' Helena nods at the phone.

'Oh, just an old school friend wondering if I'm going to a ridiculous reunion back up north. I mean, can you imagine?' I roll my eyes and take a mouthful of coffee.

'But why not? It would do you the world of good to get out and about,' Helena says wiping Adam's mouth and lifting him onto her knee.

'"Out and about"? I'm only forty-five, not some octogenarian in a care home, you know.' My attempt at levity has a bitter edge and I wish it didn't.

Helena looks at me. 'I know that, but tell me honestly, why won't you go?'

I look out of the window at the crashing waves. Think carefully about my answer. 'Because it will be filled with saddos all trying to impress each other with the huge success they've made of their lives. People will exaggerate and embroider the truth to make sure they don't seem ordinary, or worse still, boring. They'll make sure they spend money they can't afford on new clothes and make-up to show that they look good for their age, but underlying all that, there will be the stench of fear and anxiety caused by the chance they'll be caught out.' I take a breath and look back at my daughter. I'm surprised to see her hiding a smile.

'For goodness' sake, Mum. I think that's a bit pessimistic to say the least. I suppose that there will be some like that, but most will just go to catch up, remember what it was like being a kid and have a fun time.'

'Nostalgia, my dear, is a dangerous thing. I think leaving the past alone is the best idea. What's the point in raking up all the misery and angst of your teenage years and dragging it into the present?'

'I had no idea that your schooldays were so awful.' Helena reaches across the table and places a hand over mine.

'Oh, it wasn't mostly… I…' I get up and start to clear away the dishes. There's no way I'm telling Helena all about the way I was betrayed by Penny and Dan… and the consequences of that. 'Never mind. Let's just leave it now – I'm not going and that's it.'

'What were you about to say?'

'Nothing, love. Just had my heart broken when I was sixteen, but don't we all?' So much for not telling her anything. Sometimes my mouth has a mind of its own.

'And will he be at the do? The guy who broke it?'

'That's who the message was from.'

'Oh my goodness. Tell me everything!' Helena's eyes glint with the prospect of gossip.

'No, I think I'll just leave it there. Another coffee?'

'Yes in a bit when I've got this one off for a nap – he was up in the night and is almost nodding off now. Look.' Helena stands up and pats Adam's back a few times. He snuggles his head into the crook of her neck. 'When I have, we'll have that coffee and then I want chapter and verse on what happened back in the dark ages.' She gives me a mischievous wink.

I sigh and load the dishwasher. This is not what I'd planned for the morning.

Half an hour later, I feel like I'm being interrogated by MI5. 'Right… so your so-called best friend gets off with your first boyfriend, who you've been dating for a year, at a party and that was it? He just leaves you for her?'

'Yes, that's about the size of it.'

'But why? You are way prettier than her now.' Helena jabs her finger at Penny's profile photo on Facebook. 'So you must have been back then.'

'It's not just about looks, is it?'

'It is at that age.'

'Not necessarily. There are other things teenagers seem obsessed with too. Especially young men.'

Helena's eyes grow round. 'You mean sex? You wouldn't sleep with him, but she would?'

I'm shocked at how quickly Helena has latched on. 'Er… yep.'

'What a cow! Mind you, he's just as much to blame. Had you and her been friends for a long time?'

'Since junior school.'

'What a cow! What did you do, Mum?'

An image of a school toilet flashes. A scrawled note. My back pressed against cold wall tiles as I hide behind a cubicle door, my heart thumping… I blink a few times and the image is gone. I say, 'Nothing.'

Helena shakes her head in disgust and stares out at the ocean. 'That's because you're too nice. If I were you I would definitely go to that reunion just to show her how gorgeous you are if nothing else. I bet Dan's eyes will be out on stalks…' She gives me a sidelong glance. 'Not bad looking is he, for an old guy?'

'Hey, less of the old. He's only a year older than me, and I'm gorgeous don't forget.' I laugh and put my hands over my face to cover up pink cheeks.

'Seriously, Mum, it would be a break for you. And even if you don't want to spend time with Penny and Dan, there will be other people that you know. If you don't like it, just leave early – simple.'

I look at my daughter's earnest face and don't get why she's so keen for me to go. 'I really don't think it will be worth the time and effort. I haven't been back to Sheffield for years.'

'Another reason to go. See what's changed… and it would get you out of yourself. The truth is, I have been a bit worried about you lately, we both have.' Helena's eyes are sympathetic, but I feel a twinge of annoyance. Seems like Helena and Carl have been talking about "poor old Sam" behind her back.

'Why worried?' I try to make my words sound neutral, but they come out stabby and pointy.

'Don't get mad, it's just that you spend lots of time alone and brooding about Dad and stuff. You don't see your friends now and… well I think you might be a bit depressed again.'

'Oh, I see. Perhaps I should see a shrink or go back on the happy pills then?' I push my chair back and chuck the half-drunk coffee down the sink. Truth be known, I'm as mad with myself as much as Helena, because my daughter's only voiced the concerns I have already.

'Sorry, Mum. Of course I don't. I know how tough it was for you coming off those things. I don't want to upset you… only telling you what I think.' Helena comes over and puts her hands on my shoulders. 'Don't go to this daft reunion if you don't want. Like you say, what would be the point? I was only keen for you to have something a bit different to do.'

I push dark thoughts away. Poor Helena is only looking out for me. Why did I have to say the stuff about the antidepressants? Cruel. Unnecessary. It was only natural that Helena would be looking for any sign of my depression coming back. I'd beaten it, come off the tablets. There's no way I'm going back on them. Then I think about what my daughter has said about the reunion. I turn around and give her a quick hug. 'I'll consider it, okay? I think you might be right about me feeling a bit down… I wouldn't go as far as to say I was depressed…' An image of standing in the sea crying my eyes out yesterday is presented and quickly squashed. 'But maybe a trip up north would do me good.'

Helena smiles. 'I think it would, yes. Now while I've got you in a thoughtful mood, what do you think about babysitting Lord Fauntleroy on Wednesday, so I can get my hair done?'

'Oh, I'm not sure I can do that. I will be far too busy buying a new wardrobe of clothes, having a spray tan, my teeth whitened, and my hair and make-up done.'

'Yeah, right. So, I'll see you at mine for ten.'

'Yep.' I smile and hug Helena again. God knows where I'd be without her. I speak to my son Jack a few times a week on the phone, as he's at uni up country studying to be a vet, but it's not the same as having someone who you can rely on close by. Adam yells from the back bedroom and Helena hurries off.

Loading the washing machine, I wonder about my decision to think about the reunion trip. If I'm honest, it scares the shit out of me. It's been so long since I've gone anywhere on my own. Since the age of twenty I've been part of a couple. Adam and Sam, Sam and Adam, we'd done everything together, gone everywhere as a two. Now there's just the one. Sam. Sam and nobody. Sam and nobody would have to walk into a packed school hall and pretend to be confident, cheerful and in control. Why put myself through all that if I don't have to? Ridiculous.

No matter how much I try to keep busy, I can't put the thought of the reunion out of my mind… and once again, as the day draws to a close, I stand on the balcony wrapped in the blanket with a cup of tea. It's bitterly cold, but in the black sky, the stars and moon shine their light bright, making silver horses of the waves gallop into shore. Looking at the ocean always helps put things into perspective for me, and a calmness fills my chest with every breath. Reason edges into the calm and provokes a question. Isn't it about time that you challenged yourself? Since meeting Adam at uni, my plans were shelved. Well, about six months before the end of my teaching degree to be precise, when I'd fallen pregnant with Helena.

There were no regrets about having my lovely daughter, and Adam and I were madly in love, but there was no way I could pursue a teaching career with a baby. I felt the loss of my parents so much at this time. Other young mums had their parents' support, but sadly both of mine had gone. Poor Dad died at sea – a fishing trip when I was twenty – and Mum died of a heart attack not long after. I reckon it was the stress of it all. I could have finished the year at a later date, but by then I was a busy mum and was already pregnant again with Jack not long afterward. Mere contraception was no barrier against Adam's super sperm, as he'd liked to joke at the time.

Once the children were at school, I'd enjoyed many years working in the local library, but in the last few years, I knew I had to leave and pursue my writing dream. We were doing well financially; Adam's parents had left us this house and we were mortgage free. We'd moved in, sold our other house, so had a fair bit in the bank, Adam had made partner in the firm and everything looked set for a happy secure future.

I blow on my tea and wrap my cold fingers tight around the mug before taking a sip. Yeah right. Okay, I'm fine financially since Adam has gone, but the future is hardly happy without him, is it?

Then I think about my writing. Earlier I thought I'd better take on a challenge, but isn't writing my challenge? I'm quite proud of the way my first two novels have gone. The writing class and scheme I'd joined were invaluable, and last year I'd been taken on by a small publisher. Okay, I'm no JK Rowling regarding royalties, but who is? I smile into the darkness. The main thing is that I enjoy writing and judging by the reviews, my readers seem to appreciate my efforts too.

I wonder how many old classmates are published authors. I would guess at very few, possibly none. So there was a huge talking point right there for "Sam and nobody" standing in the school hall. In my book, a published author beats spray tans and white teeth any day of the week. Penny might have stolen Dan all those years ago, but perhaps she won't have that much to share about her accomplishments on the night. I heave a sigh. There I go again. Penny might have just climbed Everest for all I know, but the odds are slim. A giggle escapes as I raise my empty mug to the Atlantic. Bugger it. I'll go to the reunion and be damned.

Chapter Three

The screech of the train's brakes pulling into Sheffield station jolts through my stomach and sends my heart plummeting. There'll be no going back now, even though I seriously considered bailing out more than once when I changed trains on the almost eight-hour journey. Eight bloody hours? I could have flown to New York in the time it had taken me to get the three hundred and odd miles up north. Positively medieval. Up at stupid o'clock too, so if I manage to stay awake at the reunion it will be a miracle. First, I need to check into the hotel, grab a shower, get ready and then have some food. Perhaps there'll even be time for a nap. My phone says almost 4pm and the reunion starts at 7.30… so that will be a no, then.

At least the hotel room is nice, and I'm pleased I went for the upgrade. It had to be done really. It went with the expensive dress and shoes I bought, even though I'd initially pooh-poohed all that to Helena the other week. Helena had insisted on coming with me to choose them, and said she'd been blown away by how wonderful her old mum looked. It had been a special day. I sit on the bed and look around. I suppose getting this upgrade makes me feel special too. I can afford it, so why not treat myself? Helena had said as much while grabbing my credit card and booking the room before I could protest. To be honest, the new clothes and expensive suite boosts my confidence, and that's exactly what I need tonight.

The room service meal is lovely, though halfway through, I put it to one side. Butterflies have taken up most of the room in my stomach. A shower, full make-up and the new clothes should banish the nerves. In the bathroom, I keep telling myself that I'm just as good as anyone that will be at the reunion, better than some, but the butterflies multiply nevertheless. Perhaps that's a good thing. Actors always say that a few first night nerves make the performance shine. The fact that I'm not an actor is neither here nor there. If it helps to imagine I am, then that's fine with me. In my youth, I often pretended I was acting in difficult situations. It had been a long time since I'd needed a costume and props, but tonight I'm due on stage and I need to be in the spotlight, word-perfect.

The taxi is due in ten minutes and I'm debating whether to wipe some of the eyeshadow off or not. Is it too much… the whole thing? Do I look as if I'm trying too hard? I'd said as much to Helena last week but had been reassured that I looked just right. I dab a fingernail at my eyeliner then tell myself off and leave the bathroom. The full-length mirror in the bedroom catches my eye, however, and now I stand in front of it looking at the dress. It's red and black and very clingy. I lean forward, pout and fluff my hair. Should I tie it back? It might look more sophisticated… but is that the look I'm going for? The dress says otherwise. Helena enthused that it was fun, sexy and sophisticated, but now I wonder if I look a bit like I'm off to work the streets. The black high heels are already killing me too. Oh hell. What should I do? A glance at the clock says I should stop deliberating, there's no time to change. It's now or never.

I pay the driver and watch him drive away, while all the time wishing I was still in the back seat. Then, turning to face the school, all the fears and worries are snatched away into the dark night because it looks smaller than I remember. Well, not minuscule, but smaller than it had when I'd attended. The past was small too. I have grown, blossomed, am no longer the frightened unsure teenager that had been cheated on, betrayed. I can do this. I will do it. I am the lead in a sold-out play and about to put on another stellar performance. A smile finds my lips, I pull back my shoulders and stride down the drive to the front door of the school as confidently as my heels will allow.

Ah good, it's packed. Through the double doors in the hall, I can make out crowds of people in the midst of flashing lights, and the hubbub of voices and laughter is a roar even through the glass. I'm so glad I'd ordered the taxi to drop me forty-five minutes after the start, so I wouldn't be standing there on my own in the hall like Billy No-Mates. At the desk, I collect my name badge and pin it to my right shoulder. Sam Hennessy. It's been a long time since I've used that name. In the hall, the thumping nineties music and strobe lights on the dance floor cause a few butterflies to resurface, but this time they are caused by excitement rather than nerves, and I step inside.

A quick scan of the dance floor turns up no familiar faces, so I decide to get a drink and go into the offshoot hall where people are sitting at tables engrossed in conversation. The wine tastes like vinegar but it's better than nothing, and after a few more gulps, courage takes my hand and leads me out of the noisy hall and into relative calm. A few people glance at me and smile, though it's out of politeness rather than recognition, and I sit at a table near the back wall, a rictus grin stretching my lips. Dear God, I'll frighten anyone away with that… This is where the acting is required. Forcing a more natural smile, I nod at a woman who I half remember. Wasn't she in my science class…? Something about her fainting during a dissection is whispering at the edge of my memory. Suddenly it's all too much and I decide to escape for a bit.

As I follow the signs for the loos, I realise where I'm heading. Fuck! Why did they have to designate *this* bloody toilet as the Ladies? I push the door and hear that it still has the annoying squeak it had a lifetime ago and, inside, the old familiar smell of disinfectant mingles with tobacco. All but one cubicle is full, and women are shouting to each other – shrieking with laughter as they pass cigarettes under the door as they did in their youth. I slip into the end cubicle and slide the catch home.

My heart's thumping too fast and I can feel the cool tiles on my bare back as I lean against the wall. The cigarette smoke churns my stomach and I close my eyes. I can see a scrawled note: *Meet me at 9.15 during tutor period – usual place.* Then I'm right back there on the day after I caught Penny and Dan. The door squeaks open and Penny whispers my name outside the door. I don't answer. She pushes the door, walks in, and then…

'Oi, anyone in there?' There's a bang on the cubicle door and the catch rattles.

I'm shocked back to the present and the memory disappears. 'Yeah, I'm done now,' I say, undo the catch, and walk out.

A tall dark-haired woman hops from one leg to the other – looks a bit awkward. 'Sorry, love. It's just that the engaged sign was only half on – wasn't sure if it was occupied and I'm dying for a pee!'

'No worries.'

Shoving the past away into a locked box, I go back to the hall, order a gin and tonic and make my way to a quiet table in the corner. I take a big gulp. The wine wasn't hitting the spot and I need fortification.

'Sam Hennessy! I thought it was you at the bar but wasn't sure. Now you're in the light I can see it is.'

I look up into the beaming round face of Jason Kerr, the most boring boy in the world, as Penny and I used to say behind the poor lad's back. 'Oh hi, Jason, how are you?' I stand and shake hands to ward off Jason's clumsy attempt at a hug.

'I'm good thanks. I'm an area manager and have my own house, car and have two foreign holidays a year.'

'Blimey, how wonderful!' I swallow a giggle, make my face straight and sit back down. He sounds just the same as he did when he was fifteen, always trying too hard to impress when he had nothing of interest to share really.

'I have a wife too. No children, yet, but… we haven't given up hope.' Jason rummages in his inside pocket and pulls out a wallet. 'Here she is.'

I look at the photo of a sour-faced woman in a party hat. 'Oh lovely.'

'Yes, her name's Angie and that was Christmas last year. Are you married and what do you do?' Jason's mouth has caught my rictus grin from earlier and he puts his wallet away.

His blunt approach has thrown me. Do I say I'm a widow and that I'm a writer, or do I ignore the first part of his question, as my answer would provoke an awkward response? 'I was married but…' Now what?

'It didn't work out? Yes, so many friends of mine are on their first, second or even third marriages!' Jason tips a high-pitched giggle into my ear and pats my arm.

I fight an urge to slap him and take a drink. Why not let him think I'm divorced? It will be much simpler. Pride nudges a response. 'And I am a writer. I have a couple of novels published.'

Jason's mouth drops open and he pulls a chair up to my table. Marvellous. 'Hey, well done. I have always fancied self-publishing my memoir. But I just never seem to have the time to write it.'

The idea that anyone would stay awake long enough to read his memoir past the first page was laughable, but of course that can't be said. And why do people always say they want to write a book but don't have time? If you're serious, you make time, just like I did when I worked at the library eight hours a day. I look across the room and sigh. 'I didn't self-publish actually, I have a publisher.' The showy-off tone in my voice draws a tide of red up my neck and I feel a bit stupid. Why do I care if Jason is impressed or not?

'You do? Bloody hell are you famous? You know like…'

Don't say it, please…

'What's her name, J–'

'J K Rowling, no, no I'm not. But then very few writers are. Most of us just scrape

by, don't earn enough to make a living at it, but it's my passion… so…' Bloody hell, why do I feel as if I have to justify myself, make it sound like an apology?

'But that doesn't matter. It's a great achievement, I reckon.'

I look at him, but there's no trace of mockery in his honest brown eyes.

'Yes, it is. Thanks, Jason.'

Jason leans forward, rests his elbows on the table. 'So is there anyone else you're seeing now. You know, after your divorce. And how long have you been divorced?'

Oh no. There's a lascivious light in his eyes and he's looking unsubtly at my cleavage. Just when I was beginning to warm to him. I take a drink and scan the room for any familiar face that could be waved at and can't see one. I think I half remember quite a few but can't be sure as they are chatting and most have their backs to me. I wave at a woman anyway and say, 'I think that's what's her name… um… Debbie from our old tutor group. I think I'll pop over and say hello.'

Jason screws his eyes up. 'No, that's Sally. She wasn't in our group. Anyway, how long have you been divorced?' I feel his podgy paw on my forearm, note the lust in his eyes and a trickle of irritation turns into a wave of anger. 'I never said I was divorced, Jason. You did.' I brush his hand away. 'I'm a widow, and if you don't piss off, your wife will be too. Very soon.'

Jason scoots back in his chair, his face puce, eyes bulging. 'What the hell? I… I…'

'Not sure Sam's happy with your company, Jason, mate. Perhaps it might be best if you pissed off, like she asked.'

His voice is just the same, maybe a bit deeper with age, but I'd recognise it anywhere. I look up from the table and smile at the man behind me. 'Dan. How lovely to see you.'

Jason stands up. 'Hey! All right, Dan, my man?' He raises his hand to slap Dan on the back, but then obviously thinks better of it. 'God knows what's up with her.' He tips his head at me and sneers. 'I was only being–'

'I heard what you were being. Just do one before I forget my manners.'

Jason shakes his head and leaves. I stand up and go to shake Dan's hand, but he draws me into a bear hug. With my face against his chest, I can smell a mix of lemony cologne and clean skin. I swallow, draw away, look just past his right shoulder and intend to say, how are you, but it comes out as, 'Sow's you?'

'Me's good, and you?'

I laugh to cover my embarrassment and look at his face. The face that has aged so well, even better than his Facebook picture… and his smile. A smile that had almost got me into bed that time when he'd smuggled his dad's homemade wine into the school youth club. We'd taken it to the hay field and he'd kissed me as I looked up at the star peppered sky, warm from the wine and his touch. I'd said it wasn't the right place to make love, though, and agreed to go to his brother's house, as he was on holiday. But on the way there, I'd sobered up and changed my mind. If I'd slept with him, would we be together now?

'Better now creepy Jason has gone.' Dan's smug expression prompts, 'I could have dealt with him on my own though, but thanks.'

'Yeah, I know.' Dan nods and indicates we sit down. 'But while I was creeping up behind the pair of you to surprise you, I did hear the conversation. I'm so sorry, love. Thought you might be a bit raw and need a hand.'

Looking at my feet, I'm half-pleased I don't have to explain all over again that Adam had died, but I don't like the pity in Dan's voice. What do I expect though? How is he supposed to react? I hadn't thought this bit through when I'd decided to come here as the writer, the confident woman. How could I have not considered how to respond when people asked about Adam? Perhaps I had, but just skimmed it over. An airbrushed bright and breez, *I'm afraid my husband died nearly seven months ago, devastating, but I'm getting there… moving forward at last.*

'Sam, you okay?'

'Yeah, sorry… I did need a hand, thanks, you're right. But let's talk about something else, like how you and Penny are, what your lives have been like.' I look around the room, '…and where is she come to that?'

'She was going to the loo but was collared by Kerry Wolstenholme. She may be gone some time!'

Thank God I just missed Penny in there. It was bad enough with just her memory for company. Despite this unsettling thought, I muster a laugh at what Dan said. Kerry never stopped talking and took no prisoners. 'Perhaps I should go and save her?'

Dan shakes his head. 'I'm sure she'll be fine. Would you like another drink?'

While Dan is at the bar again, sometime later, I wonder what I'll say when he comes back. Why can't Penny be with him? Just the two of us chatting feels a bit intimate, cosy. I should be annoyed, given what he did all those years back, but as I keep reminding myself that was a very long time ago. I've told him the bare bones of my life history but not about the writing. Once was enough with Jason. Dan's told me that he's a property developer and they have no children – a joint decision – and that Penny was a hairdresser but now spends her time being a "lady wot lunches" and at the gym as his business is doing well. They have plans to get a holiday cottage in my neck of the woods, once the sale of Penny's parents' house goes through – they sadly both passed within weeks of each other – and Dan and Penny are generally happy with their life and marriage. Still… if I'm not mistaken, there is a spark of attraction for me in his eyes. He could 'do one' as he'd told Jason. He'd had his chance.

Wait, is that Penny coming through the door? Yes… I think it is. I watch as she crosses over to Dan at the bar. He says something to her and her smile freezes. Penny's head snaps round in my direction and as she raises her hand, the fake smile follows a little too late afterwards. I wave back and try not to notice that Penny must have spent more time lunching than at the gym, and that even from this distance, a road map of lines directs her features. Her hair is a cloud of fire and before she turns back to her husband, sparks of anger ignite her glare.

Hmm, a bit insecure then, eh, Pen? I watch the two have a few sharp words and then Penny shrugs and follows Dan toward my table, a drink in her hand and a rictus grin on her face. They must be complimentary, like the peanuts.

'Sam, my goodness, you are looking gorgeous!' Penny says as she kisses me on both cheeks. Her words sound genuine, but a little flash of jealousy passes swiftly across her eyes. 'I didn't think you'd really come, given the journey up from the back of beyond.'

I move my bag from a chair to allow Penny to sit. 'The "back of beyond" is the most beautiful county in the UK, in my humble opinion,' I say, hoping that I've kept the rankle out of my tone. 'And I said I was coming, I rarely go back on my decisions.'

Penny's smile falters. The rankle was obviously unmistakable, as was the look of apprehension. 'Oh, I didn't mean Cornwall wasn't lovely. It is a long way to get to anywhere from there, though, isn't it?' Penny takes a long pull of wine and eyes me over the rim of her glass.

I stare back, unsmiling. 'Yes, but I went back to my roots. My mum was Cornish don't forget, and her mother before her.'

Penny snorts. 'But you weren't born there, never lived there, did you, until you were an adult.'

I want to shout at her, wipe the supercilious smile from her podgy face. But I don't. I say in a low voice that leaves no doubt as to how I'm feeling, 'I'm Cornish. End of.'

Dan shifts in his seat and flashes a big smile. 'Okay, well, enough of that, how long has it been since we last saw each other?' He leans back and strokes his chin while looking at us both. As if he didn't know. What's wrong with him?

Penny looks uncomfortable. 'A long time… and at school here, I expect.'

Really? I can't be bothered with all the shilly-shallying and I'm furious with her anyway. The gin fortifies my resolve and I decide to clear the guff of politeness and pretence from the air. 'It was when I walked in on you both coming out of Dan's room half undressed. I was sixteen, so were you, Penny, and Dan, you were just seventeen. So, twenty-nine years ago. Thought you'd have remembered.'

Dan turns the colour of his wife's hair and takes a pull on his pint. Penny tries to hide a smile and runs an electric-blue nail down the stem of her glass. She tips her head, looks at me. 'That was a long time ago, so why bring it up?' She held my gaze, an obvious challenge.

'Hey, Dan asked,' I say, giving Dan side eyes.

'Yeah, I'm an idiot. I was just thinking of our school days… in fact, I didn't really think, did I…?'

'No. But at least it's out of the way,' I answer. 'Actually, I did see you again, didn't I, Pen, remember? It was the morning after – on school leavers' day. I asked you to pop down and meet me in the loos, like always. Said I wanted to talk about what happened.'

Penny's not smiling now. Her face is the colour of snow and she looks at her hands folded like two dead doves in her lap. 'Hmm.'

Shit. Why can't I leave it alone? A picked scab never heals. I glance at Dan, note the panic in his eyes, and change the subject. 'Anyway, as I was saying, it's cleared the air, got it out of the way. While at the time it hurt, *the understatement of the century*, it was for all the best. I met my wonderful husband and moved to the back of beyond, had a couple of children and was the happiest woman in the universe, until not that long ago.'

Penny glances up from her doves, and frowns. 'Oh, what happen–?'

Dan nudges her and flashes his eyes.

I shake my head. 'It's okay, Dan.' To Penny I say, 'I'm afraid my husband died nearly seven months ago, devastating, but I'm getting there… moving forward at last.' There. I'd airbrushed, and it sounded normal-ish.

'Oh, I'm so sorry, love.' Penny leans forward and hugs me, and all of a sudden I'm back in the playground at primary school. I've been pushed over by a bigger girl and Penny's comforting me and dabbing at my grazed knee with a tissue. We had been good mates for years, the best, until Dan… To my horror, I feel a lump forming in my throat. I pat Penny's back and pull away, take a drink. 'Thanks, don't let's talk about it, or you'll set me off.'

'No… okay. So, you have kids?' Penny sits back down, and I see that her eyes are moist. Perhaps she's so sympathetic about Adam because she stole her best friend's boyfriend and the guilt is getting to her.

'Yes, a boy and a girl. Well, they're grown now. Jack's at uni and Helena has a baby of her own. Little Adam, after his granddad.'

Penny's eyes grow wide. 'You're a granny?'

'Yeah! Nuts isn't it?' I note the derision in 'granny' but choose not to bite.

'Granny? Bloody hell. She hardly looks like one, though, does she?' Dan says to his wife, admiration in his voice as his gaze sweeps my face.

Penny fluffs her hair and clears her throat. 'Course not,' she says quietly.

I warm to her obvious discomfort. 'I do try to take care of myself. I don't go to the gym, but I do walk on the beach most days and the cliff paths. Watch what I eat too. I'm the same dress size as I was when we were sixteen.' I let my eyes sweep Penny's ample midriff and then smile at Dan. Bitchy, but I need to make a stand.

Penny narrows her eyes and says nothing.

Dan asks, 'What's your son studying?'

'Veterinary Medicine. He's always wanted to be a vet since he was a little lad.' This impresses them both – there's a number of oohs and ahhs… then an awkward silence which I fill with, 'Dan tells me you decided not to have children. I bet you've had lots of time to travel and… do stuff.' Which sounds a bit lame, but I can't think of anything else.

Penny snorts. 'Hardly my choice. Dan never wanted them, so…'

The 'so' hangs in the air, heavy with recrimination and misery. Dan looks sheepish and says, 'You kind of agreed–'

'I had no choice in the end, did I?' Penny snaps. Then her face relaxes. 'I'm sure Sam doesn't want to hear our old woes. Or mine to be exact… Last I heard, you went to uni to do a teaching degree.'

I nod. 'I did, but I fell pregnant in my last year, so it never happened. Then I raised the kids and then worked as a librarian until quite recently. Now I'm a writer.' I say this last bit into my glass as I drain it.

'A writer?' They say at the same time.

'Yup.' I can't help an ear-to-ear grin stretching my face as I answer their questions and realise that I've achieved what I came here for. Recognition, admiration – respect.

Other old friends I meet during the course of the evening are equally impressed, and I chalk this performance up as a success.

In the hotel room, I tip out the contents of my bag onto the bed and sort through quite a collection of email addresses and contact numbers from classmates who made me promise to send details of my books, and to keep in touch. Dan's is among them and I trace his name on the embossed card with the tip of my finger.

In the bathroom, I draw a cotton pad across my eyes and give my reflection a wry smile as I remember that Penny had given me a genuine hug when we'd parted. So had Dan, though he'd held me a bit too long, and Penny had pretended to stumble, so slipped her arm through his, which broke the embrace. She apologised, said she was squiffy. Penny then enthused about us emailing and calling, but I could tell she wouldn't. It was all talk. Dan was obviously attracted to me, and his wife knew it.

Because of our history this initially made me happy, but retribution was a negative emotion. No. I could do without any dramas. If Dan and Penny wanted to keep in touch, then it would be up to them. I had put the past to bed. I'd done this on my own terms at last, not theirs, and it was time to let sleeping dogs lie.

Chapter Four

It is ridiculous how much I've missed Cornwall, Helena and Adam. I was only away one night, for goodness' sake, but now I've been back a couple of days in my house on the cliff. There's a whiff of spring in the salt air, and all is right with the world. From my balcony I can see a few early surfers bobbing on the swell and I decide on a brisk walk. After that, a quick spot of housework and then cracking on with my book will be the plan for the day. I'm going to Helena's for tea too, so it's going to be a good day. Sometimes I just know when things are going to go well – there's a light feeling in my chest.

Back from my walk, I'm dusting the coffee table when the doorbell rings. 'Robert? What a lovely surprise.' I smile and usher one of Adam's oldest friends, who is also our accountant, inside, and lead the way to the kitchen. It isn't really a lovely surprise, because I want to write, but mainly because I clocked the serious look on his face when I opened the door. 'Tea, coffee?'

'We might need something stronger.' Robert's forehead is a deep furrow and he sits at the kitchen table. 'Sit down, Sam.'

I sit… collapse more like, as his grave tone makes jelly of my legs. I look at his sandy hair, stuck up at one side because of the stiff breeze he's endured while waiting for me to answer the door, and he self-consciously smooths it and straightens his tie. 'What is it, Rob? Just tell me.'

'I told you that Adam had left you comfortably off…'

I don't like the sound of this. Robert had handled all our accounts for years and he'd even organised the paying of the funeral expenses. That meant I hadn't had to lift a finger and couldn't even say what bloody accounts we had. Adam had organised all that, I'd no interest in it. Everything was paid for by standing order and I just got money out of the ATM as I needed it. Wrapping my arms around my body, I nod. 'Yes, you did. You said I had near on a hundred thousand in the bank…'

'You did have, but Adam…' Robert sighs and stares out at the ocean.

A chill creeps up my spine. 'Adam what?'

'Adam made me promise not to tell you, but he invested in a few luxury holiday cottages, down near Fistral in Newquay. He hadn't bought them, just put some money in for a short while to help a business colleague buy them. They made a decent return in the first year and he put the money in a separate account, so you wouldn't know about it. He was going to buy a business for when he retired – you know him. He couldn't have just sat on his arse. This account was the one that you had most of the hundred grand in.'

My heart thumps inside my chest and my stomach swims with nausea. 'But I thought that was the money left from his parents' savings…'

'No. That's gone.' I open my mouth to ask where it went, but he hurries on. 'He was going to tell you about the money he'd made when the time was right. It was all going to be a wonderful surprise. Anyway, what I didn't know until the other day was that he'd heard about these other cottages, he had contacts through being an architect, everyone knows everyone in the building business, and he decided he'd put a hefty deposit down on two… huge actually… with a view to buy them by mortgage. You're mortgage free on this place and so… it should have been fine because of his earnings. That was going to be a surprise too, I expect.'

'Is the deposit where his parents' savings went?'

Robert gives a quick nod. 'I'm afraid so.'

'This is nuts. I never imagined he'd do something like that without telling me.' Robert sighs and shoves his hands through his hair. 'Oh my God…' The penny starts to drop, and a scream builds.

'As I said, it should have all been fine. But, of course, he died, and the company sent a demand for the mortgage default payments. He didn't pay, how could he? There had been a direct debit set up but... I haven't checked that account since the funeral though. Why would I? I spoke to them, but there was nothing I could do. He lost the deposit and the properties. I only found out when they tracked me down last week. I have been wondering how to tell you ever since.'

This isn't going in. It isn't making sense. 'I don't understand why there wasn't any money left in the account. If there was a hundred thousand in there after the funeral six months ago, there should still have been enough to cover the mortgage payments by direct debit?'

Robert shakes his head and his jaw tightens. 'There should have been, but... I don't know how to tell you this.' I just stare at him, at his funeral-sad face. 'The thing is, the rest of it went on the stock market and the investment bombed.'

I hear what he's saying but my brain is refusing to grasp it. 'How could he invest money in anything after he'd died for God's sake!'

'Because he had a financial "expert", Liam, who'd been entrusted with investing for Adam over the last year or so. Unaware of Adam's death, Liam invested a few days after the funeral, and then again, later on.'

A half-memory surfaces of Adam telling me about Liam. But, as usual, business stuff had gone over my head and I'd not paid much attention. From a sandpaper-dry throat, I manage to ask, 'How... How much is left?'

Robert bites his bottom lip, blows air down his nose. 'Nothing in his secret account. Just under £10,000 in the one you know about.'

Hysteria bubbles in my chest and I want to release the scream, laugh and yell all at the same time. He wanted it all to be a wonderful surprise... it was a surprise all right. How could he have done this? For fuck's sake! How am I going to manage? Okay, the ten grand would tide me over for a bit, but not that long. All the dreams of writing and not having to worry about the future financially are turning into the worst nightmare right before my eyes, and there isn't a thing I can do about it. I scrape back my chair and hurry to the balcony, take deep gulps of air, try to quell the nausea rising in my gut.

I feel Rob's hand on my shoulder a few moments later and fight back tears. The surfers shimmer and blur as I fail, and then anger takes over. 'What the fuck am I going to do, Rob? All my writing dreams are wrecked, just when I had a feeling that things were about to take off. I'll have to try to get my job back at the library. How could Adam have been so stupid? Not only do I have to try to live without him, I have to scrape by while I do it!'

'Hey, he was doing it for the both of you. There was no way he knew he was going to die... He wanted it all to be a lovely—'

'Surprise. Yes, you said.' I close my eyes, take a few breaths. Of course he didn't know he was going to land me in it, but he had, nevertheless. There is only so much I can cope with. What a hellish seven months this has been.

Rob takes his hand away and heaves a sigh. 'It could be so much worse – at least you still have this place. You could sell it. Must be worth at least £800,000.'

The idea of leaving 'this place' fills me with dread. I adore it. It's all I have left of my life with Adam. Yes, I'm lonely and rattle around this big house like a pea in a drum... but sometimes, just sometimes, I think I see Adam from the corner of my eye watching TV like he used to; feet up, beer in hand. And other times I hear his laughter, his voice. Of course it's all in my imagination, but if I left this place, bought somewhere new, I'm scared that the memories and imaginings would disappear quicker than dew on summer roses.

'I don't want to do that. I couldn't bear it. The upheaval, the—' I throw up my hands. What's the use in going through it all with Robert?

'It would be hard, but it might be your best option.'

'No. I'll get a job – forget all this fanciful writer lark. It was a nice dream while it lasted.'

Robert is silent for a moment. 'You could still write in the evening, weekends?'

'Yes, I could, though it won't be the same…' I notice Robert's mouth twitch into an almost sneer, which he hides just too late behind a sympathetic smile. How must I sound? Robert just said it could be so much worse and it could. There are thousands more worse off. Millions. 'Hey, I'm just being a prima donna. Don't worry about me, Robert. And it couldn't have been easy coming round here to tell me this news.' I pat him on the shoulder and lead the way to the door. I need to be alone.

Robert stands on the doorstep and gives me a quick peck on the cheek. 'If there's anything I can help you with, night or day, you know where I am, okay?'

'I do. You have been a good friend, Robert, and I'm very grateful.'

Half a bottle of wine by three in the afternoon on an empty stomach is not one of my better ideas. All I want to do is sleep, and I've to be at Helena's at five for tea. They eat really early because of little Adam. What on earth will he think of a half-cut grandma? Coffee. I need coffee. There would be no mention of Robert's news to Helena either. That would only worry her. I'll get a job before I tell her, then there'll be no need to worry at all, will there?

One cup of coffee down, another to go. Already I'm feeling more positive. If I get my old job back, a long shot, but you never know, there would be lots of people to take snippets from for future characters in my novels. Working full-time wouldn't be bad at all, in fact… Was that my phone? I find it under a cushion and thumb the screen. I don't recognise the number. 'Hello?'

'Sam, it's Dan. How you doing?'

I sit on the arm of the sofa. What the hell does he want? So much for thinking that they wouldn't get in contact again. 'I'm good, but then it's only been a few days or so since I saw you…'

'And with any luck we'll see you again next week!'

'You will?'

'Yes. I said that we hoped to get a holiday cottage down your neck of the woods at the reunion, remember?' I did. 'The money's come through from Penny's parents' sale, and so we're going to come down and house hunt!'

No. Bloody hell, that's all I need. 'Oh… right. That will be lovely.'

'Jeez, don't sound too enthusiastic.'

'Er… I am, just not feeling too well. Touch of the flu, I think.'

'Oh, poor love. Hope you're well by next Wednesday. I'll give you a bell when we're down and we'll meet up, or we could pop over to yours?'

I force a smile into my voice. 'Great, yeah.'

I press the end call button and slump backwards onto the sofa. The positive feeling has drained into the coffee dregs; why wasn't I more assertive with him? I should have just said I was busy or told the truth. The truth is that I don't want to see them. They are my past, and I only went up north to put that to bed and show them I'm not the girl they'd dumped on back then. Right now, however, the confident writer, the woman in control I'd been last week has gone. My world has fallen apart. Again. The sixteen-year-old girl I thought I'd left behind is right here and sitting on the sofa.

Chapter Five

A fish out of water. Penny looks like she doesn't belong. Even though she's left the fast-paced bustle and noise of the city behind, she's brought its essence with her, wears it like a second skin. I hide a smile. Who wears high heels to come to Cornwall? Who wears high heels, full make-up and a tight skirt to come to Cornwall? Is she mad? Penny looks odd; misplaced. Is this her armour? Her defence against my perceived threat to her glad-eyed husband? Perhaps. There's no other explanation I can think of for her inappropriate dress. The problem is, she just looks bizarre.

Against my better judgement, I've allowed myself to be taken to lunch at The Harbour Fish and Grill restaurant in Newquay. I've been here a few times before and have never been disappointed, but today, mainly because of Penny's appearance and Dan's overly cheerful attitude to everything, I feel a bit fish out of watery too. Once again, my ability to be assertive and honest deserted me yesterday when Dan called to arrange this lunch. It was as if my resolve just melted as soon as I had the phone in my hand. Two people live inside my head and the assertive one, ironically, it seems is the weaker.

'I might have the crab salad,' Penny says, running a red nail down the menu, a pout on her mouth – also red – matching lipstick.

'I have had that before here and it was delicious,' I say, pouring some water for all of us and apologising as some of the lemon slices plop out into Penny's glass, causing the water to splash onto her skirt. Penny's glare doesn't sit with her "no probs" light response. Does she think I've done it on purpose, for goodness' sake?

'I'm more of a meat man, myself,' Dan says as if this is a reflection on his masculinity somehow.

'You like something to get your teeth into don't you, love?' Penny's lascivious wink and a cursory sweep of my slim figure nearly puts me off eating anything at all. Coming here had been a bad idea. A very bad idea.

Dan ignores his wife, which earns him one of her glares, and says, 'So, you say your house overlooks a beach, Sam?'

'Yeah. Mawgan Porth, about fifteen minutes from here.'

'We'd love a nosey later, wouldn't we, Pen?'

'Er… yes, if we aren't imposing too much.'

Penny sounds as enthusiastic about seeing my home as she would be if invited to pull her brain down her nostrils with a rusty nail. I don't want them there anyhow. I need to ring my old boss about getting a new job. I'd meant to do it every day this week, but each time I'd put it off. 'I do have a few things planned, I'm afraid…'

'Aw, really? I was so looking forward to seeing your house, we both were, weren't we, Pen?' Dan's unsubtle eye-flash at his wife elicits a lukewarm response.

'But you heard Sam. She's busy… perhaps another time.'

Something in her tone rankles me. Penny used to be my closest friend, and apart from her genuine concern at the reunion over Adam's death, she has treated me as if I was something unpleasant on her shoe. I was the person who had been in the right all those years ago. Anyone would think it was the other way around. Then I sigh. Is it any wonder after what I did? I do feel ashamed, and hate the person they made me become back then. But part of me can't help but feel that my revenge was justified. And if she is insecure about her husband, then tough. I wonder if Penny's fears are based on evidence. Once a cheater, always a cheater, don't they say?

'I can put it off until tomorrow if you both want to come so much.' I direct this at Penny with a winning smile. Cruel, perhaps… but so what?

'That's great! We won't stay ages, just would like to see the house. At the reunion, you said you adored it as it was so special.

And me being a property developer, I love to look at stunning structures.' Dan's slow smile and prolonged eye contact draws a flame up along my neck and into my cheeks.

I smile, avert my eyes, take a long drink of water and pretend to brush something off my jeans. I don't like how he's making me feel. Or I do… I can't decide.

The cool mood Penny was in before I said they could visit my house is now bone-chillingly arctic. I stop trying to make conversation with her and turn all my efforts to Dan. We are getting on really well and I can't remember laughing so much for ages. He's just as funny as he was as a kid, and we still share the same offbeat sense of humour. All the while, Penny just picks at her crab salad and drinks more wine than she ought to at this time of day. She's got that hangdog expression on her face. The same one she had when she'd walked into that cubicle all those years back. I was behind the door smoking and I grabbed her arm and slapped her hard across the face. She'd started crying, begged me to forgive her for sleeping with Dan, but I wasn't having any of it. The red mist descended, and I spun her round and jabbed the toe of my shoe in the hollow of her knee. She went down fast on both knees and banged her head on the edge of the toilet seat. I lunged forward, grabbed her long hair and forced her head into the pan and pulled the flush.

Unexpectedly, she'd just gone limp, rested her head on the seat and sobbed her apology over and over. That had made me even more furious. I wanted her to fight back so I could really hurt her. And then before I knew what I was doing, I yanked up her top and stubbed my cigarette out on her back. Penny had screamed and screamed. It was an awful sound – pain mixed with disbelief and horror. I can almost hear it again now and I try to focus on what Dan's saying, try to blot out that awful memory.

'Don't get me wrong. I like the sea as much as the next person, but I can't see the fun in living by it, miles from anywhere,' Penny drawls and points a chip at me. 'I mean, how do you cope without a big mall or shopping centre on your doorstep? Where do you get your clothes from?' She looks at my jeans and flowery blue cotton top as if they offend her.

I've shaken the memory, but the anger remains. 'I normally go through the bins.' I point at my jeans. 'Sometimes I nick stuff from scarecrows. It's amazing what a bit of washing powder can do though.' I wink at Dan and he guffaws.

'Oh, I didn't mean…' Penny says and has the grace to blush.

Yeah you did. 'Never mind. I'm not bothered about designer this or that. I just wear what I think suits me.'

'Very sensible too.' Dan nods at my shirt. 'That top looks stunning on you, brings out the colour of your eyes.'

Penny looks ready to choke on her chip and downs more wine.

'Thanks, Dan. So, Penny, where are you looking for the cottage? Round here, or further afield?'

'God knows,' Penny mumbles into her glass. 'It's Dan's domain… truth be told, I'm not really that bothered about getting one.'

'You say that now, Pen, but you'll love it. Just think, on a Friday afternoon when I've finished work in the summer, we can get a plane down here and be in the cottage before last orders.'

'Hmm. It sounds like it will take a big chunk of my parents' money though. Not sure it will be worth it… and the weather down here isn't exactly Mediterranean, is it?'

'You like holidays in the sun, Penny?' I finish my steak and push the plate aside.

'Who doesn't? Beats wind and rain any day.'

'I know it's weird, but I do love a wild and windy beach. Calms my soul. More characterful than frying on a sun lounger round a pool and breathing in other people's booze and fart fumes.' I grin, loving the way I'm provoking Penny, but can't help it.

Dan laughs. 'Me too! I get *so* bored on those bloody all-inclusive holidays Penny makes us take.'

Penny winds her neck back, snorts, and folds her arms. 'Oh, excuse me, I had no idea you hated them so much.'

'Hey, I wouldn't go that far. But I do like something to occupy my mind.'

'Yes, me too,' I say. 'I love the warm weather but I also like to go off exploring on holiday. There's so much of Cornwall I haven't even seen properly yet and I've been here nearly twenty years.'

'It's certainly beautiful.' Dan's gaze lingers on my mouth and I excuse myself.

In the Ladies, I look at my flushed face and splash it with cold water. This was so not a good idea. Dan is so obviously attracted to me that even a stranger could see it, let alone his wife. No wonder Penny's a bit spiky. Once they've seen the house they could bugger off because Dan's attention is unwelcome. Unwelcome because I like it, and that's both unexpected and dangerous. It's all to do with the past and being wronged, but then Dan was just as much to blame – why am I attracted to him? He was a shit and still is, probably. In fact, there's no probably. He's married to Penny and giving me the come on. Too long without Adam, that's all it is on my part. Lonely for a hug, a man's arms. I'm just about to leave when Penny comes in.

'Think we're ready to go, if you are.' Penny reapplies her lipstick, fluffs her hair. 'I'll just have a wee and then head to yours, yeah?'

I nod, try not to see the icy chips in my old friend's glance. 'Yeah. Has Dan asked for the bill?'

'All taken care of. Our treat.'

Before I can think better of it I say, 'You okay? I get the feeling you'd really rather not be here or come to mine. I didn't suggest it, you know.'

'Oh, I know. Dan was the eager beaver – was determined to come down here as soon as he saw you again at the reunion.' Penny sighs and closes the cubicle door. I'm glad because my reflection tells me that my face is the colour of Penny's lipstick.

'What do you mean by that?' I say to the door.

'That he fancies his chances, wants to get back into your knickers. Isn't it obvious?'

'Eh? But he…' I'm about to say that he never got into my knickers, which would be a lie. But we never actually slept together, as Penny knows, but it's all a bit academic. Penny's worried that her husband has the hots for me, and she's right to be.

'Oh please. Don't tell me you can't see him practically salivating. He's a randy old dog, always shagging around, and you're the bitch he's set on.' Penny's voice, though sharp and bitter, trembles on the last few words. She unlocks the door and comes out, tears standing in her eyes.

'Oh God, Penny. Why did you come down here if you think that?' Despite everything, I can't help but feel a bit sorry for her. She looks resigned, weary, beaten.

'Because he'd have come anyway, and I want to keep a bloody eye on him.' Penny runs the tap, gives me side eyes. 'On both of you.'

From nowhere, anger flares in my chest. 'Now wait a sodding minute. Just because you did the dirty on me years ago, doesn't mean I'm ready to sink to your level.' Who the fuck does she think she is?

Penny's unfazed. 'You sank pretty low that morning in the school toilets, didn't you?' She puts her hands up. 'Don't get me wrong. I know I deserved it. And why wouldn't you try to take him back? I would in your shoes.' She yanks out too many paper towels and chucks half on the sink.

'Yeah. Well, I'm not you.' *Thank goodness.* How can she say she deserved what I did? She was always too passive. No wonder Dan runs rings round her.

Penny folds her arms, leans against the wall. 'Miss prim and proper, yeah? If you hadn't had been back then, you might be the one married to him now. In fact, you would be. Dan told me a few years after we were married that he'd never love me the way he had you. That he'd made a mistake, just because he'd been thinking with his dick instead of his brain.'

My mouth drops open. Fuck. What do I say to that? 'But that's horrible… why did he marry you if–'

'I asked him that. He said he loved me, but just not in the same way as he had you. He knew there was no getting you back. Told me that he'd tried to find you and discovered you were married, had a kid, so no hope there. I didn't know what to do – it hurt so much, but we muddled along. I tried so hard to make him happy, but he's had lots of affairs over the years. Thinks I don't know. You see, Dan has to be in control of every little thing.' Penny gives a defeated shrug. 'Of his business – which he's made a packet in by the way – his life and, of course, his wife. It suits him to have the dutiful wife at home – a nice respectable front to present to his clients, while he does whatever the hell he likes outside the home.'

I'm incredulous. How can she live like that? 'So why the hell do you stay with him if'

'Because I love him.' Penny throws her hands up and lets them fall with a slap to her hips. 'Same old bloody story. Foolish wife thinks she'll be able to change her husband. One day he'll realise that he's been a bastard, that he's be sorry.' Then she steps forward and gives me a huge hug. 'I can't tell you how sorry I am for taking him from you. You were my best friend and what I did… it made me sick to my stomach.' She steps back and dabs at her eyes with a paper towel. 'But I adored him you see, the first time I laid eyes on him, even before he was your boyfriend. I loved him then, love him now. I'll always love him, no matter what. Stupid cow, eh? I bet you think I deserve everything I get.'

I do to an extent, but mostly I feel pity and sadness. We look at each other and Penny makes a noise in her throat which sounds a cross between a sob and a yelp. Then her shoulders shake, and she flaps a hand at her face.

I say, 'Hey, come on. We were best friends, once. Let's be friends again. I promise you I am not interested in your husband. That was all a very long time ago and Adam was the love of my life, not Dan. You did me a favour, really, because I might never have met him if you hadn't gone off with Dan.' I try a smile.

'Really? Good… but you seemed pretty cosy together just now.' Penny sighs and tries a smile back.

'We were just having a laugh – as friends – that's all there is to it.' I cross my fingers behind my back.

'On your part, not on his, believe me.' Penny's voice is distant, unbearably sad.

'Maybe not. But it takes two to tango, and I'm not dancing.'

Penny smiles again and this time it lights up her face. 'Thank God.' She takes my hand. 'Once again, please believe me that I am so, so sorry for betraying your friendship. I honestly hated myself but couldn't help it… I loved him so much, as I've said.'

'I do believe you. It hurt like hell at the time, but now it's all so much water under the bridge. And for the record, I am so, so sorry about what I did to you… Can we be friends? We had some great times, didn't we?'

'The best. And it's forgotten; we're even.'

Really? Not sure I could forget something like that. I wonder if she still has a little round scar on her back. Then I drop Penny's hand and dab at my eyes. 'Right, come on, Dan will think we've gone to my house without him.' I cock my head to one side, look at Penny through the mirror. 'You know, I could make an excuse – say there's a reason why you can't come after all?'

'No. He'll whine and beg. Best get it over with. And now I know that he's not going to get anywhere with you, I'd love to see your place! I adore Cornwall and the idea of living near the beach.'

I laugh. 'You said you couldn't see why anyone would want to, and–'

'Yeah, I lied.'

The two of us crack up laughing and suddenly it feels as if we're girls again, and all the recriminations between us and the years apart have melted away.

Chapter Six

'You weren't joking when you said this place was special!' Dan paces between the kitchen, balcony, living room and back, excitement flushing his face. 'My God, what I wouldn't give to live here!'

'I'm not selling, I'm afraid,' I say with a little laugh and place a tray of coffee on the kitchen table. I probably should, given my circumstances, but it's not happening.

Penny shakes her head at Dan as if he's a toddler asking for ice cream. 'Even if Sam was selling, we can't afford it – money doesn't grow on trees, you know.'

Dan stops pacing and glowers. 'I know that. Just saying.'

Penny picks up a mug and sips her drink. 'It is stunning though, Sam. You're very lucky. I bet getting up on a summer's morning and looking at the sea from your balcony never gets old.'

'No, it never does. Though summer bypassed me this year without my Adam to share it with.' The 'very lucky' comment was really insensitive to my mind and I couldn't let it pass.

'God, of course not. I didn't think.'

I say not to worry and remind myself that it's only me who remembers the pain of Adam's loss every waking moment. Dan's been given free rein of the place and can be heard oohing and ahhing from one of the bedrooms. Then I think I hear him go outside. I lower my voice and lean forward across the table to Penny. 'I can make an excuse about going to see my grandson when we've finished the coffee if you like, and you can get off.'

Penny shakes her head. 'That's okay. I'm enjoying being here… and what I wouldn't give to have children, a grandchild…'

I might be about to be talk out of turn, but I do wonder about the spat Penny and Dan had at the reunion when children were mentioned. 'It must be hard, Pen. Why didn't Dan want kids?'

Penny shrugs. 'He just said he didn't want them, cost a fortune and restricted what we could do.' She snorts. 'What he could do more like. He knew early on I wanted kids, but always kept saying not yet. Then after we'd been together ten years or so, he had a vasectomy without my knowledge. It was the closest I came to leaving him.'

There are a few choice words waiting on my tongue, but if I say them I'll go into a rant. What a complete bastard! And Penny must have been a bloody fool to stay after that. She is such a pushover. 'I can hardly believe it. So cruel.'

'Yes. Dan could have as many women as he liked after that, no worries of getting them pregnant.'

I grip my coffee mug and try to keep calm. Penny used to be such a self-assured confident girl, before she slept with Dan. That changed her, somehow – she never fought back when I got my revenge, and now? Where was her self-respect? She's become a doormat, a lapdog.

'I know what you're thinking.' Penny gives a sad little smile. 'How can I live like this? But it's simple, I hate what he's done to me, but I can't live without him.'

'You'd get used to it.' I know my voice is harsh, but maybe it's what Penny needs – some home truths. Some poor women have limited choice when they have a swine for a husband – the refuge or put up with it, but Penny must have grounds for a successful divorce. Hadn't she said the other week that Dan had made a mint?

Penny gives me an intense look, shakes her head. 'No. No I wouldn't get used to it. I would *actually* die without him, and I'm not joking.'

A shiver runs down the length of my spine, but before I can reply, Dan bursts in like an over-excited puppy. 'This house is perfect for a small guest house. A few tweaks to the décor and maybe a little extension and Bob's your uncle.'

I raise my eyebrows. 'That's just what Adam used to say.'

'We're in the same game really. Or was, in his case… him being an architect, me a developer. It's obvious what the best use for this house is.'

'I beg to differ. It's my home.'

'Of course it is. But your living quarters could be separate – you'd still have your privacy.'

'Get real, love,' Penny says. 'How could she have her privacy and run a guest house?'

'And why would I want to?'

Dan's face falls and he joins us at the table. 'Hmm, I suppose I'm just saying what I would do if I were you. I'm forgetting you must be well provided for – you don't work, after all. Mortgage all paid for, I assume?'

Penny slaps his arm. 'Dan! It's rude to ask such personal questions.'

It bloody well is, and there's no way I'm telling him the truth. 'You assume right. And I do work. Writing is work.'

Dan looks as if I've made a joke then makes his face straight. 'Oh yeah, course it is.' He looks away and then back, with the excited puppy expression. 'Tell you what a better idea would be than a guest house.' Penny and I glance at each other and roll our eyes. 'A writer's retreat! One of my mates worked on one in the Lakes not long back. Writers go and stay for a few days, recharge their batteries, meet like-minded people, get ideas, do some writing and have a great time. This place is ideal for one of those.'

Hasn't he been listening? I've had enough. 'Yes, I know what a writer's retreat is, but, for goodness' sake, Dan, this is my home. Can we change the subject?'

He puts his hands up. 'Never mind. Just an idea.' Then drains his coffee and steps out onto the balcony, points at some houses on the cliff opposite. 'Any holiday cottages up there?'

I lean my forehead against the cool of the door's glass after I close it behind Penny and Dan, and exhale a long sigh of relief. They were only here an hour, but it feels like three. Being polite and holding my tongue has drained me, and I need a lie down. Being with Dan in exuberant mode is like being caught in a whirlwind. He was just the same as a young man, but then I found it exciting. Now I find him ridiculously annoying most of the time. Any spark of attraction I'd felt in the restaurant has been doused. It doesn't help knowing what a shit he was, and had been for years. Poor Penny.

I put the cups in the dishwasher and think about the conversation with my old friend. Yes, Dan was a shit and no mistake about it, but then Penny must shoulder some of the blame, surely? She has indulged him from the off and let him do whatever the hell he liked. Even knows about his affairs but won't confront him. Where is her pride? The look in her eyes when she'd said that she would actually die without him scared me. What exactly did that mean? I shudder and put it out of my mind. I'd agreed to meet once more – Penny's suggestion – because she wanted to meet Helena and little Adam before they went back up north. The rest of this week would be spent looking for holiday cottages, but they'd go back early the week after and pop in to visit on their way home. Sorry as I feel for Penny, with any luck they wouldn't find a cottage and that would be the last I'd ever see of them.

Right. I can't put this off any longer. I pick up my phone to call Naomi, my old boss, and arrange to meet. I need that job, and fast.

Chapter Seven

'I can't wait to see your old boyfriend. It feels weird realising you were a fun young person with boyfriends before you were a mother and wife.'

I turn from the sea and catch my daughter's mischievous smile and cheeky twinkle. 'I see. So, when you become a mother and wife, you become old and boring?'

'No, just you, Mum. *I'll* always be young and exciting, even though I'm married with a child.'

I pretend to clip her across the head and then slip my arm through Helena's, as we walk up the beach towards The Catch café. Adam looks down at me from his perch in the carrier on his mum's back and dribbles from a gummy smile. 'You are so cute I could eat you, young man.' I laugh and dab at his mouth with a tissue. 'Oh look, you've dribbled all over your mummy's hair. Serves her right for being a cheeky monkey.'

'Baby dribble is the new conditioner, don't you know?' Helena says with a smile. Then she sighs. 'This Dan. Is he really as horrible as Penny's making out, do you think?'

'I have no reason to think otherwise.'

Helena stops and puts her head on one side. 'I have.'

'What do you mean?' I wrest a hank of windswept hair from my eyes.

'She might be so scared of losing him to you that she's made the whole thing up about his affairs. Not thought about that one, have you, Ma?'

'I can't see that…' I shake my head and make to set off again, but Helena puts her hand on my arm.

'Think about it. She lied and did the dirty on you all those years ago, she must be terrified of losing him to you now. You – a much prettier and nicer person than she is. You said it was obvious he was attracted to you at lunch that day. Makes sense for her to lie again.'

'Hmm. She seemed pretty honest when she was upset in the Ladies. You can't fake that kind of crying, can you?' I decide not to tell my daughter that Penny revealed Dan had said he'd always loved me more than his wife.

Helena snorts and sets off again. 'You're so trusting and naïve. No wonder you didn't see it coming all those years ago.'

That rankles. Does Helena think I'm dumb? 'I try to take people at face value and believe what they say,' I call after her.

Over her shoulder she says, 'Of course you do, and I wouldn't have you any other way. I'm just saying don't take everything Penny tells you as gospel.'

I catch up to her and we walk on in silence for a bit then Helena says, 'I'm a pretty good judge of character. I'll know if he's a shit or not in five minutes flat.'

I very much doubt that. 'Right, course you will. Anyway, after today I'm hoping they'll bugger off back to Sheffield and that will be it.'

'Not if they've managed to get a holiday cottage. Must have some dosh.'

'They do. But this place is coming from Penny's parents' estate.'

'Nice.' Just before we get to the road, Helena stops again. 'Mum, don't fly off the handle, but I saw your old boss yesterday in Sainsbury's.'

My heart plummets. If Naomi has splurged all my money worries to my daughter, I'll…

'Why didn't you tell me what Dad had done? I had no idea you were so badly off.'

Fuck. So much for keeping it all a secret. I take a deep breath, but it does no good and my anger spills out with a torrent of words.

Amanda James

'Bloody Naomi! How dare she tell you my financial situation? This is *not* what I wanted at all!'

'She assumed I knew.' The hurt in Helena's voice is unmistakable.

I hadn't thought of this scenario. Shit. I make my voice gentler. 'I didn't tell you because I didn't want you to worry. I thought I could get a job and then tell you. There'd be no need for you to worry once I was earning again. But there are no vacancies back at my old library, as I'm sure she told you. I'll have to look elsewhere. Plus, there are plenty of other things I could turn my hand to.'

Helena's brow furrows and the sympathy in her eyes makes me look away. 'Like what, Mum?'

'Loads of stuff. There are other libraries in Cornwall, you know, and if not then I'll work in a shop, stack shelves, clean floors. I will make it work. I always do.'

Helena tries a smile. 'I know you will… but you could just sell the house though, that would be the most sensible soluti–'

'No bloody way!' My raised voice makes a woman walking her dog glance in our direction. I see the hurt in Helena's eyes and the surprise in Adam's and silently curse Naomi. 'Hey, I'm sorry. I didn't mean to shout. I just wanted to keep it from you until it was all sorted.'

'Don't apologise. I know you did. I want you to know that I am here for you, Carl too. If there's anything at all we can do. We don't have many savings, but–'

I put my hands up. There was no sodding way I'd ever borrow money from my child. 'Thanks, love, but we're not at that stage yet, and we won't be.' I find a smile from somewhere. 'Come on then. Let's go and have coffee with my old shithead boyfriend and his lying wife you're so eager to meet!'

As we walk into the café, Dan grins and leaps up from a table by the window as if he's on springs. 'Sam, over here!' He waves us over and pulls out two chairs.

Penny raises a hand but stays seated. We wave back, and Helena says from the corner of her mouth, 'He's a bit of all right for an old guy. Can't say the same for frumpy drawers though.'

48

I give her an elbow dig and try not to burst out laughing. Penny stands up, hand outstretched. Helena shakes it. 'Hi, Penny, Mum's told me all about you.'

I cringe inwardly, then Helena gives Dan her biggest and brightest smile. 'And you too, Dan.'

Dan gets predictably flirty, saying how much she looks like me when I was younger, and kisses the back of Helena's hand. Penny rolls her eyes at me behind his back, and I laugh. Then they both say how wonderful Adam is and I ask the lady behind the counter for a high chair.

After we order, Helena gives me a cheeky wink and asks what I was like as a kid. Penny shakes her head and pulls down the corners of her mouth. 'She was a bloody nightmare. Always getting into trouble with the teachers, and your grandparents were always in school in front of the Head.'

Dan nods vigorously. 'Yeah, God knows how she didn't get expelled.'

Helena looks at their straight faces and raises her eyebrows. I busy myself with Adam so my daughter can't see I'm desperately hiding a smile. Dan is the first to crack out laughing, shortly followed by Penny. 'No. We're pulling your leg. She was the perfect student really!'

Helena smiles, though her words hold no humour. 'I knew that. Mum's told me… shall we say bits and pieces about those days. Particularly the latter years.'

I flash a warning at her and change the subject with a bright and breezy, 'Any luck with the holiday house?'

Dan grins. 'We have indeed, a lovely little place overlooking Fistral Beach!' He pauses while the waitress sets the coffee and cake on the table and my heart sinks. I'll never be rid of them now. 'Stunning views hasn't it, Pen?'

Penny looks much less enthusiastic than her husband. 'It does, but we haven't plans to buy it at the moment. We're not sure if it's right for us so we're just renting until we decide.' She stirs her coffee and offers a fake smile.

'You mean *you're* not sure,' Dan says. 'Penny's a bit wary about dipping into her parents' legacy, hey, dear?' The glare he shoots his wife could curdle milk and I share a knowing look with Helena.

Penny sighs and turns her back on her husband, leans across to Adam. 'Just being cautious that's all… one of us has to be. Anyway, if you're so determined, take it out of the business profits.' Then her face lights up as Adam slaps a sticky hand on hers. 'Oh, what a darling boy! How gorgeous are you?'

I watch Penny with Adam as I pour tea and pass a cup to Helena and Dan. Penny's cooing and giggling, a smile on her face as wide as the sky. The woman clearly adores kids and it must have been so hard for her to go through life without children of her own. I can't imagine what my life would be without my children and grandson, particularly now after losing my darling husband.

Helena blows across her cup, puts on her mischievous face and looks at Dan. I nearly choke on the cake. Oh God, now what?

'In the end, I suppose that's the secret of a good marriage though. You know, being able to compromise,' she says. Innocent enough but I know my daughter.

Dan frowns. 'Not sure I get you.'

'You agreed to rent instead of buy. The best of both worlds.'

Dan snorts and leans back in his chair. 'As I said, I want to buy, but Penny has a tight rein on the bloody purse strings. Yes, we have other money, but I need that for earmarked investments.' His face darkens in barely concealed frustration and Penny raises her cooing and ahhing a level. If she is attempting to cover the awkward silence, she's failing.

'Oh, I see. Sorry, I didn't mean to chuck a spanner in the works.' Helena turns her bottom lip down and shrugs.

I can tell that's exactly what Helena wanted to do. Of course, it's to be expected that Helena wants to hurt them in some way because they betrayed me all those years ago, but it seems a bit pointless really. What good will it do?

'Don't worry about it.' Dan waves his hand dismissively. 'You weren't to know that my wife has her own account with a shed load of dosh in it I can't access.'

Penny falls silent and I notice her back stiffen. Helena looks sheepish, as well she might, and Dan's jaw is jumping where he's clenching his teeth. When we were together all those years ago, I always knew that was a sign he was barely holding it together. Time to head things off at the pass. 'If you have a place overlooking Fistral it must be pretty special, so that's all that matters really,' I say with what I hope is a winning smile.

'Yes. Must be stunning,' Helena chips in, obviously realising she's gone too far.

The tense atmosphere unwinds a little. Penny starts talking to Adam again and Dan unclenches his jaw, digs his fork into his chocolate cake and says, 'It is stunning, yes.' Then through a huge mouthful adds, 'Nowhere near as wonderful as your mum's place though.'

'It does take some beating, hey, Mum?' Helena says.

'I wouldn't want to live anywhere else.' I allow my shoulders to come down from my ears and I tuck into the cake once more.

'Still reckon it would make a fabulous retreat though.' Dan winks at me and dabs a napkin to the corners of his mouth.

'Retreat?' Helena frowns.

Oh great. Not this again.

'Yes, I said to your mum when we visited the other day what a fantastic writing retreat it would make. I've since thought that a nice little bungalow down the end... you know, in the overgrown part of that huge garden that's not in use. It would work well. It has a great view, that end being raised as it is, and a veranda would provide a wonderful writing space with views of the ocean. That way the retreat would be totally separate and so the guests wouldn't have to bother your mum at all. Unless she wanted to offer tuition of course. It could sometimes be used as a holiday let too.'

I try to block out the animated conversation batting back and forth between my daughter and Dan. Dan's gushing about what else he would do if he had half a chance, and she's hanging on every word. Dear God. And to think that she said on the beach she'd know if he was a shit or not in five seconds flat. I try to engage Penny in conversation, but she's too smitten by Adam to say much, so I finish my cake and push my plate away, lost in my own thoughts.

'Mum, what do you think?'

I look at Helena's shiny eyes and excited expression. 'About what?'

'Haven't you been listening?' Helena heaves a sigh.

'I must admit I did switch off a bit. I heard you two jabbering on about making my house into a writing retreat – not interested.'

'But why the hell not? It would make a lot of sense to let Dan buy into your place. Under the circumstances it would be the perfect solution.'

Dan's eyebrows go up at this as fast as my stomach plummets. Dear God, she's not going to tell him, is she?

'What circumstances?' Dan pushes his plate away, leans forward.

I shake my head and glare at my daughter, but Helena either doesn't notice or chooses not to. 'Mum could use the money, what with the situation Dad left her in.' Helena sighs and gives me an encouraging smile. 'She doesn't like to say anything, being such a strong woman, but everyone needs a little help now and then, a nudge in the right direction.' She turns her smile on Dan next. 'Your plan would be ideal. There's no way Mum should turn you down if she wants to stay in that house.' Then she goes on to briefly explain what happened.

I put my head in my hands and heave a sigh. How could she? No. How bloody dare she! Dan's prattling on about fate and serendipity and then his hand is on my shoulder. 'At least think about it, love. We are old friends, so there's trust already and you know Pen and I only have your best interests at heart. If you came into business with me, there'd be no fear of losing anything. It would be a win-win for everyone,' he says in a soothing voice.

That was it. The fury I've been holding back is unleashed into the café. It's harsh, hungry and out for blood. 'Trust! That's bloody rich! I trusted the pair of you when we were kids and look how that turned out for me. The first chance you get, my first love and best friend shag each other's brains out behind my back!' I suddenly realise I'm standing up and waving my arms about. There's pin-drop silence. People are gawping, but I couldn't give a shit. Then I turn to Helena. 'And you!' I stab a finger through the air. 'How could you spill it all like that? After everything we talked about on the beach.'

Helena opens and closes her mouth goldfish-like for a few seconds and her eyes fill. Then Adam sends up a wail. He's not used to Granny shouting at his mummy. Some people have started to talk again but most are still watching the spectacle. A lump of humiliation and frustration rises in my throat and I just have to get out of here. Fast. Blinking away unshed tears, I grab my coat and bag, knocking a chair sideways in my hurry and barge out of the café. Helena calls me back and I think Dan says something about going after me. There's no bloody way I'll let that happen and I take off like a hare up the steep road home.

Once inside the house, I slam and lock the door, then slide my back down it and collapse in a heap on the cool ceramic tiles.

'That was bloody marvellous wasn't it, Sam? Not your finest fucking hour.'

My words ring hollow in the empty hallway. An ocean of tears wait, but I'll be damned if I'll let them fall. And why should I feel in any way to blame? Okay, so I'd made a holy show of myself in the local café, but only as a response to Helena's outrageous behaviour. Had she taken leave of her senses? And as for Dan? There were no words for his little speech…

God knows what Penny's reaction had been, I hadn't even looked at her, but I can bet it wouldn't have been favourable. Come into business with Pen and me, he'd said. *Him* he meant. Penny would rather eat a dead dog than have her wayward husband invest in this house. I haul myself up and head for the gin. There's no way Dan will ever get his grubby little hands on any part of this house unless it's over my dead body, and I have no plan of shuffling off this mortal coil just yet.

Neat gin in hand, I go outside, lean my elbows on the balcony rail and stare out over the Atlantic to where the navy horizon meets the azure afternoon sky. I take deep breaths of sea air and wish for the millionth time that Adam were still here by my side.

'God, why did you have to die, Adam?' I ask the bottom of my glass.

The glass doesn't answer, neither does God. I toss the last of the gin down my throat and cough as it goes down the wrong way. Banging the glass down on the table I shove my fingers through my hair and close my eyes. What a bloody mess, but no point in asking stupid questions and wallowing. Nevertheless, I say to the sea, 'You're on your own, lass, so what the hell are you going to do, eh?'

Right now, I have no clue. But one thing is for sure, I'd better hurry up and find one.

Chapter Eight

June. How can it be June already? I put the calendar back on the wall and look at the cheery picture on it. A verdant meadow speckled with wild colourful summer flowers and a glimpse of blue ocean in the distance. Underneath is written *June on the South West Coast Path*. Adam and I used to walk that path, used to stroll through meadows like that. Everything is "used to" nowadays, always in the past. Never now. Used to, and I feel useless.

Three months of job hunting has turned up a handful of possibilities, none of them libraries because the government has a pathological hatred of them it seems, what with the rate they're closing them down. Soon they will be all gone. If I'm honest, even if I'd got a post, it wouldn't pay enough to keep the wolf from the door. Adam's salary had paid for most things and without it, things looked bleak. There had only been a few shop assistant posts and a few cleaning jobs come up in the area. I'd kidded myself that if I did two or three jobs at once I'd cope, but I wouldn't. Besides, I'd be so tired I wouldn't have time to spend with Helena and Adam. And writing? Forget it.

I smooth out a fold in the calendar and heave a sigh. Time to be realistic. Time to end this idealistic "brave Sam against the world making it work" battle.

Time to sell up.

There's a knock behind me at the kitchen door.

'Helena, hi. Didn't hear you come in.' I re-hang the calendar and walk to the sink.

'Blimey, Mum, you sound really down this morning.'

'That's because I am.' I point to the kettle and Helena nods. 'Where's my lovely boy?'

Helena hoists herself up onto a worktop. 'Wonders will never cease, but Carl's got two days owing so he's taken our boy to the beach.'

'That'll be nice. Some father-son bonding time.' I try to inject some enthusiasm into my voice, but I know it sounds flat, empty, ironed out.

'No luck with the job hunt then, I'm guessing?' Helena puts her head on one side and the sympathy in her eyes kicks me in the gut. I hate being pitied.

'No. I'm particularly down today because I have made a decision to sell up.' I raise my voice above the kettle, but Helena appears not to have heard.

'You what?'

'I said I have decided to–'

'Yes, I heard what you said, but I didn't believe it. You can't, Mum! You've fought so hard to keep going and you'll get there in the end.'

That's rich. 'Eh? You said I should sell up when you first knew about my financial problems.'

'I know, but that was before I saw how determined you were to keep this place. You even turned down Dan's perfectly good offer.'

'Yes, because I was living in Cloud Delusional Land.' I pour water into the cups.

Helena jumps down from the counter and gets milk from the fridge. 'Are you saying you'd reconsider?'

'God, no. I'd rather sell than let him own part of this place.'

Helena shakes her head, fixes me with a hard stare just like her dad's. 'That makes no fucking sense whatsoever.'

'No need to get on your high horse.'

'There is when you are behaving illogically!'

'What's illogical about not wanting a controlling self-centred egotistical womaniser taking over your home?' I bang my mug down on the table and wish I hadn't. I grab a cloth and mop up the mess.

'He wouldn't be taking it over.' Helena takes the cloth and rinses it through. 'You never really listened to what he wanted to do, did you? He would own part of it, that's all. Then he'd build a bungalow in the garden and he'd run the business from that. You would be able to live a separate life if you wanted, or instead you could offer tuition. You could even run the business if you wanted more of an input… rent it as a holiday let sometimes… You and he would share the profits… He's really very flexible about–'

'You seem to have remembered an awful lot of details about it all.' I have a sneaking suspicion that there've been further conversations that I've not been privy to. Dan was deceitful enough.

Helena's cheeks colour and she comes to sit at the table. 'Yes, a few weeks back he phoned to ask how you were. He's kept in contact now and then.'

I knew it. 'He bloody what!'

Helena holds her hand up. 'Mum, he's worried about you, and since you blocked him on social media and on your phone, he's no option.'

'What's the matter with you? I thought after last time when you told him all about my sodding problems that you'd learnt your lesson. But no. No, you're having cosy little chats about my well-being behind my back with that bloody conniving snake!' I see Helena's face fall, but I can't believe my daughter is so gullible.

'Mum, he genuinely cares about you. He told me last week how much he regretted hurting you all those years ago and wants to do something to make amends.'

'The only person he cares about is himself. He told Penny that he never loved anyone like he loved me and wants me back. Didn't know that, did you? Worming his way into my property would be a very big step along those lines. He wants me to feel beholden to him. Grateful. And how do you think he'd want me to show that gratitude? Have a guess.'

'But then, as I said on the beach that day, can you believe everything she says? You told me that she puts up with his affairs, makes him out to be this controlling ogre. But what if he isn't? What if he doesn't have affairs. What if he genuinely cares about you – just as friends. Or maybe more than that. Maybe he does still love you, I don't know. But you can bet Penny's just jealous to death, terrified that he'll fall for you and so she's trying to make sure you keep away.'

'He's done a right number on you, has our Dan. You've fallen for his blarney, hook line and sinker.' *Just like I always did.* I drain what's left in my cup, try to keep my cool.

Helena carries on regardless. 'You're in control. Mum. You. Even if he does still carry a torch, you don't have to light it for him. Take his money, everything will be drawn up legally – get Robert's brother, what's-his-name, to do it, then you'll be sure. Run the business, don't run it. Whatever. But his investment in this place will mean you don't have to leave. You can carry on with your writing with no financial worries. I'll be here for you if you think he's coming on too strong.' She puts her hand on my arm. 'At least think about it… please, Mum. You'd be so miserable if you had to say goodbye to your home.'

Miserable wasn't the right word. I'd be utterly devastated. Adam is here. His essence lives in the walls, the floors, the fabric of the building. Sometimes his laughter can be heard on the breeze outside as I sit quietly on the balcony. If I really concentrate, I can feel his arms wrapped around me in the bed we'd shared. If I got a new place there'd be no sign of him. He'd be truly gone. On a bad day, sometimes I really have to concentrate to even see his face, so what would it be like if I left everything we'd shared behind? Every day would be a bad day. Bad days lead down dark roads. The kind of roads you need pills for. The pills I swore I'd never go back to.

'Mum?'

'Hmm?'

'Will you think about it?'

Would I? Thinking wasn't doing, was it? Thinking wasn't making any rash decisions. And as Helena said, I was in control. Just because Dan may or may not have romantic notions about me, doesn't mean that it has anything to do with me. His feelings were his own concern. It would be a business venture and that would be it. Robert's brother, William, was a solicitor and an old friend. He'd have my interests at heart.

'Mum?' Helena asks again, her eyes imploring.

'Okay. I'll think about it.'

***

Hard to believe that a month ago felt like the end of the world. July feels like a new start. A start not without its worries, after all, as Dan now owns twenty-five per cent of the property, but I have two hundred thousand pounds in the bank. This means that all my writing dreams are now back on track, and I'm even considering doing a few tutorials when the bungalow retreat is built. It's a new challenge and I could do with one. As long as Dan keeps his distance, all will be perfect.

I push the last bit of bacon from my breakfast onto a slice of toast and consider Dan. So far, he's been very business-like and well behaved. Penny, however, hasn't been in touch, and every time I've asked after her, Dan's been evasive. Said she was busy. In the end, Penny refused to give him the money from her account, so he had to abandon one or two of his other investments to complete the deal. This had not pleased him in the least. Perhaps they'd had a huge row about it all and Penny was washing her hands of everything. In the end I don't give a damn, it's time to put worries in the past and concentrate on the future. If Penny wants to stay with a man who she says is cheating on her and controlling, then that's her look out. We had been friends once, and I hoped we could be again, but things change. People change.

William had made a fair and good deal that had protected me and my future assets. Dan had to put his name to an agreement where if anything should happen to him or Penny, there wouldn't be a hundred relatives crawling out of the woodwork demanding a piece of my pie. When I'm gone, the house will be Helena and Jack's, less twenty-five per cent, of course, when it's sold. That would go to Dan and Penny if they survived her. There was no way she'd be forced to sell the house either, so all looked set fair for the foreseeable.

Today is the day I aim to get back on track with the writing. Until this morning I hadn't felt like it. But now the dust has settled on the deal I believe I can try to get back to normal. Okay, more tea, a packet of biscuits just in case and the laptop. On the way into the kitchen, the phone rings in the hallway. Damn. That's all I need. To my surprise, it's Penny, though I have to strain my ears to make sense of what she's saying through her hiccupping sobs.

'Penny, take a few deep breaths and have a drink of water. You're not making sense, love.'

There's the sound of water running and then a few seconds later, Penny comes back on the line. 'Dan's threatened to leave me.' Her voice is wobbly but at least she's coherent now.

'Why? What's happened?' I'm sympathetic, but part of me thinks it might be just as well.

'I...' There's another sob. 'I asked him if he still loved you and he wouldn't give me a straight answer. Then he said that I didn't love him because I refused to give him my parents' money to put into the retreat.'

I roll my eyes at my reflection in the living room mirror and wonder what to say next. 'I'm sorry to hear that, Penny. What did you say?'

'I said that I adored him, and why did he think that I'd stayed with him all these years if I didn't? I mentioned all the women he'd had, all the tricks he'd pulled, how he'd stopped me ever having the chance to be a m-m-mother.'

I sigh, flop down on the sofa. 'Yes, you'd have to adore him to put up with all that.'

'Yeah. But then he says that any woman worth their salt would have left him years ago.' Penny's voice is still heavy with emotion, but it's anger this time. 'He said that he despised me for being weak, spineless. Allowing him to do all those things and just behaving like a little lapdog. But then when it mattered, I wouldn't give him the money. And it really got to me when he said, "Poor, sad old cow. Trying to assert your control over me with that pot of money. A bit late to try to grow a pair." Then he slapped me!'

Penny descends into a fresh bout of sobbing and I have no clue how to stop it. What a bastard! Physical violence too, how can she stand it? 'Oh Penny, I can't believe he hit you – and what an awful thing to say. I'm so sorry, Pen.' I raise my voice over her sobs to make myself heard. Lame, but what else is there?

'Vile,' Penny spits and then calms down a little. 'He's a real bastard when he wants to be. I told him there was no way I'd ever leave him because I love him so much. Didn't he see that? Even though he hit me – mind you, he hasn't done that for years.' Oh well that's okay then. 'Then I explained that I didn't give him the money because I was worried he was after you.' I shake my head and closed my eyes. The poor woman is torturing herself unnecessarily. 'He just snorted at that and so I asked if now, because he'd got stakes in your place, he'd be seeing you more often, and would he try to get back with you?'

Okay, enough. 'Look, Penny, no matter if Dan does have notions in that regard, there's no way that I'd encourage it. As I keep saying, I have no interest in him whatsoever. I needed the money, yes, and now I have it. We've got a business arrangement and that's all.'

'I know, you keep saying that. But he can be very persuasive, you know.' There's a deep sigh on the line. 'But then I don't expect you to understand. Until you lost your lovely husband, everything in your life was wonderful. You have a daughter and grandchild to get you through the bad times. You've come out the other end stronger and determined to make a life for yourself. I'm just not like you.'

How dare she just assume I'm out the other end. In fact, what the fuck does that even mean? Before I can think twice, I say, 'I haven't *just* sailed through, you know. And I think I still have a bit of a way to go. When I lost Adam, my world fell apart. Yes, I had my daughter, but she was grieving too. There's only so much you can share. Too much and you both go under, sink into the black hole that Adam left. It nearly swallowed me up. In the end I turned to sleeping pills and antidepressants. Booze too, anything to stop the pain, blot out reality…' My voice trails off. Why the hell did I just share this? I'd finished with all that months ago, why go back there? Penny doesn't need to know.

'Oh, so sorry, love. I didn't mean to suggest that it had been easy.' A pause. 'So are you still on the pills and–'

'No. I came off them all ages ago. I still have a drink, but so does everyone.' I want to minimise the damage my blabbermouth has done. 'You won't tell anyone will you? About the tablets…'

'Of course not. But there's nothing to be ashamed of.'

I cringe. 'I know that. It's just that it reminds me of when I was at my lowest.' I swallow. 'There were a few times that I thought I wouldn't make it.' More than a few. And there I go again giving out more information than is required.

'Your secret's safe with me.' Great, now she thinks she's my conspirator. 'Just like mine is safe with you.'

'Secret?'

'Yeah, what I told you about him threatening to leave me. If he ever did there'd be no amount of pills that would help me. As I said before, I can't live without him.'

This again – how dramatic. 'I'm sure you'd come to terms with it in the end. I've had to go on without Adam.' I tried to make that sound sympathetic, but I've had enough of Penny for now. And to be honest, Dan's right. She is spineless – his lapdog, cringing when he slaps her, licking his hand when he's nice.

'Hmm. Anyway, I've decided I'm going to try to make it up with Dan when he gets in. Then we'll come down to you soon, have a good catch up. If he sees that I'm not worried about him and you, then things will be better I'm sure.'

Oh joy, a catch up. Can't wait. 'Yes, good idea.'

'Speak soon, Sam. Bye.'

The positive mood I had just before the phone call has buggered off. So much for getting down to writing. On the other hand, some of this pent-up frustration and grumpiness could be worked off by plotting a murder. The murder scene isn't planned for another few chapters, but I think I'll bring it forward. I can do the research at least. Yes, that's what I'll do. A good murder always cheers me up.

Chapter Nine

The first dinner party in this house without Adam will feel odd, but life must go on. My feelings are mixed though. Despite the empty space at the table, and in my heart, part of me is happy that tonight the house will be full of chatter and laughter once more. I pull out a kitchen chair and carefully lift the best crockery down from the top shelf. Daft really. Adam always used to say I should use it every day, but then when we had guests it wouldn't feel special I'd told him. A pang of longing to hear him say that again brings moisture to my eyes and I concentrate on the task at hand.

Guests tonight will include Jack and his new girlfriend, Felicity, who he met at university, Naomi, my old library boss, Helena, Carl and little Adam – though he'll probably be asleep for most of it – and Penny and Dan. The latter had invited himself and his wife when he heard about my intention to have a dinner party when they visited last week. Penny hadn't been too sure, but at the time I couldn't think of an excuse to decline them fast enough. Apart from saying that it was rude to invite yourself anywhere. Given that would make me rude, I'd said they would be welcome. When will I ever learn?

Thinking about it, though, Penny had been more like she used to be when they'd popped over for coffee last week and Dan had been as charming as ever, though not flirty which was a relief. When he'd popped to the loo, I'd asked Penny how things were between them and she'd said much better. After he'd returned from work the day Penny had phoned me, she'd apologised to him and admitted she was overreacting about him and me. She'd promised to back off and trust him. He'd apparently said he'd stay with her as long as she stuck to her word. Everything in the garden for now was lovely. I'd believe it when I saw it.

I chop onions for the lasagne and wonder if the largest dish will be big enough for eight adults and a toddler. Perhaps I should do an extra one in a small dish. Then I wonder if Felicity likes lasagne, I'd never even thought to ask my son if she ate meat. Oh God, what could I give her in case she was a veggie? I go to the fridge and am uninspired by the alternative my brain comes up with. A veggie frittata and salad? It would have to do. No point in getting anxious about something that might never happen. Jack had only ever brought one girl home and that was when he was a sixth-former. Julianna, I seem to remember. That dinner had been a disaster, as the girl had been so nervous she'd been practically mute. Adam had tried his best to joke with her and make conversation, Helena had too, but Julianna had just smiled and blushed scarlet. Hopefully Felicity wouldn't be the same. Even if she was, the others would take up the slack – Dan in particular was no shrinking violet.

All the prep done, and the table laid, I'm in the bedroom agonising over my outfit. What shall I go for, smart casual or more dressy? Smart casual, I think. Then I think why the hell am I getting so worked up about it all. It's only a dinner party. Yes, I want to make a good first impression on Felicity for Jack's sake, but there's no point in getting screwed up over it.

Eventually I'm decided on black trousers and a red figure-hugging top, I look at my reflection in the cheval mirror. Yes, I'll do. I've twisted my glossy dark curls into a chignon and carefully applied make-up. Not bad for a woman nearing her forty-sixth birthday. Suddenly the nerves are back twisting my stomach tighter than the chignon. It's because Adam's not at my side. If he were here, he'd be chilling the wine, letting the red breathe, checking they had beer too, pottering about asking me if I needed help. I watch my eyes fill with an ocean of tears, but I'm determined not to let them fall. I snatch the clip from my hair and shake it loose. Perhaps the rest of me will follow suit.

Helena, Carl and Adam are the first to arrive and Helena lends a hand while Carl watches *Peppa Pig* with Adam. Naomi arrives next and talks non-stop about anything and everything while I'm trying to concentrate on making sure the garlic bread isn't burning. Naomi is lovely, but she takes no prisoners. I've forgiven her for telling Helena about my money worries, because she hadn't meant it maliciously. That's what Naomi's like; blunt, and straight to the point. Naomi has been divorced about six months and is still single. I invited her after Dan invited himself and Penny, to make me not having a partner less obvious. Stupid really. What difference did it make?

Good, everything is ready, and the glass of wine Helena poured earlier for me is helping to relax the knot in my tummy. Naomi's conversation is now less machine-gun attack, due to her downing her own glass in less than five minutes, I guess. Perhaps she's nervous too. And darling Adam is holding court from his high chair. Just Jack, Felicity, Dan and Penny to come now. As if on cue, the doorbell jangles and all four come in together behind Carl who'd let them in. Jack hurries over and gives me a big kiss on the cheek and swings me round, much to my embarrassment. Felicity is introduced – a tall willowy blonde with model good looks. She's bubbly and smiley, and I like her immediately. Dan and Penny step forward for a hug too. Hers is warm, his is brief and rigid. He barely looks me in the eye; instead he turns on the charm and takes over from Adam in the holding court stakes.

At the table, I'm relieved that Felicity isn't vegetarian, and the atmosphere is relaxed. Any worries about awkwardness amongst the very different guests are unfounded. Adam is sleeping soundly in my bedroom and Helena and Carl are looking into each other's eyes now and then, like a couple of teenagers. It's nice to see that they are so much in love still.

Everyone else seems to be getting along well, though I keep noticing Jack giving Dan side eyes and whispering to a giggling Felicity when Dan says something a bit pompous… which is often. I've also noticed Naomi's reaction to Dan and it's much more favourable than my son's. Something else for Penny to fret about.

I can't help noticing how handsome her husband looks tonight, however. He's wearing a green shirt which is his colour, and he's acquired a light tan that makes his smile even more dazzling. His mother was Spanish, I remember, and he looks every inch the dashing Mediterranean lover tonight. Dan catches me staring and he gives a knowing smile. I avert my eyes, mortified. What the hell am I thinking? I know what a shit he is and all the stuff I've said to Penny about not wanting him is true, so I need to get my libido in check. That's all it is, lust. At least I know I still have functioning parts of my anatomy that have been dormant for some time. That thought makes me snort into my wine which I quickly disguise as a cough.

'More drinks for anyone?' I say during a lull in conversation. If I keep the drinks flowing, the happy atmosphere should continue while I'm busy. The starters are over, and I need to get the lasagne from the oven, the salad from the fridge, and generally faff about being the hostess with the mostest. I don't want to disturb Helena and Carl by asking for help either.

'I'll see to the drinks, you've enough to do, Sam,' Dan says and tops up Naomi's glass. 'I'll get another bottle.' He winks at Naomi and says to me, 'In the kitchen?'

I nod but feel uncomfortable. It's as if he's assuming the host's role and that would be like a red rag to Penny. 'Yes, but don't worry, I'll get—'

'I'll help,' say Felicity and Penny at the same time and then they burst out laughing. Jack jumps up too and starts to clear away the plates. In the end, there are too many bodies in the kitchen, but it's better than just Dan's.

The lasagne was a triumph according to Dan and everyone agreed, and my strawberry pavlova and clotted cream went down equally well. Felicity had said it was the best she'd ever tasted, and now we're in the living room with coffee and brandy. Listening to the buzz of two or three conversations around the room, I swirl my brandy glass and wonder if I've already had too much. I try to remember how many glasses of wine I had during dinner and think it was three… yes, and with this bucket of brandy too, hmm. Never mind, you only live once. I kick off my heels and tip the recliner back.

'Hey, look at our hostess relaxing there. Don't you have washing-up to do?' Dan asks with a laugh.

'That's your job, mate,' Jack says, grinning but I see little humour in his eyes.

'I don't mind mucking in, young Jack,' Dan replies, an edge to his voice.

'Let's not worry about that now,' Naomi says. 'Do tell us what you're writing at the moment, Sam. I seem to remember the other week you saying it was a suspense?'

I feel my cheeks burning as all turn expectant eyes my way. 'I don't think everyone wants to hear about that.'

'Yes we do!' Felicity says, leaning forward on the sofa. 'Jack's told me all about your books and I downloaded your latest on my Kindle yesterday. I've read the first chapter and it's really very good.'

This is music to my ears, but I still feel a bit self-conscious. 'Thanks so much, Felicity. It's great when people tell me they enjoy my work.'

'So what's the new one about then? Any juicy murders in it?' Dan asks.

This makes me laugh. 'Funny you should say that because I planned a murder scene only the other week.' *Inspired by your paranoid wife's phone call.* I glance at Penny – thankful she can't read thoughts.

'Come on, spill it, Mum,' Helena says, leaning her head on Carl's shoulder.

'I can't say too much in case you all want to read it!'

'But you don't have to say who murders who… or should that be whom?' Jack puzzles.

'Okay, okay. One character murders another and makes it look like suicide. Without them knowing, this character puts drugs in the other's drink – antidepressants, sleeping tablets etc, and then they go swimming at midnight in the sea. Once the drugs take hold, the baddie slits the wrists of this character and he or she drowns.' I notice Penny's look of distaste, but see the others are intrigued and hurry on. 'It's not gory, though, in fact the death scene is quite beautiful.' I ruffle my hair and out comes a rather self-conscious laugh. 'Well, I hope it is. As the character is dying, he or she is floating in the ocean looking up at the stars, drowsy but content, contemplating the beauty of the universe.'

'What, with their wrists slashed? They'd be howling in pain and thrashing about, wouldn't they?' Naomi says, nudging Dan with a wink as if she's making some hilarious point.

'Actually no, I researched it carefully. The character wouldn't be in much discomfort as the water dulls the pain, and they'd bleed out quickly.'

'Yeah, but they'd feel the pain in cold water. It's not as if they were in a bath tub, is it?' Naomi sticks her chin out.

What the hell's the matter with her? I'm about to reply that they'd be too far gone to do much about it anyway, when Dan says, 'You researched it on your computer?'

'Yes,' I say stiffly. Is he going to start interrogating me now?

'Right,' he says and shuffles away from Naomi a little, who's leaning against him. 'Let's hope you don't get in trouble with the law then and they take your laptop. Nice history – drugging, slitting wrists, drowning.' He laughs, and everyone joins in. I'm grateful he's lightened the atmosphere.

'Also, you said suicide. Wouldn't there be a note? The killer hasn't thought about that have they?' Naomi's slurring and seems up for a fight.

I shrug. 'You'll just have to wait and see when you read the book. Anyone for more coffee?' I look pointedly at my ex-boss.

In the bathroom half an hour later, I'm hoping my guests will be on their way shortly. I'm tired and want the house to myself again. It's been a nice evening, apart from Naomi's comments, but it's almost ten thirty and I need some sleep, so I can be fresh for writing tomorrow. I step out of the bathroom, and bang slap into Dan who's standing there outside the door.

'Bloody hell, Dan! You frightened the life out of me,' I say, pressing my back against the wall to put some distance between us. Difficult with him standing so close. He smells gorgeous and he's got that old look in his dark eyes. My body responds to his nearness and I fold my arms across my breasts.

'I wasn't sure if anyone was in there. I just put my ear to the door when you came out,' he says, tracing a finger along my cheekbone and giving a slow smile.

'Yes, it's free now.' I push his hand away and try to get past him, but he moves closer.

'Don't you realise what you do to me? I can hardly breathe when I'm near you.' Dan puts his arm around my waist, pulls me to him and nuzzles my neck.

The sensible thing to do is slap him or knee him in the bollocks, but I'm all out of sensible as his mouth comes down on mine. An all-consuming passion overtakes me and I kiss him back, hungry for more as I feel his erection pressing against my groin. Then Helena shouts up the stairs and the spell is broken.

'For God's sake, Dan, stop.' I push him away and hurry along the corridor. From the top of the stairs I see my daughter's face peeping round the banisters. 'Yes, love?'

'Just to say me and Carl are thinking of staying over, if that's okay? Adam is so peaceful in your room – we'll put the travel cot up.'

'Of course, that will be best. No point in disturbing him. And–'

Helena waves a hand at me as Carl calls from the living room and she hurries away.

I nearly fall down the stairs when I feel Dan's arms go around my waist from behind and then he plants hot kisses along my neck. 'What the fuck are you doing?' I hiss, turning around and giving him a shove.

'What you want me to do. What we both want to do.' He tries to pull me into his arms again, but I slap his hands away.

'Your wife's just down there, have you gone mad? And this can't happen, Dan. Do you hear me? Can. Not.' My voice is barely a whisper, but my anger is loud and clear.

Dan doesn't seem to notice though as he takes my hand and kisses it. 'I love you, Sam, always have. I want to look after you. Make sure that you're never unhappy again. My heart ached for you the other day when Penny told me about the antidepressants–'

What? I'll swing for bloody Penny! 'That was supposed to be confidential! And stop all this love shit. I'm going downstairs *right* now, and things will be back to normal between us. If it isn't, this fucking retreat won't happen. I know we have legalised everything, but if you so much as come near me again…' The hurt in his eyes is killing me, and I've no clue how to continue, so I turn and run downstairs. He calls my name, but I ignore him.

Penny looks up from the sofa, suspicion in her eyes. 'Is Dan up there?'

I avoid her gaze, pick up some empty cups and say to the floor, 'Yes, I came out of the bathroom and he went in. Then I checked on Adam.' Damn it. Why had I said that? It's as if I'm trying to justify my absence. And I'm lying my head off. I take the cups into the kitchen and hope Penny's satisfied.

Jack follows me in. 'Me and Fliss are in the room down the corridor, right?' he says, draping his arm around my shoulders as I run hot water into the lasagne dish.

My heart's pounding, and I try to put what Dan and I have just been doing out of my mind. 'Yes, that's right. It's been lovely to meet her at last. I think she's just perfect.' My voice comes out in a rush, sounds squeaky, unnatural.

'Good. She likes you too.' Jack kisses my cheek and I can feel his eyes on my flushed face. 'You okay, Mum?'

'Yeah, just a bit tired, that's all. It's the first dinner party I've done all by myself. Think it went well though.' My voice sounds more normal now. Good.

'It did,' Jack says, stepping to the side and leaning against the counter to watch me scrub at the dish. I give him side eyes and think he looks a bit suspicious, but that's daft. He was down here while I was upstairs with Dan. He sighs. 'Leave that 'til morning, it will soak off overnight.'

I push my hair back with a soapy hand and look directly at my son. My heart twists as he reminds me so much of his dad. 'When did you become an expert on washing-up?' I smile and flick soap suds at him.

'I learned from the master, or should I say mistress. You were a good teacher, Ma. Not just in washing-up either.'

His serious grey eyes are full of love and respect and I swallow a knot of emotion. Drying my hands on a tea towel, I say, 'I did my best.'

'Yep. And you've hung on to this place too. Not an easy task.' Jack folds his arms and inclines his head to the living room where Dan's talking about his new car. 'Shame you had to involve Knob Head though.'

'Nice new name for him.' I pull a face. 'You don't like him much, do you? I noticed at dinner.'

'Not one bit. He's just so up himself, false, arrogant, pompous. I'm just sorry that you seem to like him more than you should… Thank God you didn't stay with him when you were a kid. I would rather poke my eyes out than have him for a dad.'

I turn away to hide the tide of red seeping up my face and thankfully I'm saved from further comment as Penny comes in and says that she and Dan are leaving. She's the designated driver and has offered to drop Naomi home too. She was going to get a taxi but Penny figures that I will want to get to bed pretty soon and a taxi might take a while. Hugely relieved, I thank her and see them to the door. I'm careful to avoid Dan's eyes and turn slightly at the last minute to stop him planting a goodnight kiss on my cheek as they leave.

Alone in my bed at last, I heave a sigh and punch the pillow. What the hell had I been thinking? Yes, he'd made the first move, but I hadn't needed much encouragement. There was the booze factor, yes, but it wasn't much to blame, if I am totally honest. I'd wanted Dan, plain and simple. I've also been kidding myself these past months that I didn't. Even though Dan might be all or some of the things that Jack had called him, and my head is over him, my heart is apparently treacherous. And what did Jack mean by that comment – I like him more than was good for me? I hadn't showed it, had I?

Closing my eyes, I vow to stick to my word and keep him at a distance because if I don't, my whole life will go tits up. Dan is bad for me. I'm just lonely, that's all. The bed's too big and his arms are familiar. Hearing him say that he loved me threw me a bit, to say the least. It's been a long time since I heard those words. I turn out the light and snuggle down. Tomorrow's another day and I'll try my best to forget this disastrous evening ever happened. If Dan won't do the same, then he'll be sorry.

Chapter Ten

The end of August brings temperatures hotter than we'd enjoyed for most of the summer, a new hot tub in the grounds, and the building of the retreat. Dan had organised the last two, and in a few hours he's throwing a barbecue and celebration party for friends and local business people, most of whom I don't know. I'd invited everyone who was at the dinner party last month and a few friends – mostly ex-work colleagues and neighbours.

Mainly though, this was Dan's baby and he'd organised the caterers and a couple of chefs to man the barbecue. There will be flyers, vouchers and a raffle with wonderful prizes, three of which is a two-day stay at the retreat when it opens properly in December. For now, it has bare plaster walls and basic plumbing and electrics, but there is much to do before it's ready to welcome guests. That aside, the aim of the whole evening is to celebrate the new venture and to engage the local business community in its promotion. I walk outside to take a look and I have to admit I'm impressed how quick the retreat has gone up. Dan's skilful crew worked quickly and efficiently, and the overall effect of the Cornish stone low-rise structure is stunning.

Tracing my fingers along the wall, I have to shut down thoughts of how much Adam would have loved it. It was a year last week since he passed, and I chose to mark it by walking his favourite cliff path. Helena asked if she should come, but I wanted to be alone with his memory. I laughed and cried as I walked and cursed the night I'd let Dan come too close.

Since the disastrous evening, Dan had been the perfect gentleman, even a bit distant, which, although odd, was better than the alternative. Penny had even asked if we'd had a row the other week because of his behaviour. I'd said that he was just busy and had his mind on the job. It had been tempting to say that I should have a row with Penny for blabbing about my antidepressants, but I'd kept quiet. I'd have to let on that Dan had mentioned it to me, and then that would potentially open up a whole can of worms about when he'd talked to me about it and why.

At first, when the celebration party was mooted, I had been less than enthusiastic, but I'm looking forward to it. Things are okay with Dan, well apart from his aloofness, and I'm beginning to like the idea of guests at the retreat needing my help and advice. December guests sitting round the roaring log fire – a central feature of the retreat – sipping eggnog and discussing books is my idea of heaven. The new novel is on the way to being finished and I think it's shaping up to be my best yet. Now and then my treacherous heart catches me unaware when Dan pops round, but my head ignores it. It's perfectly rational that I have the hots for him, we have history, he's good-looking and I'm not an old woman yet. I miss the sex and intimacy I had with Adam, that's all. One day I might find someone else, but right now I'll concentrate on my new venture and writing.

'This party is amazing!' Alison, my friend from the library, says giving me a hug and nearly spills half a glass of red over my new white dress in the process.

'Hey steady on, Ali!' I giggle and guide her over to the newly built dry-stone wall edging the garden. I set my own and Alison's glass on a flat bit and take a breath of salt air. I feel squiffy already, but I've only had two small Proseccos. Oh no, actually, three, Dan topped my glass up. Dan's been helping the waiters keep everyone topped up, so he can strike up conversations about the retreat. There's no denying it, he knows how to work a room.

'Have I ever told you how bloody lucky you are to have this place?' Alison says, spreading her arms. 'And just look at this view!'

I nod and look out at a passing boat on the Atlantic, its red and green lights winking in the sunset. 'You have. And I am. Now I have a great retreat to run too.'

'And you're beautiful and slim. It's just not fair.' Alison pouts and fluffs her blonde bob.

Alison is pretty enough, ten years younger, and is fishing for compliments I think. 'Says Alison the drop dead gorgeous one.'

'Who's dropping dead?' Penny says, wandering over.

I introduce her, and we talk about the retreat, the unusually warm weather – though there is a nip in the air now – and to my slight embarrassment, how gorgeous I look.

'You see I could never wear a tight white dress like that,' Alison says. 'There are too many rolls of fat around my middle.'

Penny and I look at Alison's middle and frown. She must be a size ten at the most. Penny clears her throat and pulls her jacket over her own stomach. I change the subject.

'How's the library nowadays?'

'Boring without you. I'm still the part-time lowly assistant and general dogsbody. Naomi is okay, but you can't have a laugh with her.' Alison glances over her shoulder to check where her boss is. She's chatting to Dan, though Dan looks like he'd rather be anywhere else. 'Hmm, who's the guy she's talking to? I wouldn't mind a bit–'

'That's Penny's husband,' I say quickly.

'Really?' Alison says a touch of incredulity in her voice and not in the least embarrassed.

'Not surprised you're shocked. Why would he want me, eh? He's all over Sam like a rash. Still loves her. He'd leave me like a shot if she'd have him.' Penny's voice is full of bitterness and Alison's agog.

'Really?' She raises an eyebrow at me.

'For God's sake, Penny, let it drop. I keep telling you it isn't true! There's nothing going on and I've *so* had enough of listening to it.' I lower my voice at the end, but a few guests have turned to look. Damn it. Penny really knows how to push my buttons.

'Dear oh dear…' Alison taps her red nails on the stem of her glass, a glint in her eye, clearly enjoying the spectacle. 'Right, I'm off for another refill, ladies.' She gives Penny a wink. 'Might try my luck with Dan while I'm there.'

There's an awkward silence as we watch her walk away. I want to apologise but I'm getting fed up with Penny's constant harping on. 'Ali can be a bit blunt, but her heart's in the right place,' I venture.

'Yeah, well I think she's a right little madam and I've only known her five minutes.' Penny drains her glass and pouts. 'But then what can you do? Dan attracts women like flies round shit. I ought to be grateful he's still with me.'

'Now don't start that again. You're lovely. And sorry. I didn't mean to snap at you…'

'Me? Lovely? Kind, but untrue. And I'd have snapped at me too. I need to keep things to myself more. No wonder I don't have many real friends.'

Oh for God's sake. I can't be doing with this, and I wave at Helena as she's passing. She comes over, shortly followed, to my dismay, by Alison, glass in hand.

'Hi, Mum, great party.'

'Yes, I'm enjoying it. Where's Carl?'

'He's chatting to Jack in the kitchen and I've just phoned the babysitter to check on Adam for the fiftieth time!'

Alison interrupts with a snort. 'Blimey! Young mums, eh? My two are at their nan's, thank God. Drive me up the wall. Mind you, if I had a bloody husband at home every night like yours instead of in the army, I might be a bit less frazzled.'

'Carl is normally working, so it's nice that he can be here with me,' Helena says sweetly, but I can tell that Alison's got her back up.

'Your little one is a darling,' Penny says. 'I'd be checking on him every few minutes too. It's only natural.'

'How many have you got then?' Alison says and grabs a handful of nibbles from a tray as a waiter walks past. 'Mind you, at your age they'll be grown up now, eh, Penny?'

'I… we don't have children.'

'Lucky you! Not only do you bag the hot husband but you're child free…' Alison's laugh falters when she sees that nobody is joining in. 'Oh, sorry. I was only joking.'

Helena turns away from Alison and says, 'I was wondering, Mum, when everyone's gone shall we try out the new hot tub? I could borrow one of your swim suits.'

'That sounds like a nice idea, love. I–'

'But what would the rest of us wear?' Alison splutters, a few chewed crisps falling onto her cleavage.

Helena looks at Alison's chest and frowns. 'I was thinking just a few of us… you know, family?'

Ignoring the obvious rebuff, Alison brushes the crisps to the floor. 'Birthday suits, I expect. Skinny-dipping? That might be fun!'

Penny snorts. 'Yes, sure. Not sure that'd catch on, to be honest.' She rolls her eyes at me and Helena, and we laugh.

Alison's face darkens. She wipes her mouth with the back of her hand and sweeps her eyes over Penny's midriff. 'Perhaps not. You have to be skinny to skinny-dip, don't you?' Then she excuses herself and heads in the direction of the kitchen.

Penny looks as if someone's slapped her across the face and gazes out to sea. Helena mouths *Oh my God* at her me behind Penny's back and also makes herself scarce. I put a hand on Penny's shoulder and say, 'I'll have a word with Alison later. I'm not sure she knows how hurtful she can be some–'

'Yes. Yes, she does. And she's right. I'm a disgrace… I've put nearly a stone on since the reunion and that's because I'm worried about Dan straying again. Stupid really. Because he's liable to do that more if I'm a bloody whale. I might as well give up. He's way out of my league and I'm not sure that I have the strength to keep fighting for him any more. I'm a miserable fat cow with a miserable life. What's the point?'

My heart sinks. *Thanks a lot, Alison.* 'You really aren't a whale, Penny, and you've a lot to be thankful for in your life. Look, let me get you another drink, eh? Cheer you up a bit.'

'Make it a bottle. I'm in the mood to get completely rat-arsed.'

***

I wake with a start. My bladder's full, my head's throbbing, and my mouth feels like it's stuffed with sawdust. On the way to the loo, I glance at the clock – 7.30am. Feels more like the middle of the night. The cold toilet seat on my bare skin wakes me up a bit more and I rub my temples, wondering why I feel so lousy. Then last night slams into my memory like a wrecking ball. Bloody Penny was in a right state. I'd tried to cheer her up, but it hadn't worked, even though she'd monopolised all of my time. I'd barely spoken to any of the other guests, after about eight thirty, and had stayed with Penny in my room. Dan hadn't helped, bringing us refills every time our glasses were empty. Granted, he was trying to make sure the party was a success by keeping his miserable wife away from the crowd, so I'd taken one for the team. My God, I wish I hadn't now.

Splashing water on my face doesn't help, and I pat my face dry, look in the mirror and wish I hadn't done that either. Red-rimmed eyes in a snow-white face, framed by a bird's nest of wild dark hair, isn't a good look. What time had I gone to bed? Another wrecking ball smashes in, bringing an image of throwing up in the kitchen sink... Helena holding back my hair... yes, Helena had put me to bed. Dear Lord. What time was that? What had happened with Penny, and more importantly to all the guests? Had Dan seen me in that state? Had everyone else? Why can't I remember? A wave of shame and nausea rolls in my stomach and I lurch for the toilet bowl.

As I'm cleaning my teeth, there's an almighty hammering on the door. 'Mum! Mum, are you in there?'

'Jack? Yeah what's up?' I pull my dressing gown on and open the door to my frantic son.

He shoves his hands through his hair a few times. 'It's…' He stops, shakes his head in bewilderment and looks at me, his face whiter than my own. 'It's Penny, Mum. I've just found her in the hot tub… She's dead.'

Chapter Eleven

I stumble to the bed and sit on the edge. This can't be happening. Can. Not. It must be a weird dream or something. 'Dead?' I hear myself say.

Jack nods. 'Looks like suicide. I didn't go too close but there's… lots of blood.'

Nausea rolls again and I have to concentrate hard to keep my stomach contents where they should be. 'Oh my God…' I push myself up, force my legs to carry me to the door.

'Mum, where are you going?'

'To see her, of course.' A dizzy spell has me clutching the door handle. 'Have you called the police? Does Dan know?'

'No, not yet. I felt a bit hungover, so went outside for some air. That's when I saw her. Then I just ran to you.'

'Okay. Let me see her and then we need to tell Dan.' I walk to the back door and steel myself.

Outside, the sun's spreading a golden light across a blush sky, and the navy ocean is flat calm. I'm anything but, and want to run back inside, bury my head under a pillow and pretend this isn't happening. I drag my eyes from the ocean to the far corner of the garden. I can see the back of Penny's head resting on the edge of the hot tub as if she's fallen asleep.

The grass is damp under my bare feet as I step from the path and draw nearer. Then I can see. I can see it all. The water is totally crimson, but Penny's naked body is deathly white, her round stomach and large breasts rudely protruding from the tub as she floats on a sea of her own blood. Her eyes are closed, her face relaxed as if she is indeed asleep. If only. In shock, I draw a deep breath along with the stench of blood and retch at the bitter coppery taste in my throat. This time I can't stop my stomach coming up and I kneel on grass, helpless.

'Mum, come on, let's get you indoors.' Jack's by my side and I feel his arm through mine pulling me to my feet.

'Poor Dan… someone has to tell him.' I wipe my mouth on the back of my dressing gown sleeve and a sob breaks free.

'My God… my God!' Felicity's desperate voice from behind us makes me sob harder and then from the retreat, I see Dan emerge in a dressing gown, hair stuck up and rubbing his eyes.

'What's all the yelling about?' he says and starts to walk towards us.

Jack holds his hand up. 'Stay there, Dan. Let's go to the house and I'll explain.'

But Dan's looking past him towards the hot tub, open-mouthed, wide-eyed. Then he's running. 'Pen? Penny!'

Jack goes after him and Felicity puts her arm around me. My whole body is shaking, and through my tears, I watch Dan kneel at the side of his wife, take her face in his hands. I can't bear it and run for the house. I must phone the police, but at the door my legs give way and I slump against the wall. Felicity comes after me, helps me up and makes me sit at the kitchen table. Then she brings a glass of water. 'Just sit there quietly, I'll phone the police. You're in no fit state.'

What seems like minutes later, DI Nick Brocklehurst and DS Charlotte Jennings are sitting at the kitchen table with me, Jack, Felicity and Dan. They want to ask a few questions. And it's not minutes, it's a few hours. First at the house were uniformed police followed by a private ambulance and a doctor to pronounce life extinct. Then the site was cordoned off while CID were informed, and I felt I was in the middle of an episode of *Silent Witness* as I watched people in white overalls examining the area and taking photos. My stomach is swollen with tea and water but my brain's just about functioning as normal. Investigators are still in the garden. I sigh. Why all those people are needed is beyond me. Penny's dead; slit her wrists with one of my kitchen knives. All I want to do is sleep and when I wake, all this will just have been some awful nightmare.

'Let's start with you, Dan,' DI Brocklehurst begins, pen poised over his notebook. 'Can you tell us the last time you saw your wife?'

Dan's ashen. He rubs his stubble and sighs. 'Must have been about eleven or so when she came in. I'd seen the last of the guests to the door and I was getting ready for bed. Penny was very drunk, argumentative. She said she was going out to the hot tub as she wasn't in the least tired and she'd been waiting for the young ones to leave the tub for ages. They'd gone inside, so it was her turn. Eventually I talked her out of it.' Dan shook his head. 'Or so I thought. I said it wasn't a good idea to go out there drunk and naked.'

'And then what?' Jennings says.

'We went to bed. We stayed in the new retreat on just a mattress – no bedrooms yet because it's not finished. I'd had my share of booze too, but the mattress was comfy enough and I went out like a light. The next thing I heard was Felicity shouting in the garden and Sam crying.' Dan's voice cracks and he takes a sip of water.

'She said the young ones had gone inside? Was that you two?' Brocklehurst looks at Jack and Felicity.

'Yeah,' Jack says, handing Felicity a tissue. 'My sister and husband were in there too until about ten thirty, then they went home to relieve the babysitter. Fliss and I stayed in for another half hour, perhaps. Penny came over to chat and said she wanted to come in, but she had no suit. Like Dan, we said it wasn't a good idea, the state she was in.'

Felicity nods. 'We didn't say it like that, just said she'd be better getting some sleep. She was completely out of it. Her eyes kept closing while she was sitting on the side of the tub. Then she stumbled off in the direction of the retreat.'

Brocklehurst's pen moves swiftly across the page. 'And that was the last time either of you saw her?' Jack and Felicity nod. He turns his keen blue eyes on me and I feel guilty, even though I've not done anything wrong. 'And when did you last see Penny, Sam?'

I've been dreading this because I can't remember. More of the evening has come to me in dribs and drabs, but it isn't as clear as it should be. 'Um, I'll be straight with you, DI Brocklehurst, I was very drunk and my daughter Helena had to put me to bed.'

'Right. What time was that?'

'Oh… let me think.' I look at the kitchen clock for inspiration.

'About nine, or nine thirty,' Jack says. 'Just before Helena got in the hot tub with us.'

Brocklehurst's expression says it all. I feel my cheeks flame – I must have been drinking for England to get in such a state by that time. I scowl at Dan. It was all his fault with his bloody refills. 'Yes, about then… I guess,' I say to the table in a small voice.

'Had any of you spent much time with Penny during the evening?'

Everyone looks at me. 'Yes, I had. Me and Penny were in my room for part of it. She was upset, and I was trying to comfort her.'

'Upset about what?' Jennings asks.

This makes me feel uncomfortable. But I have to tell them. 'She was upset about her weight and worried that Dan would leave her for someone else.'

'Was there anyone else?' Brocklehurst asks.

A memory of the night of the dinner party comes unbidden and unwelcome. Dan's erection against my thigh, his mouth on mine. 'Not as far as I know. You'd better ask Dan.'

Dan speaks before they have chance, he sounds exasperated. 'No. There's no one else, Penny got it into her head that I'd been seeing other women when I hadn't. She was always accusing me throughout our marriage.'

DI Brocklehurst considers this, tapping his pen against his chin. 'What do you think drove your wife to kill herself, Mr Thomas? If indeed it was suicide.'

A murmur of shock goes around the table.

Incredulous, Dan asks, 'What are you suggesting – somebody killed her?'

'Not at all,' Brocklehurst says, evenly. 'But I'm ruling nothing out at this stage. Our job isn't to assume... and we're treating her death as suspicious for now.'

'What was her state of mind recently?' DS Jennings asks. 'You say she was upset tonight? But has she been upset or depressed long-term?'

Dan raises his arms and lets them fall in a gesture of bewilderment. 'God, I don't know.'

I shrug. 'If I had to say one way or the other, I'd say yes, she's been pretty down for as long as I have been reacquainted with her.' I explain about the reunion in Sheffield.

'But she's never talked about suicide?' Brocklehurst directs this to Dan.

'No, never.' Dan scrubs at the sides of his head with his knuckles.

'How about last night when you were talking together in your bedroom, Sam?' Jennings asks.

I wonder what to say. The truth was that no, Penny had never said outright that she wanted to kill herself, but there had been more than one occasion when Penny had said she'd not be able to live without Dan. Was that the same thing? No. But I remember feeling very uncomfortable each time Penny said it. The first time had been in the pub that day when we'd met for lunch and–

'Mrs Lane?' Jennings breaks into my thoughts.

'I'm not sure... not last night, but a few times over the last few months since we met up again she's said that she couldn't live without Dan. I said that she'd get used to it, and that I had to live without my husband, but she was adamant. Penny said something like "I'd die without him and I'm not joking".'

Dan clicks his tongue against the roof of his mouth. 'But I wasn't leaving her, for God's sake.'

'Perhaps Penny thought you might,' Brocklehurst says. 'Has your relationship been stable recently?'

'We had our ups and downs. No different to anyone else who's been together for years, I expect.'

I have to bite my tongue. It seems obvious that Dan is trying to come out of this snow-white. But then if I mention Penny saying Dan was going to leave the other week because she wouldn't let it drop about him still being in love with me, it would look bad.

'So she had no cause at all to suspect you of seeing another woman?' Jennings asks.

Dan looks like he's going to explode. His cheeks flush and a fire ignites behind his eyes, then he says, 'Okay, I'll tell you. But it *was* all in her head! She thought that Sam wanted revenge for what happened back when we were kids. Thought I was in love with her still, too.'

My insides clench and I feel my colour drain. What the fuck did he have to say that for? I listen dumbstruck as he's questioned about our teenage years and what happened between us.

'Is there any truth in what she feared? Is there some part of you that wants revenge, Mrs Lane?' Brocklehurst does the annoying tapping thing with his pen again.

'No.' My voice is barely a whisper, so I repeat it a bit too forcefully. 'I told her it was all rubbish and she said she believed me, but not Dan. She said he still loved me. I said it took two to tango and that I wasn't dancing.' My face is on fire and I look away from the shocked expression on Jack and Felicity's faces. I daren't look at Dan. Why had I kissed him at the dinner party, it all feels so wrong now. It was wrong at the time, but if poor Penny has done this because of me, I'd never forgive myself…

'I see,' says Brocklehurst, sharing a knowing glance with his colleague.

I sigh. *Great. He's taking two and two and come up with fucking twenty.*

'And are you in love with Sam, Dan?'

'No.' Dan folds his arms. I note this classic defensive pose. Marvellous. 'We told you, it was all in Penny's head.'

'Right. But if she was convinced you were leaving her for Sam, she could have taken her life because of it…' Felicity says, as if to herself. When she realises everyone is looking at her she flushes. 'Sorry, just speaking out loud.'

Brocklehurst stands up and nods to Jennings. 'I think we'll leave it there for now. We have the names and contact numbers of the other guests and they'll be questioned too – see if they can shed further light.'

Dan snorts. 'I doubt that. She didn't know any of them, well, apart from Naomi I think. And Penny stayed with Sam all evening.'

'It's surprising what can turn up, Mr Thomas,' Jennings says.

Jack sees them out and then he and Felicity go to their room to pack. They're due back at university tomorrow. They've offered to stay on, but I just want to be alone. I want to crawl into my big bed and pretend the world outside it doesn't exist.

Dan's still sitting at the table and reaches his hand across to mine. I snatch my hand away and stand up. 'What the hell do you think you're playing at?'

He frowns at me and shrugs. 'Trying to offer comfort, that's all.'

'Yeah, I know the kind of comfort you have on your mind.'

'How can you even suggest that when Penny's lying in a mortuary somewhere?' Dan's bottom lip trembles and his eyes fill.

I lean forward and hiss, 'Pity you didn't think of her the other week when you were all over me, telling me you loved me.'

Dan clicks his tongue against the roof of his mouth again and folds his arms. 'You didn't protest too much as I recall.'

'Get the fuck out of my house and don't ever come back.' My voice is cold, bitter.

'That's not going to be easy. Not with the retreat and everything,' Dan says evenly.

I know it, but if he doesn't get out of my face immediately, I'll swing for him. 'Get. Out. Of. My. House.'

The noise of Dan's chair scraping back and toppling over as he leaves sets my teeth on edge, and the slamming of the door vibrates through my legs and into my belly. Suddenly woozy, I clutch the edge of the table to steady myself. I need sleep – oblivion.

In my bedroom, I draw the blinds and crumple onto the bed, pulling the duvet up over my head. It's dark and warm and comfortable, but all I can think about is a cold slab somewhere with my old friend's naked form upon it ready for dissection. Brocklehurst said there would be a post-mortem, even though the cause of death seemed obvious. Poor Penny. Poor, poor Penny. I close my eyes, but silent tears still pour down my cheeks until at last, I feel myself drifting into unconsciousness.

Chapter Twelve

*P*enny, oh God… it's so weird to think you aren't here any more… But then you did kind of ask for it. Ever the doormat, you just allowed yourself to slip away – never put up a fight. You never did put up a fight, even when it mattered, I remember…

It's so sad, because when I think about it – you were a bit of a non-person. You pretended to be the life and soul, without much of either really. A sad spineless cow that owed everything to her husband. It was as if you sucked everything of any value from him like a leech. A big FAT leech. You stayed close, basking in his glory, hoping that some of his personality would seep into you and become yours. Make you interesting to know. Luckily, he had enough charisma and sparkle to share – but it really didn't make an awful lot of difference in the grand scheme of things, did it? You wore his reflected glory like cheap Christmas baubles on a cut-price tree.

And now you're dead and gone. Dead and gone with hardly a mark to show where you've been. No children to carry on your memory, or your line. Just as well. You were a one-off. It could have all been so different if you hadn't opened your legs all those years ago. Your husband would have been with the love of his life, and you wouldn't be dead. But you are, and that's down to you. You brought it on yourself without a thought for your poor husband. What on earth will he do without you? Who will he go to for comfort?

Don't trouble yourself too much, though… I expect he has a few ideas about that.

Chapter Thirteen

How many more times must I go over what happened? I've been here at the police station for four hours and I'm beginning to feel like I might actually be guilty of murder. They haven't accused me, but they're suspicious and it's not looking good. After all, there are still gaps in my memory from two nights ago. Could I have killed her, slit Penny's wrists? I shake my head and try not to laugh at that surreal thought. I'm not amused, just hysterical, but laughing wouldn't be a good idea would it, not with Brocklehurst and Jennings sitting across the table from me, taping my every utterance. So many questions they've fired at me every which way, until I'm not sure who I am any more. My name is Sam Lane, Sam Lane, Samantha Lane…

'Mrs Lane? Sam?' Jennings says.

'What?'

'I asked if you still take the antidepressants, sleeping tablets and painkillers that Naomi Peters told us about. The same ones that we found in Penny Thomas's system. The same ones that you researched on your laptop history that we've been looking at.' Jennings paused and flicked through her notes. 'The same history showed us you had also researched suicide in both warm and cold water by slitting wrists.'

I blow down my nostrils and close my eyes. 'How many times? That was for my suspense novel. I'm a suspense writer, I have to do research. It's not unusual. And in the book, she was in the ocean, not a hot tub.'

'Yes, Ms Peters told us this when we interviewed her. She said you told her and a few others about the novel at a recent dinner party. One character killed another but made it look like suicide.'

I open my eyes. 'Yes, so surely that means Penny's death is more likely to be suicide?'

'Why?'

'Because would I be stupid enough to commit a murder in exactly the same way as a character in my own bloody novel? A murder which I'd told people about at a fucking dinner party!'

'It could be a clever double bluff to fox us. I mean, who would suspect you, as you say?' Jennings says, patting her sleek black hair as if she's scored a point.

Fury boils up from my depths. 'A double bluff to fox you? What? We're not in an Agatha fucking Christie play, you know!'

'Calm down, Mrs Lane,' Brocklehurst says.

'Calm down? Yeah right, when you're accusing me of murder?'

'We haven't yet accused you—'

'As good as!'

'You agreed to help us with our enquiries.'

'Yes, but I've been here ages. I've had enough now, we're going round in circles rehashing the same old shit.' They stare but say nothing. 'So I'm free to go?'

Brocklehurst and Jennings look at each other. 'We'd rather you stayed a little longer,' Brocklehurst says.

'No. Either charge me or let me go. If you're going to charge me, I want my solicitor here bloody sharpish.' I try to make my voice sound assertive and strong, but I know I just sound terrified.

Brocklehurst carries on as if I've not spoken. 'You didn't answer the question about the antidepressants and sleeping tablets.'

'No. No, I'm no longer taking them. I haven't been for months. I have said this at least ten times.'

'Yes, but if that's true, where did Mrs Thomas get them from?'

'How the hell should I know? From her doctor, I expect. They couldn't have been mine, I threw them out months ago.' Even as I say this, there's a little nagging image of me tucking some behind the cleaning cloths in the bathroom cabinet. I swallow and close my eyes. Yes, I remember now. As an act of defiance, I'd written *I will beat you* on all the packages in red marker pen, but when I had beaten them, I couldn't quite bring myself to chuck the last few packets in the bin.

Jennings leans forward, gives me a smug little smile. 'The thing is, Samantha, her doctor had prescribed sleeping tablets, but not antidepressants and there was no evidence of packaging for any of those tablets. We searched the place the night it happened and nothing. Nothing in bins, cupboards, nowhere.'

'What's your point? She could have got them from a friend or off the Internet. God, I don't know. And after she'd taken them, she chucked the packets over the wall into the sea. The hot tub *is* right next to the wall.'

'She could have, but unlikely,' Brocklehurst says. 'It would be more likely that she took them and then just chucked the package in the bin if it were empty, or on the table, anywhere. She wouldn't be concerned with hiding them if she was about to take her life.'

I rub my eyes with the heels of my hands. I've no clue where he's going with this. Dan had phoned me yesterday and told me they'd questioned him for hours too. He told me to be strong and just try to keep calm if they did the same with me. I take a deep breath. 'I'm not really sure what you're getting at, Detective Inspector.'

'I'm wondering if it wasn't suicide, Sam, but murder. Wondering if her murderer put the tablets in her drinks and then once she was unconscious, slit her wrists. Just like the character in your novel. They obviously didn't think about it clearly enough though. You know, the fact that missing packaging would look odd. Because they had committed a crime and they probably wanted the evidence gone – not too bright.'

'Or she just chucked it into the sea…' I say and close my eyes again. I need to get out of here before I start screaming and can't stop.

'Hmm.' Brocklehurst taps his pen on his chin. 'Also, there's the argument you were heard to have, by your ex-colleague, Alison Hardy, and a few other guests mentioned it too during their interviews.'

There's a twist of unease in my gut. This is new. 'With who?'

'With Mrs Thomas, of course.' He looks at me as if I'm stupid. Then he consults his notes. 'Ms Hardy says that Mrs Thomas, regarding her husband, said words to the effect of, "He's all over Sam like a rash because he still loves her. He'd leave me like a shot if she'd have him." Then you snapped at Mrs Thomas, raised your voice and said words to the effect of, "For God's sake, Penny, let it drop. I keep telling you it isn't true! There's nothing going on and I've *so* had enough of listening to you fucking moan".'

My mouth drops open. I can't remember that at all. Must be yet another gap in my memory. But I wouldn't use language like that, surely. Not in front of all the guests. Drama queen Alison probably made the whole thing up.

'I- I don't remember that.'

'Really?'

'Really. I told you I'd had a lot to drink that evening and there are a few gaps–' I stop. I'm walking right into the shit there. 'What I mean is, Alison does tend to exaggerate, you know.' I hope that's covered up the first sentence.

'As I said, a few other guests corroborate her statement.' Brocklehurst sets his pen down and puts both hands behind his head, and rocks back slightly on his chair. I look at the floor. If he's supposed to be feigning nonchalance he won't win an Oscar. 'You said there are a few gaps? Does that mean there are parts of the evening that you might not remember. Things you might have done, for example?'

He was like a dog with a bone. *Shit!* Now what do I say? Once again doubts creep from my depths and tighten a grip around my heart. If I can't remember the argument because I was so drunk, I might have killed Penny and then blocked it all out… Oh God. And the tablets in the cabinet… were they still there? I feel sick.

'No. I don't know. I want to go home. I want to go home now.'

Brocklehurst stands up, says the interview is terminated, the time, who is in the room and turns off the tape. He asks Jennings to step out for a moment with him and tells me to sit tight a few more minutes.

Once the door closes behind them I lower my forehead to the cool tabletop. This is not happening, can't be. Where have Brocklehurst and Jennings gone? Are they having a conversation outside about whether to charge me with murder? My blood runs cold and I rake my hands through my hair, take a hank and twist it hard until my scalp hurts. Think. I must think what to do, to say. Before I can think anything much, the door opens and they walk back in.

Brocklehurst stands opposite and folds his arms. Jennings stands next to him fiddling with her ear. 'We've had a chat and we think it's time for you to have legal representation,' Brocklehurst says, his tone flat, his eyes stony.

Jennings stops the ear fiddling and straightens her back. 'Did you have someone in mind or do you want us to arrange–?'

'Are you going to charge me with m… murder?' My voice comes out as a whisper. My legs feel like someone else's.

Brocklehurst nods curtly. 'Samantha Lane, we are charging you with the murder of–' He's interrupted by the door flying open and a young officer steps in, waving an evidence bag containing a piece of paper. 'What the bloody hell? Can't you see we're busy, Officer Kelsey?'

Kelsey blushes scarlet. 'Yes, sir. But this can't wait – it is directly related to what you're about to say.'

Brocklehurst snatches the bag, scans the paper, rolls his eyes and then passes it to Jennings. She can't help twisting her mouth in what I think is a show of pent-up frustration. He takes her to one side and they talk in low voices. Then he comes back to the table.

'It appears we have a suicide note from Mrs Thomas. For now, you're free to go, but we will need to speak to you again when we've investigated further.'

The weight in my heart lifts and I can't get out of there fast enough.

As I hurry down the corridor, I wonder where they found the note and why they hadn't found it before. In the end, I couldn't give a damn. Nothing matters now. I'm free, and the most important thing in my head is the knowledge that I haven't killed my old friend in some drunken stupor. I'd seriously started to doubt myself as the interrogation went on, and Brocklehurst and Jennings kept turning up evidence against me. Flimsy evidence, yes, but flimsier evidence *had* been made to stick before. I've seen those TV programmes on miscarriages of justice.

Outside, the afternoon sun is warm on my face and I stand by my car for a few seconds, take some deep breaths. Thank God I'm out in the world again. The hours spent inside that claustrophobic interview room in the station feels more like days. A glass of wine and a hot meal have my name on it at home.

Just as I open the car door I hear a shout from across the car park.

'Sam! Thank God you're out! Helena told me you'd been gone for hours.' Dan arrives at my side and puts his hand on my arm.

He's the last person I want to see and shrug his hand off. 'Yes, well I was about to be charged with fucking murder. Can you believe that?' I throw my arms up, let them fall. 'That was until they found a suicide note at the last possible minute.'

Dan smiles. 'I know. I'm the one who brought it to them.'

Chapter Fourteen

Why will he never take no for an answer? I open the front door to Dan and walk back down the corridor. I've just stepped out of the shower and looking forward to that drink and meal I promised herself when I got out of the station, but no. No. Now I have to listen to what is so bloody urgent it can't be left until tomorrow. We face each other across the living room and I pull my bathrobe close about my neck.

'Look, Dan. As I said in the car park, thanks for bringing the note in, but I just need to be left alone for a while to gather my thoughts. It was an ordeal in that bloody interview room today and—'

Dan holds his hand up and goes to sit on the sofa. 'I know, I know. They did the same with me as I said. But I needed to make sure you understand a few things… just in case they call you back in.'

A shiver runs down my arms. 'Call me back in for what?'

'No idea, and it's very unlikely, now they have the suicide note…' His eyes slide away from mine. 'But you know what they're like.'

'Okay, but why can't this wait?' I say, feeling more apprehensive by the minute.

'It could, but I've been keeping something from you since that night and you ought to know really.' Dan's dark eyes fix on mine and my stomach turns over.

'The look in your eye tells me I might need a drink. Want one?' I walk into the kitchen, take a glass from the cupboard and slosh a glug of red wine into it. He comes in behind me and takes the glass. I pour one for myself and suggest we sit on the balcony.

Dan leans his elbows on the rail, looks out over the ocean and takes a breath of air. 'So peaceful here, isn't it?'

I drag a comb through my wet hair and sigh. 'Yes. But can we get to the point?'

He sits opposite me at the table, watching the comb and gives me a sad smile. 'Your hair was wet on that night too.'

My hand stills and my mouth goes dry. 'Which night?'

'The night Penny died.' He takes a swig of wine and looks at the table. 'What I'm about to say now makes me ashamed, in light of what's happened… you know, saying nothing to the police… but I have my reasons. Let me explain.' His eyes flick to mine, his stare intense. 'That night I woke in the early hours and thought I heard a woman laughing. Penny wasn't there, so I went outside to investigate. I saw that the back door to your house was open, so I went inside. There was nobody in the kitchen or anywhere downstairs and all was quiet. Then I went to your room. I heard you giggle, and I opened the door.'

'You came into my bedroom?'

'Yes… If you want the truth I wanted to see you. Needed to.' Dan stops, draws his hand down his face and looks sheepish. 'The drink had made me bolder than I would have been in the cold light of day. Sam, I just couldn't stop thinking about you. Still can't, despite what's happened. You haunt my dreams and you're in my head all the time.' He jabs a finger at his temple.

There's a tickle of apprehension in my belly. What the hell had happened when he'd come into my bedroom? I've no recollection of it whatsoever. Nothing. 'And then what?'

'And then I found you kneeling on the floor, naked apart from a pair of knickers. You were wet through and trying to dry your hair with a towel. Because you were so pissed, you kept dropping it and giggling.'

I've almost stopped listening. The words *naked* and *wet* punch into my consciousness. Fears that had whirled around my mind when I'd been in the interview room shove their way back into my thoughts and I'm desperately trying to calm my nerves. What if I was with Penny in the hot tub that night? What if I'd actually killed her – completely out of it… rolling drunk? But then, if I'd been that drunk, I wouldn't have been capable, would I? An unwelcome answer pops up – *not unless Penny was already unconscious with the drugs that you'd given her, Sam. Then it would have been pretty easy…* Then I remember the suicide note and get a grip. I've been through a lot. My brain is fried.

'You okay, love? Your face has drained.' Dan reaches his hand across the table, but I put the comb down, fold my arms.

'What do you think? You tell me you come into my room in the middle of the night, find me naked and… so what happened? Just get on with it!' I feel my face flush with anger.

Dan puts his hands up. 'Hey, don't get upset.' He leans back, mirrors my pose. 'I took the towel and put it round your shoulders. Then I got a new towel from the bathroom and dried your hair off a bit. I asked why you were wet, but you just kept laughing. Then you stood up, dropped the towel and tried to kiss me.'

My mouth drops open. Incredulous, I say, 'I tried to kiss you? Yeah right. And you what, pushed me away? Played the gentleman?'

'Yes, I did actually.' Dan sighs. 'I kissed you back at first, I'm only human after all, but then I came to my senses. I knew you didn't know what you were doing so I couldn't take advantage of you.'

I drain my glass in one and slam it down. Shit! What the hell happened that night? I rub my eyes, try to organise my thoughts. Try to remember something… anything. But all I remember is throwing up in the sink, Helena putting me to bed and then waking up feeling like death the next morning. Why can't I remember stuff? *Why?* A thought occurs, and I let Dan have it with both barrels.

'You must have been putting some drugs in my fucking drinks that night, Dan.'

Dan's face darkens. 'What! Why the hell would I do that?'

'How the hell should I know?' I get up and go to the kitchen for a refill with Dan close behind. 'Perhaps you thought you could shag me while I was out of it.' I stop, one hand on the wine bottle and whirl round, my heart thumping in my chest. 'Bloody hell… you didn't, did you?'

The look of pure horror in his dark eyes gives me comfort. 'How could you imagine I would do such a thing? You know how I feel about you. I would *never* hurt you. *Ever.*' Dan leans his back against the counter and gives me a soulful stare.

But I'm still furious. 'No. You didn't hurt me all those years ago, did you? I suppose that must have been someone else.'

I watch a tic in his cheek as he grinds his teeth together. Through a small gap in his mouth, he says, 'I've told you a thousand times how sorry I am for doing that. It was the worst mistake of my life.' Then his eyes fill, and I look away. I turn around and pour myself more wine.

'Okay. Let's not dig all that back up.' I pull a chair out at the kitchen table. He pours himself a glass and sits opposite. 'What happened after that…?' I look into his puzzled face and add, 'You know, after you'd dried my hair and fought off my advances.'

Dan leans his elbows on the table and rests his head in his hands. 'Nothing. I took off your wet knickers, made sure you were okay and put you to bed.'

My face is on fire. How completely and utterly humiliating. But I say nothing, I have no words, just sip my drink. Stare at a spot just above his head. He rakes his fingers through his hair and mutters something I can't catch. 'What did you say?' I narrow my eyes at him.

Dan gives me a level stare. 'I said I wish that party had never happened. If it hadn't, Penny would still be here.'

'Are you trying to say I drove her to suicide? Is that why you kept quiet to the police about finding me wet through?' I try to keep the tremor from my voice but fail.

'No, that's not what I'm saying at all–'

'Because if I had been with her, why didn't I have blood on me?' I stop. '…I didn't, did I?'

'No. No, of course not. I'm just saying that if she hadn't have got so drunk, taken those tablets, and then I suppose, killed herself… then she'd be alive.'

The way he'd said 'suppose' unnerves me. What does he mean? He found the note, didn't he? Before I can say that, another thought takes over. 'Talking of Penny, after you left my room, did you just go back to bed? Didn't you look for your wife?'

Dan shakes his head and turns the corners of his mouth down. 'No. That's the worst thing… I didn't want to go looking for her. I felt guilty because I'd gone to your room.' He looks into my eyes. 'I wanted you so much, you see… and I just assumed she'd be conked out somewhere. I was tired and didn't want the hassle of waking her and maybe having another argument, so I just slunk off back to bed.'

I sigh. 'Not your finest hour. Mine either… I suppose I must have been in the hot tub with her at some point, or why was I wet? Unless I'd had a shower.'

'No. The shower was dry. I noticed when I'd gone into the bathroom for a towel. I did wonder if you'd been in the sea, but you weren't particularly cold.'

'Right.'

'My theory is that you two were in the tub. You got out, and then afterwards, she did what she did… or somebody else did it to her.'

The unnerving I'd felt comes back with reinforcements. 'What? You're saying it wasn't suicide? Somebody cut her wrists with my kitchen knife?'

Dan puts a trembling hand to his forehead and then places it down on the table again. 'I'm not sure what I'm saying, but I just don't think Penny was the type to do something like that.'

I can hardly process his words. 'But *you* found the sodding suicide note, Dan!'

He gives me an intense stare and then snaps his eyes to the ceiling. 'I wrote that note, Sam. It was me.'

Chapter Fifteen

I t is as if time is standing still. I look at Dan, my heart thumping in my ears. He looks back and then reaches for my hand, but I slap it away. Hard. Anger and fear struggle for dominance in my chest and then anger wins.

I stand up, lean forward and yell in Dan's face, 'You what? Why the hell would you do such a thing?' Then anger drains as trepidation crashes into me like a wrecking ball. I back into the kitchen sink, a mishmash of thoughts whirling in my brain. *There was no note. No suicide note. On that night I wasn't tucked up in bed from nine o'clock, sleeping off the booze, I was up in the early hours. I was wet. Drunk. Why was I wet? Where had I been? No note... no note... no—*

Dan's face is full of compassion. 'I did such a thing to lead the police away from you. To protect you. Just like with me the day before, they'd had you in that interview room for hours and I was terrified they'd try to pin something on you. It was unlikely, given the fact that you'd not be stupid enough to act out a murder scene from your book in reality, but I couldn't risk it.' He stands up and steps forward, but I hold my hands up and shake my head. If he comes any nearer, I'll slap him.

He shoves his hands through his hair and leans against the table. 'I can't lose you, Sam. As I said, I had my reasons for not saying anything when the police interviewed us on the day and since. That's why I didn't tell the police about your hair being wet and I'd come to your room. Also, I was ashamed to admit I'd not looked for Penny. But if I'd told them everything I told you just now, it would have given them exactly what they needed.'

I'm incredulous. A wave of nausea rises in my belly and I turn to the sink, splash cold water on my face and look out of the window at the sea. 'You're saying that you think I'm capable of killing Penny,' I say to the waves. 'You *actually* think I drugged her and killed her.'

'No. No I don't think that at all! But I'm saying that others might. Felicity gave you a few suspicious looks when we were being interviewed that morning. And, it stands to reason the police would have been extremely suspicious of you if they knew all the details. They were about to charge you on what they had, for God's sake!'

I whirl round. 'Don't you dare talk about Felicity like that! She would never suspect me.'

Dan shrugs. 'Sorry, but while we're at it, it crossed my mind at first that Jack tried to set me up. He found her after all… perhaps he went with the scenario – they always suspect the husband. Luckily for me, and for you… there was a note.'

I would laugh if what he said weren't so terrible. 'My own son killed Penny to set you up? You're fucking nuts. Get out.' My voice comes out quiet but shaking with anger.

'I said at first. My head was all over the place… It's been an awful ordeal.'

'I asked you to leave.' I fold my arms, glare at him.

'Just hear me out. There's one more thing you don't know. Jack warned me off at the dinner party. He'd come up to the loo, saw us kissing but didn't tell you. Later he took me to one side and said to fucking leave you alone. He said some vicious things. I was angry, so said more than I intended.'

I put my hands on my face, peer at him through my fingers. No wonder Jack had had that suspicious look on his face that evening. 'Shit. What did you say?'

Dan swallows hard. 'I made it clear it wasn't just a quick grope. Said I loved you and you were the one I should have married. He said he'd rather poke his own eyes out than see me married to you, and his dad would spin in his grave. Then he pushed me hard against the wall.'

I throw my hands up in exasperation. That is just wonderful. This day is just getting better and sodding better. I grab my wine glass and take a swig. I know what Dan just said is the truth, because Jack had said the same thing the night of the dinner party when I'd commented that he didn't much like Dan.

'Why did you say all that to him? He'll think that the feeling is mutual! No wonder he's been a bit off with me. God, Dan, you're so bloody stupid sometimes. And to even *think* for one second that Jack could have killed Penny to set you up. I despair! Why would he have used the same method as in my book to cast suspicion on you? It would cast suspicion on me instead, you numbskull.'

Dan looks crestfallen. 'Yes, I know. I did say it just crossed my mind. I know it was stupid… and admitting to him I loved you was stupid too.'

Silence builds between us like a wall until I knock it down with, 'So are you *now* saying that Penny just took her own life but didn't leave a note?'

'I guess. I know I don't want to think of her being capable, but there's no other explanation.'

'But why would she kill herself in the same way as it happened in my book?'

'In some warped way to point the finger at you? She was eaten away with jealousy don't forget.'

I'd come to that conclusion a while ago, but needed to hear it out loud. It would at least mean that I hadn't killed Penny. 'Hmm, I suppose. And where did she get the drugs from?' I visualise the bathroom cabinet and fight the desire to run and search it.

'I have no bloody idea.' Dan slumps on a kitchen chair.

I put down my glass and rub my eyes. This is getting too much. I think about the suicide note. 'Where did you tell the police you'd found the note, and didn't they think it was odd you only *just* found it? Also, what about her fingerprints? Can they test paper for prints? If they can, then they'll find none except yours.' In saying this last sentence, a warning bell that had been sounding faintly since Penny's death had been suggested as murder by the police grew louder. Could Dan have killed her? He had the motive. He was in love with me. He would have also collected all her parents' money she'd previously kept from him.

Dan nods. 'Yes, they can test paper – I looked it up. I told the police I found the note inside my wallet folded up neatly at the back, next to my money. I hadn't used it since she died. I'd stayed at the cottage, shopped online. But then I'd taken it out this morning. The notepaper was torn from a sheet of paper she'd used for a shopping list earlier. Her fingerprints would be all over it. I wrote the note in a shaky hand as if she were drunk. Printed it – that disguised my handwriting too. It doesn't name you, Sam, but it says she was sick of always worrying about me not loving her – worried I'd leave her for someone else. Said she was sorry if her death caused me any pain, and she loved me, but she just couldn't do it any more.'

I watch his face as he tells me all this, he seems distant, unmoved. A chill runs the length of my spine. The earlier warning bell is deafening now. If he's this cold, calculating and good at deceiving, it wouldn't be beyond the bounds of reason to suspect that *he'd* killed Penny. In his twisted mind it could mean that him and I would live happily ever after and go skipping through the tulips. But why make me think that I could have done it? The wet hair, the drunken wander round the garden in the early hours? I can't take any more for now.

'I see. I don't know what to say to all of that. I do know I need to be alone though.' I walk from the kitchen, open the door to the hallway. 'Can you leave now. I need to process this.' I keep my gaze on the floor as he moves past.

At the front door he pauses. 'I did all this for you, Sam. Remember that. The suicide note makes sure that nobody will suspect you now, even if they did at the start. Not the police, nor friends like Alison and Naomi… not even family members.' He holds his hands up when I glare at him. 'Not that they would… just saying. You're free from blame now and all suspicion, love.' He goes to touch my shoulder, but then drops his hand and leaves.

An hour has passed since he left, but I can't move from the chair on the balcony. Wild fears and dark thoughts are in degrees of free-fall, tumbling churning and then surfacing again like some putrid smell. Deep down, I don't really think Dan can have done it. He's determined, ambitious, takes what he wants. But murder? No. My mind's just lurching at anything at the moment. No wonder, is it? And me? Am I to blame? Of course not. But if I'd been out of it – perhaps Dan had slipped drugs into my drink because he thought I'd agree to have sex with him? Would he stoop so low? Had I been on some weird trip – couldn't tell reality from fantasy... gone out to the hot tub and...?

Suddenly I'm on my feet and racing for the bathroom, my heart thudding in my chest. Flinging open the doors I chuck out painkillers, insect repellent and plasters until I find the plastic box I used to keep the antidepressants in. There it is, tucked under a face cloth under the back shelf where I know I hid it. I remember the shame I felt at the time. The weakness in me that meant I couldn't throw the last few packets away. With a shaking hand, I pull off the lid and look inside. The box is empty.

Chapter Sixteen

It's nearly the end of November, but still I feel like the night Penny died has just happened, even though it's nearly twelve weeks ago. It's like I'm stuck in a terrifying Groundhog Day scenario, or I'm a demented hamster trapped in a wheel, trying to escape from a soul-crushing existence. Just when I think I'm making headway, there I am, slap bang in that fateful day again.

I pour boiling water into a cup and mechanically stir the teabag round and round. Morning has somehow seeped into afternoon and I can't really remember how that happened. I'll have to snap out of this before next week when the first guests arrive at the retreat. Dan rings every day and sometimes pops round to see how I am and tries to discuss plans for the guests' schedule, or some trivial detail about décor. More often than not, I fob him off or won't let him in – say I've got a migraine. I contact him by email instead and send reassuring texts to say that I will be available to greet the guest and yes, of course, I'll be able to discuss their writing with them, perhaps even do a bit of tuition.

I point blank refuse to discuss anything else though. Anything important like my feelings, because if I give him an inch, he'll wedge open the gap in my armour and tip his heart into mine, perhaps even think he can declare his everlasting love and devotion. So I've kept him at arm's length, acted cool, been professional and shut him out at every turn. Much worse than worries about Dan and his heart-tipping is my inability to carry the burden of guilt about the missing antidepressants around for more than a few hours without collapsing into chairs, sofas, or beds in order to stare into nothingness.

Sometimes this staring into nothingness involves booze and, on a rare occasion, sleeping tablets. The slippery slope I was on just after Adam died is waiting in dark corners and in the middle of the night. So far, I've narrowly avoided losing my footing, but it's only a matter of time before I'm sucked down into the black pit I was in, and this time I'm not sure I'll be able to crawl out. I'm not sure I'd even want to. At least then I won't have this constant nagging in my ear that I done it. I killed my old friend Penny.

The tea is way passed builders' now. It looks more like beef soup, but I don't care. A glug of milk will sort it. I would pay big bucks for such a simple remedy for my problems. I know there are none, however, and I take the tea and my big woolly blanket out onto the balcony for a breath of fresh sea air. A few brave surfers bounce and slap over the grey breakers near the water line and a stiff offshore breeze whips waves further out into stiff peaks. Why do surfers insist on braving this kind of weather? Must be nuts. But I can see the attraction too. The exhilaration of mastering the mighty ocean, albeit it fleetingly, must be worth it.

I wrap the blanket tightly around me and lean against the railings, one hand around the handle of the mug, the other keeping hold of the blanket because the wind is trying to take it off. Though looking at the surfers, my mind's working overtime, yet again. Objectively, I feel that I didn't kill Penny. There would be a deep sense in my heart of hearts of knowing the truth, if I had. Hopefully there would be. But there's enough doubt to plague my nights and days. The doubt is based on the state I was in that night, the missing tablets… and past experience.

I did a vicious, spiteful thing to her that day in the toilets. A malicious, premeditated and cruel thing. Much as it shames me, I have to admit to myself it felt good at the time. Revenge was swift, merciless and righteous. Penny and Dan had betrayed me, made me feel worthless, inferior, unloved. And that had unleashed evil – an all-consuming hatred. I have never done anything like that before or since, thank God. But what if it had happened again? Had being with Penny somehow triggered the old Sam? I shut those thoughts down.

On the surface I'm functioning, but Helena, and to a lesser extent Jack as he's away at uni, knows there's a problem. Just like Dan, I've kept them at arm's length, but it's more difficult with family – particularly my daughter. Once or twice I've made excuses not to see little Adam. Not because I love him any less or find him a nuisance, but because I don't want him to see me cry, or I find myself staring into nothingness when he's visiting.

The tea tastes like the inside of a kettle and the tannin strips my tongue, so I set it down on the table and bite into the chocolate digestive. Half of it lands on the floor which is covered in sand blown from the beach. Typical. In frustration, I fling it over the side and almost immediately a seagull swoops and carries it off. How wonderful it must be to fly. To just spread your wings and take off to wherever you liked, unfettered by worry, or gravity. I sit at the table and rest my head on the cool wrought iron top. I need a drink… a cold G&T with a slice of lime and a handful of ice. Then I notice the time. It's only 1pm. One o'clock or not, I ought to be showered and dressed, not wandering about with dirty hair, in pyjamas and an old grubby dressing gown.

This has to stop.

Has to.

Is it time to face the music and ask Doctor Grayling for some antidepressants as well as sleeping tablets? They helped last time, but do I really want to go down that path again? *Though what's the alternative, Sam? To crash out of control through the endless days, hoping someone has a safety net, catch you when you fall? The slippery slope won't wait forever.*

Interlocking my fingers, and stretching my arms up, I look up at the sky through the gaps in my fingers – then the vast expanse of grey cloud pulls me into nothingness. I shake it away and watch a few seagulls suspended from invisible strings gliding past and the call of the gin bottle grows louder. No. I won't give in to it. Can't. Think nice thoughts… Jack is coming up tomorrow, Felicity at the weekend, so that will be good. Jack suggested they came for Christmas lunch too, along with Helena, Carl and little Adam.

The retreat will be open on Tuesday with three interesting guests, so life could be much worse.

Focus.

Focus on those things instead of some crazy fantasy that you were involved in somehow ending Penny's life. But what about the missing antidepressants from the "hidden" place in the bathroom cabinet, Sam? What about those? The likelihood of Penny taking them, or even Dan was slim. When would they have done it? How did they know they were there? Then a memory surfaces – I'm taking a long pull on a cigarette, watching the end burn red hot, grinding it out into white yielding flesh, the sound of screaming… The jangle of the doorbell snaps me out of yet another downward spiral and I hurry to answer it.

Alison is on the doorstep wearing a black padded coat with fur round the hood and after a sweep of my dressing gown and unwashed hair, she puts a sickly sympathetic expression on her face. From behind her back she whips a bunch of multi-coloured flowers and thrusts them into my hands. 'I know you keep saying you're fine on the phone and not to visit, but I know you're not. I just had to stop by and see you, hon.' The sickly expression adds a wobbly smile.

Stop by? Has she become American in the last twelve weeks? I'm in no mood for Alison's fake comfort and a barrage of searching questions. But can't refuse her entry… unless I can think of an excuse. 'Hey, that's so kind of you, Alison. But I am truly fine. The house is a tip and I was just going to have a shower and then do a bit of shopping. I've nothing much in. Thanks so much for the flowers.'

'Don't worry about that, lovely. I haven't come to be entertained. Just a cuppa will do, and if you've no tea bags I'll have water.' Alison's through the door and down the hall before I can draw breath. She stops at the kitchen and turns around. 'It's you I've come to see, not the state of your house.' Then she walks into the kitchen and grabs the kettle. 'Tea or coffee?'

Ten minutes later, I feel like an intruder in my own home. I'm nursing a cup of tea that tastes of nothing, while Alison's rushing about my house plumping cushions, sweeping floors and stacking the dishwasher. All the time she's doing this she's chucking seemingly innocent questions over her shoulder at me. 'And the police say it was suicide then, the final verdict, like? Bet you were bloody relieved given that they had you in for questioning and that?'

'Yes, they called me a few weeks back.'

'But why would she do it, though?'

'Not really sure.' I put the cup on the coffee table and pull my dressing gown tight, wrap my arms around myself. I'm feeling vulnerable and afraid. It's obvious Alison is just after the juicy gossip, and I'm worried that my head's in such a mess that I'll say the wrong thing.

She comes to sit on the opposite sofa and takes a sip of her drink. Then she tucks her blonde bob behind her ears and assumes a benign curious expression, but in the big blue eyes there's a thirst for news – naked and desperate. 'What did the note say? There must have been a clue in it.'

I shrug and look down at the chipped varnish on my toes. When did I last paint them? 'Um… not really, she'd just had enough of it all…'

'On that night she'd deffo had enough of the hot husband fancying you, hadn't she? I couldn't believe how rude she was to you. No bloody wonder you ripped her head off.'

My head shoots up at this and heat floods her cheeks. 'I didn't quite rip her head off… did I?'

'Yeah.' Alison's eyes flicker with excitement. 'And I don't blame you. God knows what he saw in her when he could have had you back then. I chatted to him at the party, you know, later on? And he told me how you'd met. He was a bit drunk, to be honest.' Alison does a fake laugh. 'But weren't we all? Anyway, he said that you were his girlfriend and he'd left you for Penny. He didn't say why, but he went a bit red.'

Great, get to the point, why don't you. Now what do I say? 'It was all a very long time ago, Alison.'

'But Penny said he still loves you to me that night, didn't she? Do you think she topped herself because she thought you and him would get back together?'

I have just picked the cup back up but bang it down now. 'For God's sake! No. There's nothing between us.'

Alison blinks and sits back a bit. 'Hey, don't get upset, chick. I was just trying to piece things together. And Naomi was going to come instead of me until I persuaded her not to. She's even worse than me for being direct.' She tries a smile, but I don't answer it.

'I think that's debatable.' I shut my eyes, pray that she will take the hint and fuck off.

'Trust me, she's worse. Anyway, I'm really here just to see how you are, hon. And if I were you I'd grab that Dan one with both hands. Why not? You're both free agents *now*, aren't you?'

Something about the intonation of the word 'now' tells me so much. It's clear that Alison thinks that me, Dan, or perhaps both of us know more than we're letting on. Perhaps she even thinks the suicide verdict was wrong. I open my eyes and stare directly into the other woman's greedy gaze.

'I'm tired of talking about this now. Either change the subject or leave.'

Alison's mouth drops open. 'Oh, sweetie. I really didn't mean to upset you. Look, let's change the subject. I can see how things are with you.' Her eyes sweep my appearance again and this time there's no hiding the disgust behind sympathy. 'No wonder you're so stressed.'

'No. Let's not change the subject. Can you leave now? I want to get showered and go shopping like I said before.' I stand up and walk to the front door. I hear her snort of derision but at least she follows.

At the door, Alison turns and says, 'I'm sorry if I upset you. I don't like leaving you like this – you know when you're struggling with… life.'

Anger that has been so desperate for release in my gut slowly rises up to my chest. I daren't allow my mouth to open or it would be out, free and dangerous. I just nod and push the door open.

'Why don't you go to the doctor's? See if they can give you something for anxiety and stuff?' Alison gives a little smile, but her eyes are cold. 'You know there's no shame in it.'

That is the last straw. I put my face inches from hers and say in a low voice, 'Why don't you go to the fucking doctor's and ask if they can give you something to help increase the size of your pinhead brain? Now fuck off and don't come back here again!'

Alison's face drains and she scrabbles out of the door and down the path. 'You're bloody nuts, you are! I wouldn't put anything past you!' she shouts over her shoulder.

I slam the door and lean back against it. That wasn't very smart was it, given that Alison will be turning the sails of the rumour mill in the community before I can draw breath. But right at this minute I don't give a damn. It was worth it to see the shocked expression on her nasty little face.

The kitchen clock says three thirty and I'm still in my dressing gown pondering on what I said to Alison and all the rest of my problems – again. Ideas of a shower and then shopping somehow disappeared into a glass of wine when I wasn't looking. The glass is empty and it's too late to go shopping. It will be dark in half an hour and it's bloody freezing out. Best just chalk the day up to experience and stay in nightclothes. Lunch didn't happen thanks to Alison's arrival, so another glass of wine and a microwave lasagne, possibly with a side of garlic bread sounds tempting.

Halfway through the meal, the doorbell jangles again and my stomach rolls. My fork clatters to the plate. No. That's all I need. It would probably be Naomi come to see if I'm okay after Alison's chapter and verse. In other words, to get more gossip. I consider pulling on some clothes but really can't be bothered. I'll not allow anyone in anyway, no matter who it is.

Jack's standing there. His big smile fades as he takes in my appearance and concern floods his face. 'Mum? You okay?'

I feel like I'm the child. A child who's been doing something naughty – bad, and been caught out by the adult. The hall mirror reflects the sorry state of my dishevelment. There's lasagne on my chin, my dark hair looks slick with grease and is sticking up all over, and dark circles float under the blue of my eyes. In an unnaturally high-pitched voice I say, 'Jack! I didn't expect you until tomorrow.' Before my son can answer, I modify the tone – go for thrilled. 'It's wonderful to see you. Come through, it's freezing!'

Shit! Why didn't I have that bloody shower?

In the kitchen I pick up my glass and bottle, put them on the counter, but Jack's already seen the evidence. He nods at them. 'Starting early, eh?' He leans against the wall folds his arms, looks at me.

There's not a scrap of humour in his eyes and I tell myself to keep calm. Okay, yes it was early to be boozing, but I'm the parent here. 'I skipped lunch as I was engrossed in my novel.' I sweep my hand down my body and give a sheepish grin. 'As you can see. You know what I'm like when I'm writing. Just fancied a glass with my food to celebrate finishing three chapters today.' I'm gabbling, so stop. Why am I apologising, telling lies? What's it to do with Jack anyway?

Jack nods, but I can tell he's not convinced. He points at the kettle. 'Want a cuppa?'

'Yes, that'd be lovely. What brings you here a day early?'

'I had a bit of free time and thought I'd surprise you. It's been a while since I was here.' He turns and shoves his hand through his hair the way his dad used to, the floppy dark blond fringe falling over his grey eyes and my heart squeezes as it always does. He looks so much like Adam.

'Missed your old mum, then?' I want to walk over and give him a hug but given the state of me, he might not welcome it.

He shrugs. 'A bit. Don't get big-headed.'

I do a fake laugh. Then a silence swells between us until the pressure of it hurts my chest. 'Tell you what, love. Leave my coffee,

I'll go and get cleaned up and have some later.' I hurry from the kitchen and say over my shoulder. 'There are biscuits in the top cupboard if you fancy some.'

After the shower, I feel more refreshed and able to put on my "normal mother" act. I dry my hair and put concealer under my eyes, a bit of eyeliner and mascara and I look much more like my old self. Except there is no old self, is there? Not really. Just the shell of the woman I once was. Then I tell myself off for wallowing and paint on a big smile as I enter the living room. The TV is on and Jack's watching *Danger Mouse*.

'*Danger Mouse*?' I say, sitting beside him on the sofa and giving him a quick hug. 'Not a bit old for that?'

Jack gives me a genuine smile. 'You're never too old for DM. It's really funny, you know. Mostly aimed at adults, 'cos some of the humour's quite subtle.'

'If you say so,' I say with a giggle in my throat.

Jack smiles but then he flicks the TV off and shifts to face me. 'Mum. I'm not going to beat about the bush. I'm a bit worried about you.'

The buoyant mood developing in my chest drains away. *Great. We're going to have a big bloody discussion about my life, are we?* I settle back in my seat, conceal my irritation and try to make my voice light. 'Why, love?'

'The way you looked when I arrived.' He holds his hands up as I start to answer. 'Yes, I know you said you'd been writing and lost track of time. But you looked dreadful. Your hair hadn't seen shampoo for a few days and…'

'What do you mean, I *said*? Don't you believe me? And my hair was washed yesterday, thank you.' I feel my colour come up at yet another lie.

'Mum, I'm not attacking you. Just worried. Helena said the other day that she's worried too. You've been in your dressing gown late afternoon when she's popped round a few times, and you don't see little Adam as much as you used to.' Jack puts his hand on my arm, gives it a squeeze. 'We love you, that's why we're concerned. You do know that?'

The love is plain to see in my son's eyes and mine moisten, so I look away from his gaze. I'm torn between anger at being caught out, and the desire to let the tears come. He's right. I am a mess. And Helena has noticed too. I knew my daughter was worried, but I'd managed to fob her off – or so I'd thought. Helena had seen through my excuses not to have Adam as well. How humiliating.

I sigh and pick at a fingernail. 'It's been so hard since Penny's death. I-I feel partly to blame.'

Jack sits back, crosses his legs. 'How on earth did you arrive at that?'

'It happened here, for a start. I was so out of it that night. So out of it. It's hard to look outside now without seeing her in the tub.' My voice trembles and I swallow hard.

'God, Mum.' He takes my hand. 'Yes, it must be – I get that, but why are you to blame? Okay, you were out of it, but she was worse. You didn't see her later, you know, after you went to bed. She was wasted – her pupils were the size of Jupiter.'

'But if she was so bad, how did she have the gumption to do what she did?'

Jack gives me a strange look, releases my hand. 'No idea, but she must have, mustn't she?'

I shrug. I need to shut up now before I say too much. 'I guess.' Everything feels muddled, nothing makes sense in my head any more. I used to have thoughts in logically ordered lines, now they resemble spaghetti. And I'm acting crazy, losing friends, family. They are all worried about me. What am I going to do?

I feel Jack's hand on mine again and he stops me worrying at my nail. I'm not even aware that I still had been. 'Has *he* been round lately?' The way Jack says 'he' leaves me in no doubt as to who he means.

The elephant in the room is at last being let out into the wild then. Good, it was about time. Not an easy topic, but it's better than the one we're on. Another moment and I'm sure I'd have blurted everything out to Jack. 'You mean Dan?'

Jack nods.

'Look, he told me that you'd seen us the night of the dinner party – you know, kissing.' I glance up quickly and then away as I'm too embarrassed. Jack looks angry. 'He also told me what he told you about loving me and that you pushed him against the wall–'

'Ought to have done more than that. Taking bloody advantage.' Jack's voice is calm, but his agitation is unmistakable.

At the risk of upsetting him further, my instinct is to be honest. 'To be fair, I kissed him back. I'm not proud of it and I shouldn't have encouraged him. It was a moment of weakness, but I assure you his feelings aren't reciprocated.'

'I should bloody hope not! He's a scumbag, a womaniser too according to Penny. She told us when she was pissed. He thinks he can do exactly he what likes.' Jack jumps up and paces the room. 'I'm furious with Dad for leaving you in a position to go into business with that shithead!'

I stand and go over to my son, put a hand on his arm – stop his pacing. 'Hey, come on, love. He's not that bad. He's been nothing but kind to me since it happened. I don't speak to him half the time, don't even let him in when he comes around, but he never fails to ask after me and–'

'That's because he wants you!' Jack shakes off my hand and glares. 'Can't you see that? Just steer well clear, Mum. I don't trust him.' Jack marches off into the kitchen and I hear him pour a glass of wine.

I follow, a sob in my throat. I've never seen my son so angry. Inside there's an argument raging about whether to tell Jack that it was this so-called scumbag who saved my skin. That he wrote the suicide note because he would do anything for me. But the wild look in Jack's eyes stops me. No. No, that would be madness. God knows what can of worms would be opened. The can of worms might lead to a further investigation and me ending up in prison.

'He only wants the best for me, love. He knows we can't be together, but he wouldn't do anything to hurt me.'

Jack sighs, shakes his head, looks out the window at the dark sky.

Then before I can stop myself, I blurt, 'He was the one to convince me that I couldn't have killed Penny.' Then the enormity of that statement hits home. How the hell is Jack going to react to that? He doesn't know about Dan writing the note, does he? What the hell am I thinking?

The look on his face is a cross between incredulity and shock. 'What? How the hell could you have? It was bloody suicide – the police have the note.' He sounds like he's talking to an idiot.

I think fast. 'I know, I know. But I was in a right state after the police released me. They'd fired questions at me for hours. I know there was the note, but I was too upset to focus. I thought I might have been so out of it that night, I'd done it somehow to get revenge for when we were teenagers.'

Jack shakes his head again, takes a drink.

Again, I speak before thinking. 'Did you think it might have been me, who killed her, did Felicity? You know, before the note was found?'

Jack sets the glass down and pulls me into his arms. I rest my head on his shoulder and with relief, sink into the comfort of his love. He says tenderly, 'Oh, Mum. Of course not. That's just nuts. Totally nuts.'

I sigh, nod and say I know it is. But left unsaid is, *it would be, if there wasn't an empty box in my medicine cupboard where the antidepressants used to be.*

Chapter Seventeen

The weekend has gone better than I could ever have expected, but as I wave Jack and Felicity off and close the front door, I let the wall support my weight as a tide of tiredness washes through me. The strain of being my old normal self in front of my son and his girlfriend, my daughter and her husband and little Adam has taken its toll, and now I'm exhausted. Perhaps my BAFTA will be announced soon though, because Jack mentioned how much better I seemed than on Friday when he'd arrived impromptu.

I'd also had a heart-to-heart with Helena about not seeing her and my grandson as much. I'd told her the truth in part – that I'd been sad and out of sorts since Penny's death and found it difficult to keep cheerful all the time. Little Adam wouldn't understand why his grandma was being a misery and I didn't want to upset him. All true. But Helena needn't worry any more as her mum was feeling so much better now. I also felt ready to meet the new guests for the retreat and quite positive about the future. Not true.

Flopping down on the sofa I close my eyes. There is one positive aspect to my life though. In the early hours, I woke with a new story in my head and jotted the bare bones down on the pad by the bed kept for exactly those moments. The pad had been sadly neglected for many months. Instead of my usual suspensy types, my brain had produced a turbulent love story set in Cornwall. An ill-fated relationship would start in the summer with lots of angst and heart-searching for the characters into autumn. But it would end at Christmas with a healthy dollop of sentimentality and feel-good endorphin inducing twinkly stuff. There isn't enough twinkly stuff in the world by a long chalk, according to me. I could do with twinkly stuff in my own little world. I'm starved of it.

The old saying 'alone in a room full of people' had never been truer for me this weekend. While acting all sparkly and full of the joys, loneliness kept coming up and layering across my shoulders. Little bricks of loneliness, one upon the other, until I felt bowed under its weight. While I was pleased that my children were so happy with their partners, seeing them together made me acutely aware that I was very much alone. Each hug, kiss, loving look between each couple made me long for the past. Long for Adam. Long for twinkly stuff.

I sit up and slap my hand on the side of the sofa. *This is no good. Get your arse up and open a new document. Crack on with the story. Take your mind off your woes. Wallowing is not an option. You are a woman, not a hippo. Actually, is it rhinos that wallow in mud? Does it bloody matter, Sam? Go do some writing!*

The writing room is warm and inviting. It has a view over the sea which helps inspiration, normally; however, there were times of severe procrastination when I would become distracted and watch the waves. This afternoon feels procrastination free, though. Maybe the lies are working. Perhaps I'm beginning to believe them. The future's bright, a new story is waiting at the tips of my fingers, and all thoughts of missing antidepressants have been buried with the past.

Not a good analogy. Burials present an image of Penny's white coffin adorned with the red roses Dan placed lovingly on top. I hadn't stayed until the end, it was too heart breaking. Penny was too young to die. Far too young. Who could have possibly predicted this terrible ending when we had been the best of friends, laughing, carefree, the world at our feet? Who could have predicted how we would have become caught up again in each other's lives after so long, with disastrous consequences for one of us?

I push these thoughts away and open a new document. My old novel had been 60,000 words in and had taken hours of work. But it had to go, obviously, after Penny had opted to... Damn it! I need to stop bringing everything back to that. Okay, the title of the new one – I type *Christmas in Cornwall* and then the doorbell jangles. *Fuck!* Why am I constantly plagued with unexpected bloody visitors! There's no wonder I can never get on with anything positive while there's a line of fucking people hanging on the doorbell every five seconds!

I wrench open the door, my temper's so hot I'm almost hyperventilating...

It's Dan looking expectant with a piece of paper in his hand. Bollocks. He's not coming in. No way.

'Hi, Dan, I'm just starting to write, so can we do this another time?' Rude, but hey ho.

He pulls his neck back and frowns down at me. 'Blimey, you look like an angry tiger. What's up?'

'Nothing, apart from the fact that it's the first time I've sat down to write in I can't remember when, and by the time I've stopped explaining this to you and you have asked more sodding questions, I'll have forgotten what the hell I'm supposed to be writing about!' To my horror, I feel hot tears fill my eyes and my mouth trembling. Dan looks so hurt and shocked. Why am I being like this to him?

His eyes flood with sympathy and he steps forward, puts his hand on my shoulder. 'Hey, love. Sorry to upset you, I really didn't mean to. There's more behind it than the writing, I can tell.'

No. He can't be nice to me or I'll just crumple. Try as I might, I can't speak. I just shake my head. Then I go to close the door on him except I can't, because he's got one foot inside and his hand on my shoulder.

'Let me come in, we can have a cup of tea and I'll lend an ear. I'm good at that.' He puts his other foot inside and closes the door behind him.

How bloody rude? I swallow away tears and make my eyes small. 'Come in, why don't you?'

'I can tell when you need a friend. Now we're going into your kitchen and you're getting stuff off your chest, okay?' Dan walks past me down the hallway.

'Not much choice, have I?' I mutter to my reflection in the hall mirror. For once I'm dressed and looking decent. That has to be a bonus.

Dan's tactics are practically see-through. For ten minutes he's not asked me what's wrong, just talked about the papers in his hand – they need my signature to agree to the building of a small swimming pool and another hot tub to replace the hole in the concrete that's out there now. I had asked for the original hot tub to be removed soon after Penny was found. There was no way I was ever going in it again, I couldn't bear to even look at it. One of the times Dan had contacted me a few weeks back, I'd agreed to the pool idea. It would make the retreat even more appealing apparently. And I couldn't care less. I'm sure any second now, he'll shelve his businessman head and chuck me a searching question in a nonchalant way when he thinks I'm off guard. He always used to do that. But I'm ready for him.

'Biscuit?' he asks, shaking the tin at me. I decline and drink my tea. Dan crunches into a chocolate chip cookie and says from the corner of his mouth, 'I must say you look a bit calmer now than when you opened the door to me. What's been bothering you, Sam?'

There we go. I can still read him like a book. 'I told you, I was trying to write.' I look over the rim of my cup at him. I've been avoiding doing this so far because of his disarming handsomeness. But now I take in his eyes, his face, and see he looks like the personification of twinkly and so desirable I nearly choke on my tea. It must be the mood I'm in. Still, it will help with the new novel. I put the cup down and push back my chair. 'So if that's all, I'd like to continue with my day.'

Dan guffaws and biscuit crumbs spatter on the table. '"I'd like to continue with my day"?' he mimics in a voice like the Queen's. 'Please. You're cracking me up.'

At first, I want to slap him but then I realise how pompous I sound and burst out laughing. Not a little giggle but a big guffaw much huger than his. And I can't stop. Laughter grips my stomach and squeezes it so hard that I can hardly draw breath, but, somehow, I do and laugh and laugh and laugh. Until I realise that I'm not laughing any more. I'm sobbing instead, and Dan's arms go around me, draw me into the comfort of his chest and I'm gone. I'm a snot-bubbling shaking out of control mess.

'Hey, hey, baby,' he says into my hair. 'Tell me what's wrong, sweetheart.'

Baby and sweetheart are not what he should be calling me at all, but I can't help but squeeze him tight, lean into the strength of him. I can't say anything for a while but then I can't stop talking. My stupid heart overrules my head and between gulping sobs, out come my worst fears as well as disclosure of the missing antidepressants.

Dan is silent for a while, then holds me at arm's length. 'Right. Now let's sit you down and get you a glass of wine.' He thrusts a handful of tissues from the box on the counter at me. 'There's no way you did anything, do you hear me?'

I take the wine he hands me but don't drink. I need a clear head, particularly with the way he's making me feel. 'If I didn't, how do you explain the missing tablets?'

'There are a number of explanations for that.' Dan pushes a lock of hair from my forehead and I sit back a bit on the sofa. Put some distance between us. 'Number one is that you misremembered where you put them. You might have thrown them out and just forgot. The second is that Penny took them.'

A gut feeling tells me the first one isn't viable. I know in my heart of hearts I didn't throw them away. I say, 'No to the first. The second one – how the hell could she have taken them? When would she, and how did she know about them and where they were?' Before I know what I'm doing, I swallow a big gulp of wine. Is there any wonder?

'How did she know about them?' Dan raises an eyebrow. 'That's easy. Because you told her, love. She might have just gone for a snoop on the off chance you had some left. It doesn't take a rocket scientist to imagine they'd be in the bathroom cabinet.'

Listening to Dan's rational reasoning is reducing my anxiety by the moment. What he's saying does make perfect sense. Except for one thing. 'That night she was out of it though, wasn't she? If she'd gone rifling through my cupboards there'd be stuff all over the place – on the floor. Everywhere. When I looked for the tablets everything was as it should be. And wouldn't someone have heard or seen her?'

Dan ponders on this a moment, looks at me over the rim of his glass. I look away. His eyes are mesmerising. 'Not if she'd done it another time. Perhaps she'd planned it and took them weeks before.'

'Really? Would she have been so cold and calculating about taking her own life?'

'I have no idea – but it's certainly possible. She could have taken them the night of the dinner party for a start. She knew about them before then, because she told me, and I stupidly mentioned it to you. You know, when we were upstairs that night and we–'

'Yes… no need to elaborate, Dan.' My face is on fire at the thought of what we did. And he's right; Penny could have taken them that night. A warning voice whispers in my ear as he gives me a slow smile. Dan could have taken them that night too. Then I tell myself off. Dan wouldn't stoop so low. I need to accept that Penny took her own life and that's that.

'What are you thinking?' He puts his head on one side, smiles again.

'Oh, I don't know. What you say makes sense. I just wish I could stop thinking about it all and worrying. It does help to have told someone about the missing antidepressants though.' I drain my glass and flop back on the sofa.

'Of course it does. And I'm here to tell you to stop worrying, sweetheart. I would stake my life on the fact that you had absolutely nothing to do with Penny's death.'

I ignore the sweetheart bit. 'But how can you be so sure, even when I'm not?'

Dan moves closer and the skin on my arm tingles as he brushes against it. 'Because I know you, Sam. I know you would never do anything like that, no matter how drunk you were. You're a good person, one of the best. I believe in you one hundred percent.'

I can't look at him, because that's not true, is it? I sigh and come to a decision. I've told him everything else, so I might as well go for the hat-trick. 'The thing is, Dan, I'm not a good person. Or, at least I wasn't once. I did a terrible thing. The day after I found you with Penny...' I swallow and look at my hands. 'I told her to meet me in the toilets and–'

'Flushed her head down the bog and burnt her back with a fag. Yes, she told me.' Dan's mouth turns up at one side. 'It was no more than she deserved after years of being besties with you. I deserved it too, and I would have taken it – gladly.'

'No, it can never be justified.' I sit back, fold my arms, though I can't conceal my relief at his reaction.

'It can. We shat on you from a great height and I'll always regret it. Always. I love you, Sam. Always have, always will.'

I open my mouth to protest but Dan gives me a long hard look and then his lips are on mine. My arms come up to his chest in a half-hearted attempt to stop him, but it's not what I want. I kiss him back and then suddenly we're lying on the floor; his hands are all over me and I'm in danger of giving in to what we both want so much. Then behind Dan's shoulder, I see a photo of Adam on the mantelpiece and my passion cools immediately. I scoot out from under him and stand up, straighten my clothes.

Dan looks up at me, desire aflame in his eyes. 'Sam? What's wrong... I thought–'

'Yes, and so did I. But it's not right. It can't happen.'

'But why?' He sits up, buttons his shirt.

'Penny, for one! If we do this then she'd be right, wouldn't she? Imagine what everyone would say? Jack, Helena, everyone.' I throw my hands up and they fall with a slap at my hips.

Dan pulls a face. 'Right. You only stopped because you're worried about what people might think?'

Did I? I don't know, but I know it's not happening. 'Maybe, but I'd like you to leave now, Dan. Thanks for helping to get my head straight and for believing that I could never have been involved in Penny's death. But I beg you to keep what I told you today a secret... and we can't do this ever again. Okay?'

He stands up, brushes a hand over his jeans, and heaves a sigh. 'If that's what you want. Though I can't pretend my feelings for you will change. And, of course, I won't tell anyone about the missing drugs. Who would I tell and why? I've just told you I love you, for God's sake.' He looks at me, a pained expression on his face, then he turns and heads for the door.

I follow him, feeling like someone has pulled the plug out of my heart and all the twinkly stuff is leaking down the drain. My head takes over and tells me that it's for the best and it would be a disaster if we got together. I couldn't face my children for a start and–

Dan turns at the door and he cups my face with both of his hands. 'If you change your mind I'll be waiting. I'll always be waiting.' Then he places a gentle kiss on my forehead and opens the door. As he steps through he says, 'I'm off to Sheffield later to sort out some business, but I'll see you Tuesday afternoon when the first guests come, okay?'

'Yep. It's a good job they're not local and know about Penny, I bet it would put them off. Hope they don't somehow come across any old newspapers.'

'Eh? How could they? Old news now. Local rags are yesterday's chip paper.' Dan laughs and runs his hand through his hair. 'Remember those chips we had as kids at Jim's Big Fryer on a Thursday after youth club?'

The memory makes me smile. 'God, yes. A sneaky fag, a can of lager shared between us and some chips. The height of sophistication.'

'Good times though, Sam.' Dan gives me a tender smile. 'Anyway, you ready for the guests, yeah?'

The idea of guests both thrills and scares the hell out of me. I say of course I am, nod and wave, then close the door behind him. In the living room I pick up his wine glass and press my lips to the rim, inhale the lingering notes of his cologne. Enough. My focus needs to be on the new business and writing. Twinkly stuff is what you make it and I'm sure it will be great looking after the new guests and helping them with their writing journey. I like meeting new people, or did before my life was turned upside down after Adam's death. Now with all the Penny stuff I realise I've just retreated from life and too far into my shell. A shell filled with slippery slopes, darkness and despair.

I put Dan's glass in the dishwasher and make myself a promise. I promise to find the positive mood I had about starting the new book before Dan turned up, and crack on with it. I also promise that this afternoon will be a new start. There'll be no more going back to dwelling on Penny and all that goes with it. Samantha is out of her shell now and she's staying out.

Chapter Eighteen

It's December, it's Tuesday, and I'm feeling good. I have kept my promises and am ridiculously pleased that four chapters of *Christmas in Cornwall* is tucked away safely on my computer. I'm up, showered, breakfasted and dressed in new black jeans ans a red smart-ish jumper. I'm wearing make-up and it's only 8.30am. The three guests are due at about two o'clock and I need to get a few extra bits in for the retreat. I had a look yesterday and it's almost perfect, but needs a few home touches. My mental list has candles, nice soaps and cake on it. Dan has sorted the rest of the food and drink – a home delivery yesterday made sure the guests will want for nothing. There will even be a caterer to provide all their meals, so I don't have to worry about that.

Dan's very good at organising, I've found. He'd phoned to check that the food had come yesterday and finished by saying that all I'd have to do now is look beautiful and swan around being the author. That made me laugh. He does tend to make me laugh. I swill thoughts of his face down the sink with my coffee dregs and set off for Newquay.

It's 1.30pm and I'm still faffing about in the retreat. I have put out the candles in various places three times and I'm now about to pick them all up again when Helena and Adam come in. 'There you are! We've been wandering around the house, yelling for five minutes, haven't we Adam?'

Adam laughs and holds his arms out to me, a much-chewed Minion toy I bought him for his birthday in his hand. 'Mandma!' he says and my heart melts. Nearly fourteen months old, wilful and into everything, he's too adorable for words. Helena sets him down and he toddles towards me on stout little legs giggling all the time. I scoop him up and shower him with kisses until he thrusts the soggy Minion in my face. 'Kiss Minion?'

I pretend to kiss it and say, 'I'd rather kiss you. You're so much cuter.'

''Uter. Me,' he says as if he understands. For all I know he might.

I laugh and say, 'Yes, you. Very cute indeed.'

Helena's about to say something when the front door opens and in walks Dan and three strangers. Obviously the guests – they're early. Two women and a man all around my age at a guess. I know their names and that one of the women has had a short story published, but that's all. Helena stands to one side and ushers them through, and as the man passes, she inclines her head at him, gives me a wink and mouths something I can't make out. She's obviously passing comment on the guy's looks. He's incredibly handsome in anyone's book. Very tall, bright blue eyes, blond curly hair and a wide smile. Helena's mouthing something else so I look away as she's making the colour rush to my cheeks.

'Sorry we're a bit early,' Dan says. He sweeps his arm to one of the women. She's black, plump, has intelligent dark brown eyes and a warm smile. 'Sam, this is Lydia, she's from London and can you believe has never set foot in this fair county before?'

Lydia laughs and holds her hand out to me. 'I know. Scandalous. But what I've seen so far is stunning, even at this time of year.'

I shake her hand. 'It is. In fact, I do like it in winter more than summer sometimes. The crowds in summer mean that so many places are out of bounds. I'm not complaining though – everyone should visit Cornwall.'

Dan introduces the other woman, a red-haired pale-faced lady by the name of Emily from Nottingham who looks a bit timid. Her eyes are flitting about the place like a pair of butterflies and she gives a nervous laugh when I shake her hand. 'Pleased to meet you, Sam. I read your book on the train. Really enjoyed it.' She ends with the nervous laugh again.

'You did? Well, that's certainly nice to know. Thanks so much.'

Before I can say more, Dan introduces the man, a little flippantly, I feel. Perhaps he's intimidated by his height, though Dan's not exactly short. 'And this giant is Harry, from Bristol.'

Harry takes my hand in his enormous one and gives me a lovely smile that lights up his face. 'So delighted to meet you, Sam. I've yet to read your book, but it's on my Kindle.' To Dan he says, 'And at six foot four, I'm hardly a giant.' His smile stays put but I think Dan's comment has irritated him.

Lydia raises her hand. 'Just to let you know I'm not the odd one out. I've downloaded one of your books too,' she says with a cheeky wink. I immediately warm to her and can tell we'll get on.

'Reading my book's not a compulsory requirement for your stay here, you know,' I say with a laugh.

I introduce Helena and Adam, and Harry comments that I don't look old enough to be a grandma, which brings my colour up again. Dan swiftly changes the subject and suggests he show them around the retreat while I make tea. After they've gone from the living area Helena whispers in my ear, 'Someone's got an admirer, Mum.'

'Me? Who'd you mean?'

'Hot Harry, of course,' she says, a giggle in her voice.

'Oh please.' I flap my hand at her. 'And what were you mouthing at me when they came in?'

'You were just saying how cute Adam was and I was saying that another cutie had just walked in.'

I shake my head and give her a withering look. 'You need to behave, or you'll end up embarrassing me in front of him.' I straighten the already-straight candles again.

Helena widens her big blue eyes and does her pouty look. 'Don't see why. I was only saying to Carl the other night that if you found someone else I wouldn't be sad. Dad's gone and you're not an old lady… well, not yet.' A twinkle in her eye belies the serious tone.

I point a candle at her. 'That's enough, young lady. Now why don't you run along while I swan about being an important author, hmm?'

Helena laughs, gives me a hug and picks up Adam. He thrusts the Minion in my face again and waves a chubby hand as his mum carries him out through the door.

I put the candle down and clasp my hands behind my back to prevent them from fiddling with anything else and stick the kettle on just as Dan leads the guests back in. Lydia comes over, leans against the big rustic kitchen table and shoots me a big smile.

'My gosh, Sam, this place is perfect! I knew we were close to the sea, but just not how close. I think I'll come again when the pool and hot tub are built in the summer. I can just imagine how wonderful it would be, sitting in a spa, a glass of fizz in hand looking out over the ocean.' She turns and gazes wistfully out of the patio doors to the place where a tarpaulin now covers the hole that used to house the hot tub.

I smile, say it will be wonderful and take cups out of the cupboard. I'm careful to avoid Dan's eye. I wonder if he's got the same mental image as I have – of Penny swimming in a sea of her own blood.

Emily and Harry are equally complimentary about the retreat and I begin to feel more relaxed as we chat in general terms about writing. We sit on the large L-shaped sofa arrangement in the living area, Dan lights the wood burner and the room takes on a rosy glow. I sit back and realise I'm pleased that I decided to go with Dan's crazy idea of this place. Even though the last few months have been hell, I really hope everything is starting to come together now. I daren't count my chickens, of course. Chickens have a habit of getting their necks wrung.

Dan's now explaining that the three of them will be expected to get their own breakfast from the well-stocked fridge and cupboards, but a light lunch and dinner will be provided each day by a professional caterer.

'Proper luxury,' Emily says. 'And a whole five days to do nothing but write. Heaven.' She takes a sip of coffee and flushes. It's as if she's not used to speaking in front of people much.

I try to encourage her with a smile and ask, 'Always great to have head space to write. Do you work full-time?'

'You could say that.' Emily's eyes moisten and my heart sinks. 'I look after my aged parents who both have dementia. I'm an only child so…' She ends on a shrug and sighs. 'Still, I have managed to get respite and I'm going to bloody well make the most of it.' She does the nervous laugh again. 'Pardon my French.'

'Oh, bugger your French,' Lydia says, her eyes glinting with passion. 'You have a right to be fed up. I know you love your parents, but it must be so hard to give so much of your time. This sodding government needs to put more money into helping people like you instead of pouring it into bombs for Syria and…' She throws her hands up. 'Sorry, it doesn't take much for me to get my dander up nowadays.'

'I totally agree with you, Lydia,' I hear myself say. I'm so indignant on behalf of poor Emily and see her life in bold relief now I know something of her background. She's been stifled and trapped all her life – a little songbird in a cage unable to truly sing and unlikely to be released anytime soon. Or that might just be my writer's imagination taking over. I do feel for her though. 'Never mind, Emily. I'll do all I can to make your stay here a good one.'

Emily gives me a shy smile and Harry says, 'We all will. And Sam, will you be doing a tutorial in the next few days?' His expectant blue eyes search my face.

'I will, certainly. Although I thought I'd wait a couple of days until you decide what subject you think would be most beneficial. For instance, would you prefer one on structure, plotting, what makes a good opening, ending et cetera, or would you prefer open questions?'

'Perhaps a combination of all of that?' Harry answers, looking to the others for confirmation.

Dan stands up and collects the cups. 'Might be as well to settle in for a day or two like Sam suggested before you decide. And talking of settling in, it might be an idea to go to your rooms and get your bearings… or take a walk to the beach, just suit yourselves.' To me he says, 'Come on, Sam. Let our guests have some of that head space, eh?'

I say goodbye and follow him out, slightly irked at the way he took over just then. Outside on the path to my house I say, 'Who appointed you leader of the gang?'

'Eh?'

'One moment we were all chatting and the next you cut it dead, whisk us out of there. Why?'

Dan rolls his eyes at me. 'Better me being leader than Harry. I can see he wants to rule the roost, so I thought I'd make sure everyone knows he can't. The last thing poor Emily needs is someone else controlling her life. Right, I'm off to make sure that Debbie Preston, the caterer, is all set for this evening. Actually, think I'll pop down to her café instead of phoning.' He gives me a brief smile and then strides off to the house.

As I watch his ramrod straight form go inside, it suddenly hits me. He's jealous of Harry. But why? Because he's incredibly handsome, tall, funny? What? Dan's a good-looking man too and when he feels like it, disarmingly charming… so is it because of me? Does Dan imagine that Harry fancies me, poses a threat? My heart says yes. On the one hand, I find that endearing and on the other, very irritating.

Inside he's pacing while talking on the phone. I flop down on the sofa and think about a possible tutorial for the guests. I'd quite like just a Q&A session to begin with. It would help me to ease into it and find out more about their writing backgrounds. Dan ends his call and flops down opposite in an armchair. 'Catering's all sorted.'

'I thought you were supposed to be going to the café?'

'Can't be bothered. I feel like I've been running around like a headless chicken for days making sure this venture runs smoothly.'

The tone of his words implies he's fed up with it already. I cross my legs and say, 'Don't forget this "venture" *was* all your idea, Dan.'

My short shrift has his brow furrowing and shifty eye movements. 'Not complaining, just tired.'

And the rest. I want to say, but don't. A mischievous impulse surfaces, and I pretend to flick through a magazine while dropping a casual, 'The guests seem nice, don't they? I'm looking forward to the tutorial… I think Harry has already got a short story published, if I remember rightly.'

Dan's expression becomes stormier. 'No. That's Lydia. He's had nothing published. Thinks he will though. On the way back from the station he was telling us all that he's chucked in a twenty-year teaching post to do supply, just so he can have time to write more. Can you imagine? Hardly the most sensible thing to do, is it? Must have a big ego.'

A giggle builds in my chest and I suck the inside of my cheek to stop its release. I knew it wasn't Harry that'd been published but one of the women, but it was worth it to get Dan's ridiculous reaction.

'On the contrary, I think it is sensible. You only get one life after all – why waste it doing things you hate?'

'"On the contrary", is it? Gosh, darling, you're really getting into the hammy writer's role now.' Dan smirks and I don't like the look in his eyes. He can piss right off, actually. I've had enough of him today.

'I am indeed. And if you're tired I won't keep you. I'm sure I can handle it from here. Besides, this isn't the only venture you have on your books, is it? Thought you were involved in building some houses up north.' I stand and lead the way out.

At the front door, he turns and frowns so hard his eyebrows knit together. 'Yes, I have a few things on the go, but I like helping round here too. I'll be up north tomorrow but will be back the day after and I'll pop over to see how things are.'

I give him what I hope is a sweet smile and say, 'There's really no need. I'm looking forward to spending time with them all and getting to know them better. You'd just be in the way – you know, not knowing anything about writing.'

His eyes flash and he makes a noise in his throat that's a cross between a growl and a cough. 'I'll come anyway. I take care of the practical stuff and I need to make sure all is well.'

I laugh and mock in an upper-class accent, '"All is well, don't you know?" Now who's hamming it up?'

Dan gives me a withering look and leaves.

I bang the door behind him and march down the hallway. Serves him right. I won't be bossed about in my own home and I certainly won't put up with jealous little boys who think their favourite toy is under threat of being stolen. How bloody dare he? From the study, I get one of my books and some notes on my latest work in progress and set off for the retreat with a spring in my step. A few days of writing talk with like-minded people, bliss. Something tells me I'm going to enjoy this new venture.

Chapter Nineteen

I've decided that even when the three guests have gone I'll keep in touch on social media and email. The last few days have been so rewarding. I've realised my teaching dream in a way, because of the tutorials, and the confidence building inside me because of this new challenge has given me a very much-needed boost. I haven't even considered having a drink in the mornings and I'm excited to start each new day. Penny's been the last thing on my mind, thankfully. Dan phoned to say he'd been delayed on another project and he would be here the day before the guests leave instead. That suits me. He'd only spoil everything.

Harry has been very attentive, so I think Helena and Dan, though he never actually said anything, are right about him being attracted to me. It's nice to have male attention other than Dan and all the baggage that goes with him. Harry's a lovely guy and we get on well. Nothing will come of it though, how could it? He lives and works three hours away. Not at the ends of the earth, but it is in terms of making a relationship. Besides, I'm not sure if I want that type of commitment.

As I walk across to the retreat this morning, I laugh at my ponderings. There's been no mention of a relationship so far. Just my wild imagination running away with me.

Lydia, Emily and Harry are laughing at something while having boiled eggs and toast as I walk in. They have gelled as a group and promised to keep in touch with each other afterwards, as well as with me.

'Sam, come and join us!' Lydia says, jumping up. 'Would you like tea? There's plenty in the pot.'

Lydia, I've discovered, works for the Labour Party in admin and publicity – hence the swipe at the government the other day. She's such a grounded and genuine person and when I think of the three, I'll miss her company most of all. Emily has come out of her shell too, and her writing shows real promise. They are all very different writers, but I'm convinced each of them could do well with a bit more experience and practice.

We sip our tea and I tell them my suggestion for the morning's activity. Walking on the beach, listening to the sounds, smelling the air, seeing the colours and shapes and then doing some free writing when we get back. We won't talk or discuss our feelings, just let the environment speak to us and hopefully pull some stories out of our hearts.

Harry leans back in his chair and does his big disarming grin. 'I think that's a bloody great idea. How much does where you live influence your writing, Sam?'

'Only about ninety-nine per cent, Harry,' I say with a laugh. 'The ocean speaks to me, calms my spirit, soothes my troubles. Well, most of the time.'

I see the sympathy in all their eyes and wish I'd not said the last bit. They know about my loss, not about Penny of course, that might make them run for the hills. But they do know about Adam. I shared a bit about my background on the first evening, and of course Adam is a huge part of it.

For December it's quite mild, just a little breeze, and a cold but not unpleasant one greets us as we step onto Mawgan Porth beach. The tide's way out and a few white horses gallop along the shoreline. The horizon draws itself a line of sea green under the grey sky and a few seagulls yell at each other from the dunes. I suck in a big breath of ozone and suggest that we set off at a brisk pace. I also remind them that we shouldn't talk if we can help it – just listen to the sounds and look at the beauty of the place.

At first, we walk in single file quite far apart, then I notice Harry is hanging back a bit from the two women and soon he's by my side. He gives me a big smile and his bright blue eyes reflect the clear patch of sky breaking free of the heavy cloud. I smile back and then look towards the ocean as the breeze picks up and blows my hair across my eyes. Harry's still close by – too close. Then his hand brushes mine, on purpose? I've no idea, but I think yes, so I move away a bit and walk faster. He speeds up too and then he says, 'I know we're not supposed to talk, but we're observing the beauty of nature, and well… you are so beautiful, Sam.'

My breath catches in my throat and I cover my shock with a laugh. I say, 'Is your next line, "do you come here often?"' I glance up at him and see that his eyes are serious.

'Sam, I mean it. You are beautiful inside and out and I'd like to get to know you better. We've only a few days left so–'

'So it might be better to leave it at that.' I look back to the ocean. 'You live in Bristol remember?'

'It's not on the moon. And I feel like we've made a connection already. How about you?' He puts his hand on my elbow, slows my pace.

I stop, look up at him, study his face. He shoves a hand through his tousled blond hair. His cheeks are pink. Bless him, he's self-conscious. And do I think we've made a connection? Probably, but it can't work… can it? 'Um… in a way. I do like you, Harry. You're funny and intelligent, we share a love of writing, so yes, a connection.'

Harry's eyes become intense, holding my gaze until it's me who has pink cheeks. 'It's more than that. As you know I find you very attractive and love being in your company, Sam. Can I take you out for dinner tonight?'

I shake my head and start walking again. I've noticed that Emily and Lydia have looked back a few times at us and I'm conscious that the whole writing exercise might be ruined if they see us chatting away. 'Let's leave it, Harry. We're supposed to be silent,' I say over my shoulder and pick up my pace.

Then I hear his feet thudding on the sand behind me, and he leans in, whispers in my ear. 'Then say yes and I'll shut up.'

The mischievous look in his eye makes me laugh when I don't want to and to shut him up I say, 'Okay, just dinner, yeah?'

He does a fist pump and a silly little dance on the spot. 'Yes! Can't wait.' Then he sets off at a jog towards the ocean and leaves me wondering what the hell I've just done.

It's late afternoon and the writing exercise has gone really well. We're sitting round the log burner, having shared our writing and thoughts of how the day has gone and sipping hot chocolate. I settle back on the sofa and notice Lydia flashing me with her eyes and inclining her head towards the kitchen. I frown, and she mouths something unintelligible then goes to the kitchen. Harry and Emily are discussing their work, so I get up and follow Lydia.

Lydia's in there leaning against the sink, her arms folded, a glint in her dark eyes. 'Let's be knowing then,' she says in a low voice.

'Knowing what?' I mirror her pose.

'What's going on between you and Handsome Harry.' She flashes a grin.

My heart sinks. Great – nothing gets past her. I rinse my mug out under the tap and decide to tell her. 'He asked me out for dinner tonight at the Two Clomes and I said yes.' I notice her eyes dancing in merriment. 'And it's just a dinner as friends, before you get any ideas.'

'Yeah, right.'

'It is.'

'So why not have dinner here with all of us? We're all friends.' Lydia raises an eyebrow and turns her mouth to one side.

She's got me there. I heave a sigh and shrug my shoulders.

'Dan will have something to say about that when he finds out.' Marvellous, she's noticed Dan's attention to me in the short time she's known him. Lydia's really warming to this now. Her voice and manner are gossipy. All she needs is a garden fence.

'Dan isn't my boyfriend, Lydia.' I run cold water into my mug and take a big gulp to cool my hot cheeks.

'No, but he wants to be.' She turns both corners of her mouth down. 'It's all right for some. You've two gorgeous men on the go and I've none. One marriage and two long-term relationships on the rocks behind me and no eligible male on the horizon at the mo.'

'Lydia, believe me or not, I am not romantically involved with either of them and I don't intend to be.' I set the mug down in the sink. I want to be out of there, away from her scrutinizing gaze before I say something I don't want to. 'Okay, I'll say my goodbyes to the others, I'm off for a bath. See you tomorrow.'

'Okay.' Lydia winks and gives me a playful nudge. 'Have a wonderful evening with your… er… friend.'

Lydia's treated to my best withering look as I flounce out the door. Once clear of the retreat though, I giggle. If the truth be told, which it won't be, apart from to myself, I'm really looking forward to meeting Harry later. It's such a long time since I've felt excited about going on a date with a man. Years and years. Then I remind myself it isn't a date, it's just dinner with a friend. Next, I sort through my wardrobe and panic about what to wear. Nothing too sexy, but nothing too staid. *For goodness sake, Sam – just wear what you feel comfortable in. It's dinner with a friend – just a friend.*

The wine is going to my head faster than a speeding bullet. How could I have been so stupid to have two glasses on an empty stomach? Nerves, that's why. Harry looks even more attractive in the soft glow of the low lights and open fire. He's wearing a light blue shirt and dark trousers, smart casual, and he's hanging on my every word as if I'm the most interesting person in the world.

The sharing starter of sun-dried tomato bread, feta cheese and olives arrive, and I fall on it like a starving dog. When I look up, I notice humour shining in his eyes and he points at my chin. There's a dribble of olive oil on it and crumbs all over my low-cut lacy green top, I want to disappear into my seat. What must he think? I wipe the oil off and take another drink of wine. Oh dear.

'Nice to see good food being appreciated,' he says, tearing his bread in half between his even white teeth.

'Yes, that's what it's for. Can't see the point in picking at it to be polite.' I give him a little smile and cast my eyes round the pub just to avoid his amused expression.

'You look gorgeous tonight, Sam,' he says and gives me a slow sexy smile.

I swallow. 'Even with oil on my chin?'

'Even with oil on your chin.' Harry takes a pull from his pint, his eyes never leaving mine. Then he puts his glass down, smiles and his eyes crinkle at the edges. 'In fact, it's hard not to lean across and kiss you.'

Okay that's it. I can't talk like this on a half-empty stomach. I'm out of practice and feeling flustered. The thing is, I want to kiss him too.

Toilet.

Yes, that's what I'll do – go to the toilet and cool off a bit. I do a nervous laughter and excuse myself.

After a quick wee, I dab water on my face for a few minutes and check my make-up. Then I go back in the cubicle, put the lid down on the loo and sit on it, just to get my head together. I'm acting like a teenager on her first date. It's time I started acting like an adult. If I want to kiss him I should just do it and get it over with. I'm free, single and apparently very attractive, so what's stopping me? An image of Dan's hurt face presents itself, so I flush it down the loo and walk back into the bar.

As I come around the corner I see a figure in a dark green hoodie and black jeans, his back to me bending over our table talking at close quarters with Harry. Harry looks angry, or is it fear on his face? What on earth? Then my way is blocked by three loud young men singing at the top of their lungs as they bustle out into the cold December night. When I start to the table again I see Harry's alone. He's staring at his pint but looks up as our main course is set down.

I sit down opposite, thank the waitress and ask Harry who he was talking to just now.

A shake of his head. 'Oh, just some guy asking if I could give him a few quid. Some sob story about his kids having no Christmas presents.'

Harry prods a piece of fish around his plate but doesn't eat. Something tells me he's lying, or at least not telling me the whole truth. I stab a prawn. 'And did you?'

He looks up absently, irritation in his eyes. 'Did I what?'

'Give him some money?'

'No. Said I didn't have enough on me.'

The change in Harry is unbelievable. He's gone from an attentive, happy, flirty guy enjoying his evening, to being withdrawn, grumpy, even. I put a forkful of food in my mouth and speak out of the side of it. 'Right. Well, he can't expect anything else really, not just coming up to you when–'

'Look do you mind if we cut the evening short, Sam? I'm feeling unwell, a bit of stomach ache. Hope it's not a bug.' Harry pushes his untouched plate away and folds his arms over his chest. His eyes dart around the place like an unsettled butterfly. Very shifty.

Now I know he's a liar. And not a very good one. But what the hell is the matter with him all of a sudden? I lose my appetite and shove my plate to one side too. 'Oh dear, that's a shame. Shall we go now?'

'Hey, finish your food first if you like.'

He sounds about as sincere as a used car salesman. 'No, it's fine. We'll go. I'll get the bill.'

'My treat.' He's already standing up, walking to the bar. Harry looks perfectly all right to me – no sign of the stomach ache now.

'Will you be okay to drive, you know with your stomach bug?' I say at his shoulder as he hands over his credit card.

'Err, yep. I'll be fine after an early night, I suppose.'

I nod and slip my coat on thinking, yes, you will because there's nothing wrong with you apart from whatever that man said while I was at the loo. I consider asking Harry outright what the real problem is as we drive back home but I can't be bothered. If he wants to play weird games, he can play them with someone who gives a shit.

Harry walks down the side of my house to the retreat with only a brief goodnight to me. I pull my coat tight against the cold wind and put two fingers up behind his back. I fish in my bag for my keys and unlock the door to my house – just as Lydia pops out of the darkness dressed in pyjamas and a duffle coat. 'Bloody hell, Lydia, you scared the poop out of me!'

'Sorry! I've been waiting to ask how your date went but saw Harry's long face as he came in.'

'Yes, it was a bloody disaster. Do you mind if I go in now, I'm cold and tired?' I push open the door and hope she'll take the hint. I'm in no mood for a chat even though she is a lovely woman.

'Oh that's a shame…' She shifts the weight from one leg to the other, her normally pleasant expression replaced by anxiety. 'Dan didn't show up by any chance, did he?'

I turn on the threshold, frown at her. 'Dan? No, why?'

A look of relief washes the anxiety away. 'Oh that's good. I was worried that Emily put her foot in it when he came over earlier.'

'Dan came over? But he's still in Sheffield.'

'Came back early. He wanted to check how we all were and asked where you and Harry were. I was about to say I didn't know, but Emily said you'd gone out for a meal together. She hasn't twigged that Dan's in love with you, so didn't think it was a problem. I'd told Emily the pub you were going to earlier and she told him that too.'

I close my eyes and picture the hooded man again. Could it have been Dan? Doubtful. I'd never seen him in a hoodie and he looked smaller somehow. But there again, I'd only seen him for a few seconds, and he was leaning over… It was possible. I open my eyes and smile at Lydia. 'Don't worry about it, Lydia. I'll tell you everything tomorrow, Now off to bed with you!' I pretend to scutch her round the ear, and she laughs and says goodnight.

I pick up my phone and almost press Dan's number but decide against it. I'll ring him in the morning, sound him out. I'll speak to bloody Harry first though, I want an explanation. I don't give a shit about a relationship, but I need to know what on earth happened. Though right now, all I want to do is have a shower, take my make-up off and this ridiculous too-sexy top, and get a good night's sleep.

A good night's sleep evaded me, because I was too busy lying awake and puzzling over last night's debacle. So, at eight thirty I'm up and dressed and striding down the path to the retreat. I knock on the door and Emily opens it. 'Hi, Emily, I just want a quick word with Harry before we start today's Q&A session.'

I go to step inside, but she shakes her head. 'You'll have a job, Sam. He packed up in the early hours and left.'

Chapter Twenty

Voicemail again. I chuck my phone at the sofa cushion and curse out loud. Harry's too cowardly to even speak to me on the phone – unless he's on the motorway of course. I'll give him a few more hours and try again, though I know in my heart he won't answer. Emily and Lydia found a note propped up next to the kettle when they got up. I unfold it and read it again, hoping to find a clue in the scant explanation that I missed the first few times.

Morning girls,

Sorry to cut my time here short, but I have to go home – family stuff. Loved meeting you both – promise to keep in touch! Xx

No clue. I remember Dan saying Harry was divorced and had a ten-year-old daughter who he shared custody of. Perhaps there was something wrong with her? Yeah right. Perhaps the moon's made of green cheese too. I sink down on the sofa and go over the morning's events. Lydia wanted to know chapter and verse what happened last night to see if it had a bearing on Harry's premature departure, but I couldn't go into it. I just said we'd not really got on and let's leave it at that. I can't face a Q&A session either.

Aware I'm picking at the skin of the side of my nails, I busy myself with cleaning the kitchen. An unsettled churny feeling is giving me indigestion and it's because I can't think straight. Perhaps I shouldn't have spilt it all to Helena when she phoned earlier, but I needed an ear. She said it was a shame about Harry, and she wouldn't be surprised if Dan had been the hoodie man or at least sent a hoodie man to warn Harry off. She ought to be a writer with that imagination. Dan wouldn't go to those kinds of lengths, would he? Actually paying someone? My children really dislike Dan. I can see why to a point, but they don't know him like I do. She told me to have a day off – that there was no obligation to do anything for the retreat. I know she's right, but I hate letting people down. I've no enthusiasm today though, so what's the point? Tomorrow's their last day, so I'll make it up to them then.

On the balcony, I wrap a woolly blanket around my coat, jam a hat on my head and pull on gloves. It's one of those crystal-sharp December afternoons but as cold as death. The cliffs sheltering the beach are stark against the thin blue sky and the sea is deeper than sapphire. This view never fails to take my breath away and despite recent events, I do feel positive and on the up. Harry's still not answering his phone, so he can piss off, but Emily and Lydia have made great progress and thoroughly enjoyed their time here and my input. Just one cloud is on the sunny horizon – a phone call to Dan, I can't do it in person, it's too embarrassing. He might be hurt too if he's had nothing to do with Harry's change of mind and I can't bear looking into his sad eyes.

'Hey, Sam.'

Oh dear. He sounds flat, off-hand. 'Hi Dan, how was Sheffield?'

'Sheffield is Sheffield and business is business.'

Dan sighs and I can hear the TV in the background. Must be at his holiday cottage. 'Right, yeah. So are you coming over to say goodbye to the guests?'

'No. I'm too busy,' he snaps.

'What on earth's up with you?' I say indignantly, knowing full well the answer, but I don't know how to broach it.

'If you must know, I'm hurt that you went out for dinner with that knob Harry.'

His voice is quiet but the bitterness in it could curdle milk. 'I see. How did you know?'

'Emily told me.'

'Hmm.'

'I knew he had the hots for you, but I honestly thought you had feelings for me, and wouldn't have fallen for his debatable charms.'

'I wouldn't have if you hadn't behaved as if you bloody own me! We aren't in a relationship, Dan, and it annoys me that you think you have *any* say in what I do with my life!' That's a surprise. I hadn't intended to say any of that, nor to yell down the phone.

'Right, so you went out with him to piss me off – teach me a lesson, eh?'

I watch a middle-aged couple walking in the sea, holding hands, splashing through the waves in their wellies and I think about what he said. He's probably right, but I did fancy Harry too. I liked the attention and–

'Sam?'

'To an extent, I suppose, yes.'

'Hmm. So… you wanted to make me jealous? That's encouraging.'

The smile in his voice rankles and I remember why I phoned. 'It's all immaterial now anyway because he's buggered off. He was fine at dinner last night until I went to the loo. When I came back, there was some guy in a hoodie talking to him, but before I could see who it was, some drunken hooligans blocked my way and the hoodie man had gone. Harry said he was just after change to buy his kids Christmas presents, but Harry had altered. He'd become irritable, distant… we left the food and came home.'

'Really? Told you he was a knob. Thrilled that it was a disaster though.'

Dan sounds genuinely surprised, but then he's a good actor. 'You don't know anything about this hoodie man, do you?'

'Eh? Like what?'

'Er it wasn't you, was it? Or did you send someone to warn Harry off?' Heat creeps up my neck as I cringe at my words.

Dan laughs. 'Can you see me in a hoodie? And I might be jealous and pissed off that you went out with Harry, but would I go to those lengths? It's not my style.'

I know he wouldn't. For one thing his pride wouldn't let him. And can I see him in a hoodie? 'Sorry, Dan. It's just that when you said Emily told you I was out with Harry, I thought you might have come to find me and…'

'Please. Give me some credit. I'm desperately in love with you, but I'm not desperate enough to do something like that.'

'No. I don't suppose you are.'

'Give me a few hours to finish some work and I'll pop over. I'll bring a bottle of wine and cook us something at yours. You've yet to sample my culinary arts.'

This is a bad idea. I'm feeling vulnerable and I might not have the strength to keep pushing Dan away. 'I was planning on an early night, actually. I'm going to do some writing and have a long bath after dinner.' The couple on the beach are kissing and I have to look away. There's an ocean of tears filling my eyes and a lump forms in my throat.

'Okay. Perhaps another time,' Dan says, the defeat in his voice obvious.

'Yes, see you, Dan.'

'Not if I see you first,' he says quietly and ends the call.

We used to say that often to each other when we were going out all those years ago. It was one of our daft jokes. The poignancy of that and the couple on the beach kissing adds to the lump, and I feel hot tears pouring down my cheeks. Angry with myself, I dash them away and set off for the study. A good dose of cheery Christmas writing is what's needed. A shame I didn't start *Christmas in Cornwall* in the spring as I could have published it this Christmas. Never mind, next year will have to do. There're more ideas buzzing for my next novel too. Just all a bit tangled up at the moment – like my heart strings.

The contents of my fridge and cupboard are decidedly uninspiring. My stomach growls at me so I decide to get a takeaway. I deserve it – I've done three chapters without a break and cooking is way down on the list.

As I ponder over curry or Chinese, the doorbell rings. No way. If it's Lydia or Emily wanting me to join them for a drink, I'll have to be rude. I'll be the life and soul tomorrow, but tonight's just for me. I paint on a smile and open the door. To Dan. Great. He's got a bottle of wine under his arm and a bag of groceries in one hand, in the other there's a bouquet of red roses as big as Jupiter. Must have cost him a bloody fortune, but then he has one, doesn't he?

'If the wind changes your face will stay like that,' he says, giving me a lovely smile.

I close my mouth and force a smile back. 'Bloody hell, Dan. I don't know what to say – I just wanted an early night and a takeaway.' I do wavy arms at his gifts and then I fold them across my chest, try to make my voice assertive. 'I *did* say that on the phone earlier.'

'Yes. But when I said I was desperately in love with you but that I wasn't desperate enough to pay someone to warn Harry off – I realised I *was* desperate enough to ignore what you said on the phone. And if you send me away, then so be it. It's only food, wine and flowers. Not the end of the world, and I'll respect your choice with no hard feelings.' I get a sheepish grin.

How the hell can I be mean enough to send him away after the effort he's gone to? Besides, I don't want to send him away. I want to pull him into my arms and kiss him. Before I can talk myself out of it I do just that. He's so surprised he drops the flowers and we both bend to pick them up at the same time, banging our heads. We laugh, and he follows me into the kitchen. He sets the groceries down and then we just do intense staring at each other for a few moments. I break his gaze by slipping out of my clothes. He pulls me to him in a bone crushing embrace and then caresses my breasts, drops kisses on them and every part of my body. I rip off his shirt and start to unzip his jeans, but he stops me and carries me to my bedroom. For an instant I wonder if I'm doing the right thing, then he steps out of his jeans and joins me on the bed – I stop wondering.

I wake to a delicious smell coming from the kitchen and my stomach forgets about growling and roars instead. Sex on an empty stomach has made me even more ravenous and I slip my dressing gown on and hurry along the corridor. I can't believe I just fell asleep afterwards, must be the release of all that tension. I must admit, I feel bloody wonderful. It's been such a long time since I've made love like that.

As I walk into the room, I see Dan in his boxers and shirt, tasting something on a spoon, and then he dips it back into a pot on the stove. I tiptoe up behind him. 'Caught you! You're supposed to rinse it under the tap – don't want your germs, do I?'

Dan jumps and I burst out laughing. 'Fuck! You scared the shit out of me!' He turns around, grabs me round the waist, hoists me over his shoulder, and sits me on the kitchen table. 'Now, sit there and wait to be served. Won't be long.'

'What are we having? Smells like chilli.'

'That's because it is. But not ordinary chilli – it's got a secret ingredient and I'm making lemon rice too.'

'Never heard of lemon rice, and what secret ingredient?' I catch the bit of garlic bread he chucks at me and scoff it down in one.

'If I tell you, it won't be secret, will it?' Dan flashes a smile and then turns back to his cooking.

A warm glow floods my chest and contentment spreads throughout my whole body. This is what I've missed. This is the sparkly twinkly stuff I've yearned for, the intimacy, the togetherness. It's the little things in life that are the most important. They're actually the big things, but we don't always realise it until it's too late and we've lost them along the way. If Dan and I make a go of things, I promise to treasure each little thing and keep the memory safe in my heart for rainy days and old age.

At the table, I attack the chilli like a starving dog which reminds me of last night's disaster of a meal. What a difference a day makes, twenty-four little hours. I hide a smile and ask Dan how he made the aromatic and flavoursome lemon rice.

'Once again, I can't tell you. It's one of the secrets I'll take to the grave.'

'Whatever, Trevor. It's delicious anyway,' I say, through a mouthful of it.

'Like me, eh?'

I roll my eyes at him. 'Like you, yes.'

'Don't roll your eyes. You're the one who pounced on me, tore my clothes off and ravaged me to the point of exhaustion. You must have found me a bit attractive.' He winks and pours more wine for us both.

'Yep. You're not bad, I suppose.'

'You're okay too, I suppose.' He points his fork at me. 'And it's only taken me nearly thirty years to get you in the sack.'

He's being funny, but it's not really, is it? Because immediately there are unwelcome images of him and Penny coming out of his room half-dressed, of me breaking down, of him saying he's sorry and of her – bright red and guilty as sin. I fall silent and eat my food.

'Oh God I'm such an idiot,' he says putting his fork down and stroking my hand. 'It just came out. I didn't think, really.'

'Forget it. The past is the past and this is now.'

Dan slips from his chair and kneels at my feet, takes my hand and kisses it. 'Please forgive me. This has been such a perfect, if unexpected, evening.' He gives an endearing shy smile. 'That was the past like you say, but I want to be part of your future so much. Can I be?'

I'd be bloody furious if he wasn't after tonight. My bridges are burnt, my guard is down, and I don't care. I like the fact that it is. 'Not sure, Dan,' I say. 'You have to prove your worth, mate.' I smile, push my plate away and lean back, letting my dressing gown fall open to the waist.

Dan's eyes fill with lust and he kisses my neck, my breasts, moaning, 'Am I proving my worth now?'

I lift his mouth to mine, taste the spicy chilli and wine on his lips and breathe, 'Not yet. How about we have a full rerun of earlier, just so I can make sure.'

Chapter Twenty-One

A week before Christmas and it's getting harder and harder to keep Dan and my relationship a secret from my children. Helena came round unexpectedly early one morning last week to see if I could babysit Adam as she had a cancellation come through at the dentist. Dan had to stay in the bedroom until she'd gone. Even then it was tricky, because little as he is, Adam's really sharp, and he can say a few words quite well. He repeats names, so I hope he didn't say Dan to his mum. She didn't mention anything though, so I guess he didn't.

I make the bed, trace my fingers over Dan's side of the bed and can still smell him on the sheets. I catch my reflection in the mirror – a love-sick schoolgirl with splashes of pink on her cheeks looks back as she remembers her recent night of passion. The word 'love' brings me up with a start. Not sure it's that yet, but all the old feelings from years ago are back, and I certainly loved him then. I miss him like crazy when he's not here too – that's a sign this thing we have is more than infatuation. Dan was up and away early this morning as he had business in Exeter, and I'd told him I wish he wasn't going. Then he said he'd get a few more people on board to help out in the new year so he can spend more time with me. He's so thoughtful.

My morning coffee is strong and hot, just what I need to get my head together and think about Christmas again more rationally. Dan says we should just tell Jack and Helena and get everything out in the open. He's right, I know he is, but there's a chance Jack and Felicity won't come over for Christmas lunch as they promised if I do. Helena will feel uncomfortable if that happens too. She's not as against Dan as Jack is, it was her that encouraged me to let him invest after all, but I know she'll be devastated that another man is on the scene. She adored her dad. I told her that Dan had nothing to do with warning Harry off, but she seemed unconvinced. Anyway, whatever happens, Christmas will be ruined. I'm wondering if I should just not say anything until the day, and then drop casually into the conversation that Dan's coming over for lunch, an hour or so before we're due to eat. Then if there's an argument we can have it out of the way before Dan arrives. Yes, that's what I'll do. I finish my coffee and set of for the study.

Christmas morning, I'm beginning to regret my decision to leave the big reveal about Dan and me 'til just before lunch. It's bad enough that Dan had to spend Christmas Eve alone, because Jack and Felicity are here, but he did it without a murmur. He's being very cloak-and-dagger about my Christmas present though. He says I can't have it until New Year's Eve. I make a start on the potatoes and wonder what it could be. He'd better not have gone overboard as I've only got him a new shirt and some aftershave.

Felicity comes into the kitchen and picks up a bag of sprouts. 'Need a hand, Sam?'

I want to say no that's fine, but I could do with some help, actually. Helena usually comes over early to help but she didn't offer this time. 'Only if you're sure. You haven't come here to be put to work.'

Felicity twists her long blonde hair into a scrunchie and laughs. 'You make it sound like I'm a maid in *Downton*.'

We're laughing as Jack comes in. 'Any chance of a bacon sarnie, Ma? I'm Hank Marvin.'

'When aren't you? Just let me finish these potatoes and I'll make you one.'

'I can do it. Just wondered if we had bacon.' He chucks a sprout at me and I splash water at him. Then my heart sinks. This light and cosy atmosphere will likely disappear in a while once I've told them about Dan.

An hour later, Helena, Carl and my darling Adam arrive, and I scoop him up for a big hug. Then we gather round the tree and watch him open his presents. He's more interested in the boxes than the toys, but it's so lovely to see his little face light up every time he opens one. A pang of hurt, sharp and keen as it was the first day I lost his granddad, pierces my chest and I take a gulp of sherry to warm it away. Adam's missing so much. Why did he have to be taken so early? Then guilt creeps in. I haven't been thinking about him too much lately, have I? Especially when I'm in bed with Dan.

'Penny for them, Mum?' Jack says, slipping his arm around me.

That makes me think of poor Penny too. Great. This needs to stop and now is as good a time as any to tell my family my news. 'Um, I'm wondering how to begin really. Here we all are enjoying precious family time on this special day… but there's someone who's missing.'

Helena nods, leans across on the sofa and pats my hand. 'Dad's always here with us, Mum. It hurts like hell at times like this, but I can feel him in spirit.'

Shit. I was going to say Dan was missing, but now it would sound awful after what she said. 'Yes. So can I, love.' I take another gulp of sherry. 'There is something else though. I've invited Dan for dinner. He's on his own now, of course, and well…'

'You've what!' Jack snaps, turning from the fireplace to glare at me.

'Mum, no. You know we can't stand him,' Helena says, her eyes filling.

Carl gives her a warning look. 'It's not up to us, love.'

Felicity looks embarrassed and turns her attention to Adam's musical toy.

I expect this from Jack, but Helena? 'I know Jack's not keen, but you said you thought he was okay. You encouraged me to let him invest in this place.'

'But not take Dad's place so soon. I could cope when I thought you just needed a bit of, you know – comfort.' Her cheeks go pink and she flaps a hand at my surprise. 'Don't look like that, I know he's been creeping round here most nights. We do only live down the road, Mum.' *So that's why she's not been as friendly recently.* 'And Adam's *Dan, Dan, Dan*, when he comes home after the days you look after him – it hardly takes an Einstein.'

'You never told me!' Jack says to his sister, throwing his hands up.

'No. That's because I thought it was a bloody fling!' Helena says, opening her arms wide and sticking her neck out. 'But this sounds more serious now – Christmas dinner is family time.'

Adam looks at his mum and his chin wobbles. 'Mama?'

Carl picks him up. 'It's okay, sweetheart. Mama is just playing. Ooh look. Shall we play with your ball outside?'

Adam laughs and points at the door. 'Ball.'

Carl says, 'I'll take him out for a bit, and when I come back I expect calm. If Sam wants to invite Dan for Christmas dinner, it's up to her. If he makes her happy, then so what. Isn't she allowed happiness?' He jabs a finger at Helena and Jack. 'And it's about time you two stopped acting like a pair of stroppy teenagers.' He grabs Adam's coat and leaves the room.

I have never been fonder of Carl than right at this minute. He's absolutely right. I won't be bossed about and dictated to by my own children. Aware that the situation still needs careful handling though, I say, 'Carl's right. Dan makes me happy and…' I turn to my daughter. 'He will never ever take the place of your dad, love. Nobody could. But don't I deserve some happiness? I don't want to go through my life alone.'

Helena looks at her hands and sighs. 'Of course you deserve happiness, Mum. It just feels really wrong that Dad…' Standing, tears trickle down her cheeks and mine copy hers.

I go to comfort her but then Jack says, 'Yes, be happy, but why him? He's a womanising, self-centred, controlling piece of shit!'

'Jack!' I say, shocked at his vehemence.

'Hey, that's a bit much, Jack,' Felicity says, going to him and putting her hand on his arm.

'No it isn't! There's something about him that I can't put my finger on… besides what I've just said about him, I mean.' He shakes off Felicity's hand and paces the room. 'I just get the feeling that he's out to claim you, as if you're some long-lost prize that's eluded him for years and he can't stand that. No. He has to win at any cost.'

'But why do you feel like this, you've hardly seen him.'

'I've seen enough. Have you forgotten how he betrayed you when you were kids? And all that bull about him helping you to see that you hadn't killed Penny, when you were going through that really bad patch, even though it was a sodding suicide! He'll have put that idea in your head somehow, so he could play the hero. He fucked with your mind while you were at your lowest after Penny's death, Mum. He's total scum.'

As Jack's talking I'm reminded of Dan saying I was wet the morning after Penny killed herself. At the time I'd admitted to myself that Dan might have just made that up to make me think I'd had something to do with it but dismissed that out of hand when the antidepressants weren't in my cabinet. *And* I knew that the suicide note was a fake. What if I *had* killed her after all… or what if *he* had? Okay, there's no way I'm digging all that up again. I've moved on. We've moved on. The wet hair? I might have been in the hot tub with her for a while, but then she killed herself – stole my tablets one time when she was at mine and downed them on the night. Tragic, but that's what happened.

'Let's leave it now. Can't you see how upset your mum is?' Felicity says, coming over and putting her arm around me.

Helena takes my hand. 'Yes, sorry, Mum. If you've chosen Dan, then we'll have to respect it whether we like him or not.' She does flashy eyes at her brother. 'Won't we, Jack?'

Before Jack can jump in, I say, 'It's early days anyway. We might not last, but right now we're good for each other. Let's just see what happens, hmm?'

Jack glowers at us all and knocks back the remains of his sherry. 'Okay. Anything for a quiet life – I'm doing it for you, right?' He points an imperious finger at me and I want to slap it away. 'But don't expect me to be all sweetness and light when he gets here. Might be as well to tell him to leave me alone today actually.'

'Just be polite, Jack. That'll be enough.' I get up and go to check on the turkey while assessing the whole situation. It could have gone worse. Not much, but worse. At least they didn't all jump up and leave en-masse.

'That must have been one of the most uncomfortable Christmas dinners in the history of Christmas dinners,' I say to Dan after closing the door behind Jack and Felicity.

'Could have been worse, love.' Dan takes me in his arms and kisses my cheek.

'But they've all left and it's only half four.' I pull away and head for the wine bottle. 'I mean how lame is the excuse that Jack and Felicity are staying at Helena and Carl's for a few days to catch up. They might as well have just said we can't stand to be under your roof now Dan's here.' There's a tremor in my voice and I bite the inside of my cheek. I don't want to blub.

'Hey, sweetheart. It's all new – a shock to them. Give them time to get used to me.' He takes our drinks into the living room, settles on the sofa and puts his feet up.

He's right. I'm expecting miracles. 'Yes, okay. Just wish it could be all of us here together.'

'This time next year, we'll be one big happy family.' Dan pulls me onto his lap and kisses me.

'You think?' I say and rest my head on his shoulder. It's nice that he's thinking so far ahead. Planning for the future with him would have scared the hell out of me a few weeks back, but now I find it comforting.

'I know it for sure.' Dan strokes my hair. 'Trust me, I'm a magician. If I can't make it happen, nobody can.'

I keep quiet. I honestly think that this is too tall an order even for him. Why can't things just be simple? I look into his soft brown eyes full of love for me and decide as long as I have him, I don't really care.

Chapter Twenty-Two

Dan is spoiling me and I love it. Waking to the smell of a cooked breakfast is one of my favourite things, especially after a night of mind-blowing lovemaking. With a giggle in my throat, I sit up in bed and stretch. Hopping out of bed, I fling open the curtains onto a wonderfully sunny morning and a glimpse of blue sea. Just the morning for a brisk walk on the beach, and it's New Year's Eve – a time for reflection, and of new hopes and dreams for the next twelve months. Let's hope it's better than this one has been. Apart from being back with Dan, the one fantastic highlight.

In the bathroom, I run the shower and let the hot jets of water wake me up properly. I think about how happy I am, but wish my family felt the same. They've been conspicuous by their absence all week, and they're off doing their own thing tonight too. Jack and Felicity are in Exeter for a party, and Helena and Carl are just having a quiet one. They've been up during the night a bit this week with little Adam apparently. This is probably true, but Helena sounded really distant when I phoned yesterday, I remember. Jack said he was in a rush when I phoned him too – couldn't end the call fast enough.

Wrapped in a fluffy towel, I sit on the bed and try to stop my initial good mood evaporating like the steam in the en suite, but it's not working. Yes, I keep telling myself that I don't need anyone but Dan, but that's not true. It's just something I say to protect my battered heart. I want things as they used to be with my son and daughter. They mean the world to me. So what am I going to do, give up Dan? No. No way.

Perhaps I'm just feeling vulnerable – it's the time of year when emotions run high, isn't it? Maybe we need to just give it time, like Dan keeps saying. My children, I've discovered, don't love me unconditionally, or at least their actions lately suggest that they don't, and it hurts. But Dan does. For now, that will have to be enough, and much more than many people manage in a lifetime. I've had two wonderful men in my life – so very lucky. Dan hurt me once, but he's promised he'll never do anything like that again and I believe him. With a smile in my heart, I get dressed, dry my hair and hurry into the kitchen. Perfect timing, as he's setting our breakfast on the table.

We're on the beach in wellies, padded jackets, scarves and gloves, splashing in the waves and laughing like loons. Dan picks me up and threatens to drop me in the Atlantic and I shriek my head off, bringing startled looks and smiles from the surprisingly many people walking here this winter afternoon. He turns quickly, nearly loses his footing, and I demand to be taken back to dry land. He complies, sets me down and kisses me. His lips taste of salt and the Christmas cake we had after lunch, and I can't remember when I was last this happy. It wasn't so long ago that I watched a couple in wellies kissing on the beach and it brought me to tears. I have them now – tears of happiness.

Dan looks at me, takes my face in his gloved hands and knits his brows. 'What's wrong, darling? Why are you sad?'

'I'm not sad,' I say, brushing away my tears. 'I'm ridiculously happy.'

'Good. And I hope to make you much happier in a few minutes.' He gives me a slow mysterious smile and then takes my hand, leads me up the beach to the dunes and we sit down on a big flat rock.

'I don't think I could be any happier, Dan.' I gaze out at the beach scene and heave a sigh of contentment. 'Well, I could if Helena and Jack were more–'

My words stop as he gets on one knee on the sand before me. From his pocket he pulls a little green velvet box and opens the lid. There's a light of hope in his eyes and an uncertain smile on his face. My heart rate rockets and my stomach flips over as the orange afternoon sun, low in the sky, sets a cluster of sapphires and diamonds on fire.

'Sam, the first and only love of my life. Will you do the honour of marrying me?'

Words fail me. I have so many, but none feel right and slide back down my throat before they get to my tongue. I'm so shocked… in a nice way, but marriage. Marriage already? 'I… Dan, I don't know what to say.' I look at him and smile, but I can't see his face properly through my tears.

'It's too soon, isn't it? I knew it would be, but I can't help myself.' He gets off one knee, sits back on his haunches. I wipe my eyes and see his fingers are trembling as he holds the ring box. 'I want you to be my wife. I want us to live together, to share the rest of our lives. Hell, I always did, until I made that stupid mistake with Penny, thinking with my dick instead of–'

My finger on his lips stops his gabbling. 'Hey, don't bring all that up now.' My eyes search his face. He looks so vulnerable and so much like the young man I fell in love with all those years ago. The breeze ruffles his spiky dark hair and his uncertain smile is back. Right now, I know what I want to say and so I'd better go ahead and say it. 'I think this ring is the best Christmas or New Year present I've ever had, and I love you so much…' I stop and twist my mouth to one side, try to look downcast.

Dan puts a hand over his mouth and shakes his head. 'I feel a "but" coming on.'

'I nod and purse my lips. 'But…' He raises his eyes to the clouds and I see his Adam's apple bob once or twice – it'd be cruel to keep this up any longer. 'I have to tell you that I'd be honoured to be your wife.'

Dan lowers his eyes and his mouth falls open. 'You would?'
'I would.'

With shaking fingers, he plucks the ring from its box and slips it onto my third finger. It fits perfectly. I hold it up to the sun and watch the light bounce of the stones. 'It's so beautiful,' I whisper.

'Just like you,' he says, a tremor in his voice. Then he springs up from the sand, pulls me up too and dances me round the beach yelling, 'She said yes! Yes! She said yes!'

People stop, laugh and point, and a few dogs bark. I laugh too and say, 'Hey, calm down. People will think you're nuts.'

'I don't care!' he says and hoists me up in the air.

A knot of people nearby clap and I make Dan put me down. I wave my thanks to the people, and as we walk past them up the beach, they ask to see the ring. Many 'oohs' and 'ahs' follow and by the time we get to the café, I feel like I'm walking on air.

'How perfect is today?' I sigh and dip a spoon into the fresh cream on top of my hot chocolate.

'The perfectest day ever,' Dan says taking my ring finger and twisting it to the light. 'And I've thought of the perfect location for our big day. What do you think about Watergate Bay Hotel? We could have the reception there too – such a stunning view over the ocean.' Before I can process that, he adds, 'And how about February or March?'

'What? You mean for the wedding?'

'No for a road trip. Yes, the wedding, what else?'

'Well, it's a bit soon – it's January tomorrow. There's too much to organise. A dress to buy, a cake to order…' Not to mention breaking it to the family. God, that *will not* be easy. It might take me until March to pluck up courage.

'I'll do all that… apart from choose your dress.' He gives me a big smile. 'It doesn't have to be a grand do unless you want it to be. I just want to marry you as soon as possible and get on with the rest of our lives.' He looks up to the left. 'Mrs Samantha Thomas has a nice ring to it, don't you think?'

My smile is non-committal. I've been Sam Lane longer than I'd been Sam Hennessey before that and another name change feels weird. Besides, it was Adam's name.

Dan frowns. 'Unless you want to keep your name? No pressure.'

'I don't know, Dan. It's so sudden and I need to process it, okay?' I put my hand on his and he nods.

'Yep. Of course you do – I'm just over excited, that's all.' A big smile stretches his face but doesn't quite reach his eyes. That's his controlling nature I suppose. He'll have to curb that once we're married.

In an attempt to lighten the atmosphere, I say, 'I'm thinking a Givenchy dress, a bit like Meghan Markle's, or I should say The Duchess of Sussex. The train should be about ten feet long too. Five bridesmaids, a pageboy – Adam of course – and a quartet to play us in. As you know, Jamie Oliver's Fifteen restaurant is on site, so I'd like to have him to personally create the wedding breakfast and be there to meet all the guests. A honeymoon in… oh, let's say Hawaii might be nice. Can you sort all that in time?'

Dan laughs, and I think he's back to his happy self. 'You can dream on, sweet cheeks.' Then his face becomes serious. 'But, Sam, if you do want a grand do I'll wait until we can organise it even though I want a wedding soon. As you know, I have quite a bit of money and if your dress costs thousands, then I'll be happy to pay it to make your day exactly as you want it.'

Bless his heart. 'Don't be daft. I'm just playing with you. I'd not feel comfortable spending a fortune on a wedding. Just a small cosy one at The Watergate with friends, and *hopefully* family there, will be perfect.'

He takes a swallow of his hot chocolate and dabs his mouth with a napkin. 'Hmm. You're worried about telling your kids, aren't you?'

'Dur, yeah. Can you imagine their reaction?' I take a sip of my drink and the hot chocolate tastes too sweet and cloying, as an image of Helena and Jack's faces – shocked, angry and reproachful – appears in my mind.

'They won't be pleased, but they'll come round. They'll have to.' Dan shrugs as if it's a fait accompli.

'Let's leave that alone for now and talk about the wedding and the rest of our lives.' I blow him a kiss.

'Suits me.' Then he twists his mouth to one side. 'There is one thing that's been bothering me.' Oh great, what now? 'Where will we live? I'd like to think it'd be at your house as you know how much I love it… but might that upset you, with the memories I mean.'

My heart swells with sadness and I look into my mug, blink away tears. My darling Adam and I moved into the house full of hope and happiness. I've not had time to consider where Dan and I would live after the wedding. It's all so new. But yes, it might be upsetting to have Dan living in Adam's and my house. With a napkin, I wipe my tears and sniff and shrug. I don't have the words.

'Sorry, love. I didn't mean to make you sad.' Dan leans his elbows on the table and puts his head in his hands.

I tell him not to worry and we sit quietly for a few minutes to ponder the problem. Then I say, 'It will be hard at first, I think. But I really can't imagine leaving it behind and moving elsewhere either. In a way that would be worse, as if I'm just abandoning the house, the memories and… Adam. I'll never do that, you know. I'll always love him too, so if that's going to be a problem–'

Dan reaches out a hand to mine. 'Hey, hey of course not. I'll always have a place in my heart for Penny too, we can't just wipe them from our lives, nor would we want to.'

I try a smile. 'Okay, so that's settled. We'll live in the house on the cliff.'

'Yes, my darling. And we'll decorate the bedroom – make it more ours. Hell, we'll decorate the whole place if you like.'

There he is again, organising – controlling. I give him a wink. 'Let's just wait and see.'

It's two weeks into January and yesterday I plucked up courage to break the news about getting married to my children. I wasn't brave enough to do it face-to-face, plus that would be difficult as Jack's at uni and Helena doesn't seem to have much time for me now. She tends to rush off when she drops Adam two mornings a week, and when she picks him up she always can't stay long as she's "a ton of this that and the other" to do. I can understand Helena's short of time – she's started a part-time job at a garden centre in Newquay, just to have a bit of a change, as she puts it. I remember how hard it is being a young mum and can see why she needs a break. Still, I know my daughter, and the rushing about is mainly an excuse not to talk to me about Dan.

Dan's up north for the next two days and I'm in the study attempting to write for the first time since a few days before Christmas. But what do I expect? Since then I've lived in a whirlwind of emotion so shouldn't reproach myself. My fingers hover over the keyboard but I just stare at the words *Chapter Seven* for ages, while my mind drifts back to yesterday's phone conversation with my kids.

Both were gobsmacked. Predictably, Jack was furious and ended up putting the phone down on me. He did phone back ten minutes later to apologise, but he was cold and distant. Polite – like a stranger. He's sorry if he upset me but I must realise it will take some time to get used to, and we'll speak again in a few weeks. I'm convinced Felicity had made him call back. She's ever the peacemaker. Helena was just sad. Terribly sad. She broke down on the phone and said she wanted me to be happy, but she couldn't talk about it. Of the two responses, I think hers hurt me the most. Why can't they see the good in him? It's not as if I'm walking into this with my eyes closed. I know he's a control freak, a go-getter, and has been deceitful, but he's also tender, caring and loving. Am I being naive? I honestly don't think so because I've seen the worst of him, know him inside out, and the more mature me can handle him much better than my sixteen-year-old self.

The cursor after the chapter heading is winking at me as if to say, 'You've got no clue what to write, have you?' This is no good – I either get on with it or do something else. Linking my fingers together, I bend them backwards to crack my knuckles and type. *The twinkling fairly lights on the tree reminded Gemma of Christmases past. Her eyes filled with tears, as the grief of missing*

Adam... Adam? I should have written Mark. Okay, I need a break. No point writing in this bloody mood.

The cliff path is a quagmire, and some parts from Bedruthan back to Mawgan Porth have been treacherous. It has rained almost constantly for the past four days, so what did I expect? Because the sun came out today, and I needed to get away from the computer, I thought I'd chance it. Going out to Bedruthan was better as it was uphill, but the slopes coming back are a different matter. Never mind, I'm on the home stretch and the walk in the fresh sea air, stunning views of the churny ocean and the rugged coastline all around, has done me the power of good.

Nearing the intersection of the path which is a shortcut to my place, to my right, I see a bobbing head as a figure climbs the muddy path up from the beach. It's familiar. I look again – yep, Alison. She's *not* what I need right now, or any time, actually. I quicken my pace but my legs go from under me, and I sit down in the mud with an undignified 'Oomph'. My bum's sore but nothing worse than that, and I scramble to my feet, desperate to get away before I'm spotted.

'Sam? Hey, Sam! You okay? You went down like a sack of spuds.' Alison waves and bounds over to me like a bloodhound following a particularly juicy scent.

The "before I'm spotted" ship has sailed then. 'Hi, Alison!' I say, in my most cheery voice. I give a half-hearted wave and groan inside.

'You want to be more careful at your age,' she says with a giggle and tucks her blonde bob behind each ear.

'Hmm yes,' I say and flap a hand toward my house. 'Can't stay to chat as I've got a ton of things to do.' I sound like Helena.

'Oh just stop for a moment. It's ages since I saw you.'

Yes, I think. It was a few months back when I told her to piss off when she popped round unexpectedly. Talk about a thick bloody skin. 'It has been a while,' I offer. She says nothing but smiles and looks at me expectantly with those green miss-nothing eyes. Uncomfortable, I add, 'How are you, anyway? I didn't know you walked the cliff paths.'

She laughs like it's the funniest thing she's ever heard. 'Not really me, is it? But after Christmas I was horrified to find that I'd put on nearly half a stone! I'm going to make this walking lark a regular thing.' I look at her svelte figure in red leggings, black polo neck, walking boots and grey padded jacket and say I would never have guessed. 'Aw, that's a lovely thing to say, hon.'

'Anyway, I must go, as I said–'

'You seen anything of Dan?' She puts her head on one side and a lascivious light comes into her eyes.

'We're business partners, so yes.' That's all she's getting.

'Wish I had. He's bloody gorgeous, isn't he?' I sigh and look away to my house again wishing I were inside with the door locked. 'Mind you, strictly between us, I saw quite a lot of him a few months back – if you know what I mean?'

My head snaps back round to see triumph in her eyes and pouty lips. What the fuck? My voice comes out as a croak. 'No. What do you mean exactly?'

'Isn't it obvious? Though he did tell me not to breathe a word to anyone – you especially.' A peevish expression sharpens her features. 'Obviously still thinks the world of you.' Then she does the annoying laugh again and I want to slap her. 'I would have kept quiet if he'd not been such a shit the next morning. Talk about Jekyll and bleeding Hyde.'

I must have misunderstood. She has a husband in the army... I feel like I'm in some surreal dream... Alison's mouth's moving and she's gesticulating, laughing, and I'm hearing her words, but they aren't registering in my head. All of a sudden I say, 'Wait a minute. Are you actually telling me you had a one-night stand with Dan Thomas a few months ago?'

She looks at me as if I'm an imbecile and speaks slowly. 'Well, yeah, hon... course that's what I'm saying. Me and Soldier Boy have split. Not sure you know.' Then she flicks her bob from behind each ear. 'But like I said, the next morning Dan was like a different man saying it was a mistake, one of his worst. Cheeky bastard.' Alison folds her arms and pouts again. 'I mean, how do you think that made me feel? I was so furious I said I'd tell you if he kept going on, and he said that I'd be bloody sorry if I did. I mean, really!' The laugh again. 'Thing is, I do like bad boys and he is evil. Good in bed too…' Her voice has taken on a dreamy quality and she gives me a wink.

My stomach turns over and I think I'm going to be sick. No. No, Dan, how could you! 'Right… I must go,' I hear myself say and try to force my feet to move. My legs are trembling though, so I just stand there taking big gulps of air.

Alison's face looms close to mine. 'What's up, hon? You've gone ashen. Here, give me your arm, you're trembling all over.'

I yank my arm away. 'I'm fine!'

'Hey, only trying to help. It's not because of what I said, is it? You don't still fancy him secretly, do you?'

I look at the glee in her eyes and the desire to slap her becomes overwhelming. She's loving this. Before I can stop myself, I thrust my neck out and yell, 'You could say that! We're getting married!'

It's her turn to go ashen. She takes a step back from me and wraps her arms around her middle. 'Oh, Sam. I didn't know…'

'It's not common knowledge yet, that's why. I only told my fucking family yesterday!' I take a step forward, my hands itching to close around her scrawny little throat. Then I register fear in her eyes. Good. One more step and a shove to her middle and she'd be flying over the edge of the cliff and into the sea. This thought brings me up with a start and I turn round, fury giving my legs the strength they lacked a few minutes ago and march away up the hill.

'Sam! Sam wait!' I hear her huffing behind and her feet thumping on the path.

'Leave me the hell alone, Alison!'

'No! Please wait! I have to speak to you.'

The urgency in her tone slows my pace and I whirl round to face her. 'What?'

She's standing there breathing hard, her face a mask of concern. Genuine I think for a change. 'Please believe me that I'd never have said anything if I'd known. I was just showing off because I knew you'd had a thing with him years ago. Trying to make you jealous, I suppose.' A quick shake of her head. 'Stupid bitch that I am.'

'I can't disagree with you there,' I snap and give her daggers.

She appears not to hear and babbles on. 'And even though he's totally hot, I wouldn't touch him with a barge pole really, even though I said all that stuff just now, 'cos the look in his eyes freaked me out when he said I'd be sorry if I told you. Shit – my mouth just runs away with me sometimes. Now I've found you're getting married to him I'm really worried he'll want revenge. *Please* don't tell him what you know about us, Sam.'

Alison looks like a frightened mouse, makes a change from a cat that's got the cream. I've no sympathy for her though. She hurts people all the time with her casual spiteful words and nasty gossip. Poor Penny was on the receiving end the night she took her life. My stomach churns when I think of this bitch and Dan together. I shake my head.

'Just fuck off, Alison, before I do something I'll regret.'

I turn back and run up the hill. She calls my name a few times, but I keep running.

Chapter Twenty-Three

How I got through yesterday without ringing Dan and giving him hell down the phone, I don't know. Mr Merlot and Miss Gin helped big time though. My mouth still feels like a sandpit even now. Weak, is what I am. The past three months or so I've told myself I've turned a corner, moved on, become strong. But one setback has me retreating, dependent on a crutch. I drew the line at sleeping tablets, but for a fleeting moment they were an option even though taking them would have been disastrous on top of all the booze.

I look at the kitchen clock – Dan's due back at two, only ten more minutes. It will take all my strength to keep calm, ask him exactly what happened and when, but I'm determined to do just that. When it happened is the key thing for me. If it was while we were together that will be it – over and done, bye-bye, Dan. If not, I'll have to think very carefully. If he lies, I'll have an idea. I don't always, but he normally lets himself down in some way.

A knock at the door. I get up slowly and exhale. Come on, Sam. Time to show your strong side. I'm glad I haven't cut him a key yet, even though he's been nagging for weeks. I want to open the door – let him see my expression – be in control.

Dan's standing there, pulling a daft face. 'Why hello, pretty lady. Can I interest you in some double glazing?'

I turn and walk back down the corridor without a word.

'Sam? Sam, love. What's up?'

In the kitchen, I lean my back against the sink and fold my arms. 'There's something I need to ask you.'

He drops his overnight bag on the floor and slips off his grey suit jacket, a puzzled look on his face. 'Sounds serious.'

'It is. But let's have a quiz. I met someone yesterday walking the cliff path out here. Said she'd put weight on over Christmas and needed a new fitness regime. Walking the cliffs is her preferred choice. Guess who.'

Dan scrubs his hair with his knuckles, loosens his tie and turns his mouth down at the corners. 'No idea, love.'

He looks guilty already. There are damp patches under the arms of his light-blue shirt and he's making a big show of scraping the chair out from the table to sit down.

'Let's make it a bit easier then. She slept with you a few months ago. A one-night stand.' My voice wavers slightly on the last word, but the strength I wanted doesn't fail me.

Dan puts his hand to his mouth and irritation turns to anger behind his eyes. Then he heaves a sigh and looks at the floor. 'No point in denying it, you deserve the truth. What can I say – it was a moment of madness.' He raises his hands and lets them fall with a slap on his thighs.

'A moment of madness before, or after we got back together?' I scrutinise his face.

'God, absolutely before! Why would I look at her when I had you?' His eyes are open, honest.

'So *when* did it happen?'

'It was when I'd come round here and you told me about the missing antidepressants. Later we kissed, got really close then you pushed me away at the last minute, said it couldn't happen. Not ever, remember?' I sigh and nod. 'That evening I was leaving for Sheffield on business but needed to pop into town for a few bits. That's when I ran into Alison in a car park. We chatted for a while and she gave me the come-on big time.' Dan gives me a sorrowful look. 'The rest as they say is history.'

'What? You went to hers instead of Sheffield?'

'Yes. I phoned and said I'd be there the next day instead.' He rakes his fingers through his hair and draws his hand across his stubble. 'I was frustrated, love, needed some comfort. Sex. That's all it was. I had no feelings for her.'

I glare at him but inside I'm leaning towards forgiveness. I do believe him, his body language is open, honest. 'You told her to keep her mouth shut.' I sigh and sit down opposite. 'A pity she didn't – I've been going out of my mind here since yesterday afternoon.'

'Yes, little bitch!' Dan's face darkens and his eyes become coal chips. 'Why the fuck did she tell you? Must have been just to wound – cause trouble.'

I'm startled by his fury. 'She was showing off. She had no idea we were getting married, obviously. Once I'd told her, she was frightened to death that you'd go bananas. I was furious of course – tempted to push her off the bloody cliff.' I give a fake laugh.

'Really? I'm not surprised. And she should be frightened to death I'd go bananas, little mare. I'm going round there now to have it out with her–'

'Er, no, you aren't.'

'Why not? She's deliberately upset you for no reason just because she's spiteful and jealous.' Dan stands up, slips his jacket on.

'Dan, she didn't know we are getting married. Now calm down.'

He steps towards me and opens his arms. 'I'm so sorry, sweetheart. Has this changed anything?'

Has it? In a way. He's supposed to be desperately in love with me, yet after I rejected him he promptly goes into town and shags someone else. But he was a free agent, and if it was just sex – a physical need… 'I can't pretend to be happy about it, but we weren't together at the time.' I fill the kettle and put two cups out.

He looks like a man on death row that's been pardoned. He takes his jacket off and comes over to me, slips his arms round my waist from behind as I make the tea. 'I love you so much, Sam,' he says into my hair. 'I'd give anything to take that night back if I could.'

'Okay, let's just leave it. Tell me about your trip.' I unhook his arms, I'm not ready to go back to normal straightaway.

We talk about his business, the weather and possible honeymoon venues. Then he goes to have a shower and I take my tea out onto the balcony. Some dark clouds are muscling in on the scene from the south, threatening to bury the blue horizon. It's still bright enough for a January afternoon though, and I watch a few people take the path up from the beach that Alison was on yesterday and breathe a sigh of relief. Thank goodness Dan didn't cheat on me. If he had, we'd have been over. A future without Dan is unthinkable, after even such a short time of being together. Hopefully that's it now – no more dark clouds and nasty surprises to spoil our blue horizon.

***

It's unseasonably warm for the beginning of February, and from the terrace in the garden there's blue skies as far as the eye can see. I kick a bit of rubble from my garden chair and sit down at the table. Sunday brunch in my beautiful home, in my beautiful Cornwall with my beautiful man. How lucky I am. The rubble and dust have got on my nerves a bit this week, but you can't build a swimming pool without a JCB and workmen. Dan showed me the drawings of what the whole area will look like in a few weeks. A large kidney-shaped pool, then a decked area with a hot tub under a covered structure which can be raised in good weather. It's very glamorous and so different from the old one. It would have to be to keep the memories at bay.

Dan comes down the path carrying a tray, a look of concentration on his face. The cups rattle together, and he stops to balance them out. 'Need a hand?' I half stand ready to help.

'No. All good.' He arrives at the table, kicks two bits of rubble away, and places the tea and toast down. 'Now for the brunch. Want brown sauce or ketchup?' he tosses over his shoulder as he hurries back.

'Brown sauce please!' I sip my tea and smile to myself. This is what life's all about isn't it? The little things. We've decided to still live apart until the wedding, though he's here more than at his cottage. Old fashioned, yes. But we like that.

He's soon back with the food, and we eat in contented silence for a few minutes. 'You actually made these hash browns from scratch then?' I say through a mouthful of them.

'No. I made them from potatoes. No idea what scratch is.' Dan laughs, and a bit of bacon falls from his mouth onto the table.

'Oh please stop. You're making my sides split,' I say, deadpan. But then can't stop a giggle.

'Shouldn't give up the day job?'

'No. It would be nice for you to work less though.'

'After we're married I'm going part time.'

I look at him to see if he's joking. No sign of mischief in his eye. 'Really?'

'Yeah. I thought three days would be just right. Then I can pamper you, help at the retreat and be a regular perfect husband. No more trips up north either – Malcolm can handle stuff in Sheffield.'

'But that's wonderful!' I plant an eggy kiss on his cheek and he makes a big show of wiping it off with a bit of kitchen roll.

'It is, isn't it? But then I am too.' He smiles, and I prod him in the arm with my fork. We finish our brunch and push our plates to one side. 'What do Helena and Jack think of the new date for the wedding?'

I look out at the ocean and sigh. I wish it was still going to be the end of March because there's so much to do, but The Watergate had a cancellation, so we've moved it to the beginning. Shall I tell him the truth about the kids' response, or the edited version? Edited. 'Jack was his usual self. Said he might not be able to make it as he's in the middle of his dissertation. Helena said whatever suits us. Not much else really.'

'Hmm. Could have been worse, I suppose.'

It was. Jack said he and Felicity had decided not to come as it would end in a row. He was busy too though – he couldn't afford the time off. Helena said she still couldn't get her head round it but she, Adam and Carl would be there. I was her mother, so what else could she do? 'Yes, it could. And I can't wait for the pool to be built.'

'You'll have to for a little while. They think early April. It'll be heated so we'll be able to test it out even if it's chilly.'

'And the hot tub?'

'Same time.' Dan looks at me, a sympathetic smile on his face. 'You're not apprehensive about it, are you? You know, having another hot tub after last year.'

I shake my head. 'It will be very different, so no. There's no sense in dwelling on the past I've decided. This is our new start, and I'm really looking forward to it.' And I realise it's true. I rarely think about Penny now, which might sound callous, but it's not, it's self-preservation. 'What's the latest on the guest situation?'

'Booked up from mid-April to the end of June.' He drains his cup and sits back in his chair, obviously thrilled about it.

The thought of wall-to-wall guests for six weeks or so horrifies me though. Being with Dan feels like I'm caught in the midst of a tornado. My head's already spinning because of the wedding being moved forward. It's only four weeks away. Now this! I fold my arms and say, 'What? We'll barely have come back from the honeymoon and then I'll be straight into organising tutorials. I was hoping to have a spell of working on my book. I've not had much chance with wedding preparations lately.'

He holds his hands up. 'Hey, don't worry. I'll be here more, don't forget, and tutorials aren't obligatory. You can spend as much or as little time with them as you like.'

This is Dan all over. Why hasn't he consulted with me before booking so many? I want to share my writing experience, but not full time. The idea of him doing more means taking control too. Before I know it, I'll be redundant. This needs nipping in the bud. 'The honeymoon will have to be put back. I'm not that bothered as you know.' I fling my arms out to the sides. 'I mean, look where we live. What more could we ask?'

He turns his mouth down at the corners. 'But Hawaii is somewhere you've always wanted to go.'

'One day, yes. But let's postpone until we have everything just as we want it here. The pool, hot tub, the retreat running like clockwork. I find that prospect more appealing than three weeks away, honestly.' I stroke his cheek, give him my best smile. Dan's only fault is his controlling nature, I've found. The other problems Penny had with him won't be mine – I know he won't cheat on me because I'm the woman "who got away". He has me now, so it's just this desire to direct my life I need to sort.

Dan lifts a hand studies his nails. 'If that's what you want.' He's aloof, disgruntled.

'It is, for now, darling.'

He turns to me and a sunny smile comes out from behind his cloudy expression. 'Okay. How can I refuse? Whatever makes you happy makes me happy.' Then he kisses me, and I do a little victory dance inside my head.

Chapter Twenty-Four

Slipping into my new jeans and jumper, and checking my reflection in the bedroom mirror, a thrill of excitement bubbles in my tummy, because today Helena and I are going to Fistral Beach Hotel for a spa and lunch. I realised last week I've no chance convincing Jack to come to the wedding, but I hope to make Helena a bit happier about it. Today we can relax, and I'll try for a heart-to-heart. It's been far too long since we had time just us on our own. Must be a good few years, even before little Adam was a twinkle in her eye.

I hold my swimsuit up, is it too tatty? No, it'll do, but I must get a new one for the new pool.

As I'm leaving for Helena's, trepidation surfaces about the day, and I squash it down. Everything will be cool. It's all thanks to Carl. Helena wouldn't have agreed if he'd not convinced her. My idea to phone him last week and get him on board had been inspired. He's such a nice guy and so accepting of my relationship with Dan. My job is to get his wife to feel the same.

'Definitely one of my better ideas, this,' I say as Helena and I lay side by side on treatment beds having a pedicure.

'Definitely, Mum. I can't remember when I've felt so relaxed. I'd lay down my life for my boy, but it's nice to have a break from him too!'

'Absolutely.' My stomach adds a growl and we both laugh. 'Can't wait for lunch after all the swimming and treadmill work you put me through.'

'It'll do you good. You spend far too much time on your bum behind the computer.'

'Cheeky, monkey. I'm an author, don't you know?' I say in a snooty voice and we both laugh. This is what I've missed – some lovely mum and daughter time. Another thought elbows in though. How am I going to raise the subject of Dan? Will talking about him ruin a perfect morning?

The lunch is delightful, and a glass of Prosecco makes the whole thing a bit special. I've not broached my husband-to-be so far though. I decide to just drop Dan into a conversation about the merits of mixed salad leaves as opposed to iceberg lettuce. If it's not done now, it never will be.

'I've picked out a dress for the wedding, but I'd be grateful for a second opinion… you know, if you have time next week.' It'd hurt when Helena had refused to come dress shopping with me. Said she had loads to do, but we both knew the real reason.

She dabs at her mouth and shifts her cool blue eyes from my gaze. A few moments pass, but Helena says nothing, just fiddles with her raven hair and takes a few sips of her drink. Eventually she looks at me, studies my face. 'You know I'd love to, but if I'm honest, the whole thing's really killing me – twists my gut.' She jabs a finger at her belly for emphasis.

My gut registers the jab. Not going to be easy then. 'Hey, because I'm marrying again doesn't alter the fact that I loved your dad. I'll always love him 'til the day I die.' My eyes fill, and I swallow a lump in my throat.

Helena sighs and her eyes are moist too. 'Mum, I want you to be happy – I honestly do. But I don't think Dan will make you that. He's too self-centred, controlling, and all the things Jack said about him.' She holds a finger up as I'm about to say something. 'I know I said he was nice in the early days, and encouraged you to go into business with him, and you would have lost your house if not, so I did have a method in my madness. But I've seen his true colours since. Just little things he says and does.' She puts her hand on mine and gives it a squeeze. 'I don't trust him, Mum.'

What do I say to that? There's nothing to say really. She's my daughter and I love her, so I'll just have to accept her views. 'Okay, love. I can't make you like him or the fact we're marrying. And believe me, I'm grateful you're coming to the wedding.' Unlike your brother is left unsaid, but it's loud in the conversation nevertheless.

'Of course we're coming. You're my mum and I love you too.' We look into each other's eyes, mirror images apart from the crow's feet edging mine. Then she shakes her head and downs her Prosecco. 'Oh fuck it! Look. I'll come with you to see the dress, the cake, and Christ knows what else, but don't expect me to be sweetness and light to him on the day.'

I do a fist pump and give her a big hug. She smiles, and I clap my hands in glee – pull a daft face. We both crack out laughing and I order more drinks. Thank God we're getting back to normal. It's been awful without her.

At reception I pay for our extras and turn to leave when I notice Helena on the steps outside chatting to Celia, a librarian friend of my old boss Naomi. Not seen her for ages, Naomi either, come to think – though I'm not particularly sorry. I put my purse away, pick up my stuff and go out to join them. As I approach, I notice the two of them look very serious.

Celia gives me a wave and shoves her glasses up her nose. 'Hi, Sam. Just telling your girl here about poor Alison.'

'Poor Alison?'

'God, it's awful, Mum.' Helena says grimacing. 'I can't pretend to like her, but nobody deserves that.'

'Deserves what?' A seed of ice plants itself in my chest and it's growing roots and branches.

Celia says, 'She'd started walking the cliff paths, trying to get fit apparently. Anyway, last week she was on her way back, when she heard someone on the path behind her. She turned round and saw a jogger, but didn't think much of it until this jogger ran past and elbowed her off the bloody cliff!' Celia's voice goes up a few octaves – shrill, grating.

I can't speak. I can't breathe. My mouth drops open and I look from Celia to Helena and back. Eventually out of my mouth croaks, 'Oh my God. Is she hurt badly?'

Celia snorts. 'Hurt? It's a wonder she isn't dead. Lucky for her a strip of mossy grassland jutted out from the cliff about twenty feet down. She landed on that, there were some big stones on it, but at least she didn't hit the jagged rocks on the beach. If she had, that would have been the end.'

Helena continues. 'She was taken by air ambulance to the Royal Cornwall, been in a coma, but she's out of it now. They put her in one for a bit because of her head injuries. She's got severe bruising, a broken collarbone and a fractured hip. But she's alive. Tough as old boots, eh?' She winks at Celia.

'Good job,' Celia says then nods at the hotel. 'Anyway, must get in there for my treatment. I'm having my massage. And after the day I've had I—'

'Is she okay – you know, mentally – with the head injury?' I ask, trying to keep the panic out of my voice.

'Seems to be,' Celia says. 'She was able to tell the police that she thinks it was a man, tallish, but not the detail because it was a dull day and coming up dusk.'

'Didn't she see his face?' Helena asks.

'No. She thinks it was a man, but she can't be sure. They had a hoodie drawn tight round their face and were looking down.' Celia looks up to the left. 'Dark green, I think she said it was, and black jeans. Anyway, see you soon – take care.'

Helena slips her arm through mine and we walk to the car. She's chatting about how awful it all is, but I can't cope. I want to scream and keep screaming until I wake myself up. Because this *has* to be some terrible nightmare, doesn't it?

Chapter Twenty-Five

Alison's a jammy bitch. Anybody else would have plummeted quietly to their death but no. Not her. She deserved to die almost as much as Penny, but she miraculously survived. How does she get off trying to break up a beautiful and loving relationship? A relationship she could never aspire to because she's a conniving spiteful little troll. The answer is obvious. She was jealous and thought she could take what was rightfully someone else's. When she found she couldn't, she set out to try to destroy it. Alison comes across as a larger-than-life character, a femme fatale gathering men like moths to a flame. But she's just a sad bitch whose husband left her for someone else. Is there any wonder?

God it felt so good, the power-surge coursing through my veins when I pushed her over the edge. I heard her gasp in shock as she tried to suck air and failed. Then I watched her flailing arms, her body bouncing off the side of the cliff and heard the satisfying thud when she hit the ledge way below. Okay, she should have landed on the jagged rocks, but even though she didn't, you'd think the fall would have killed her. She must have the luck of the devil. Seems like she didn't recognise me though, which is a lifesaver. If she had, there'd be some very difficult questions to answer, particularly given it's not so long since Penny's sad demise.

Let's hope Alison doesn't start to remember bits that she shouldn't. Because if she does, I'll have to make sure I finish what I started. Nothing will stand in the way of my happiness. I've suffered too long, it's time for some smooth waters on this choppy ocean.

I think I'll pop along and visit poor Alison soon… see how the land lies.

Chapter Twenty-Six

Dan's fresh from the shower and asks if we might go out for dinner as he fancies that new restaurant in town. I can't face eating; I can hardly breathe after what Celia told me this afternoon. I've only just mustered courage to come home – been walking on the beach mulling everything over and over in my head. I can't let go of the fact that Dan was jealous as hell about Harry. Then a man in a dark green hoodie and black jeans was in the pub talking to Harry that night. Afterwards, Harry goes all weird and leaves without a word to me in the early hours. Next, Alison tells me she had a thing with Dan. Dan's furious – and a few weeks later she's pushed off a cliff by a man in a dark green hoodie and black jeans. Dan has to be involved somehow. Has to be.

He's standing there now, looking like butter wouldn't melt and good enough to eat. A towel round his waist, his hair damp, love in his eyes. I say, 'No, I don't want to go out, Dan. I've had a hell of a shock this afternoon.' I sit down at the kitchen table, put my head in my hands.

I hear the opposite chair scrape out across the floor tiles and his hands on mine gently removing them. Dan lifts my chin, looks into my eyes, his face a mask of concern. 'Tell me, love, what's happened?'

'A friend of Naomi's was at the spa, she told us that Alison was pushed off the cliff path by a man in a dark green hoodie and black jeans.' My eyes never leave his, they slide away. His cheeks redden, and he lets go of my chin, rubs his face, shakes his head.

'Oh my God. That's awful, is she hurt?'

'Yes, but not dead, luckily. Ought to have been by all accounts.' My voice is calm, though my insides are anything but. He's rubbing his face again, pinching the bridge of his nose.

'Is she in hospital?'

'Yeah. They put her in a coma because of her head injuries but seems like she's okay now. Must be, to be able to say the attacker wore a dark green hoodie.' My voice sounds less calm and I clench my jaw, wait for his response.

'Must be. Who would have done something like that?' Dan stands up, walks to the sink and looks out of the window at the night sky, except the light's on and I can see his reflection in the pane. He's biting his lip.

I thump the table and he spins round, a frown drawing his dark brows together. 'Aren't you listening? He wore a dark green hoodie, Dan.'

'So what? Why are you yelling?' He sticks his neck out and flings his arms back.

'So what! The guy who spoke to Harry in the pub that night wore a dark green hoodie, you remember Harry. He's the one who fancied me, but after that night buggered off as if the dogs were after him. And Alison. She's the one you fucked and warned never to tell me or she'd be sorry. After she *did* tell me, you were beside yourself with fury. Remember?' I stand up quickly and my chair falls backwards with a clatter. 'Come on – you must remember her, Dan!'

He shoots me a bewildered look and scrubs his hair with his knuckles. 'You're saying I had something to do with Alison?'

I thrust my neck out too. 'Well, did you?'

'Fuck no!' His cheeks are aflame, and his eyes are angry but shifty at the same time. He shakes his head, pinches the bridge of his nose again. 'How could you even think such a thing?' Dan turns round, marches into the living room.

I follow him, and he flops down heavily on the sofa. 'How could I think such a thing? It's a bit of a coincidence, don't you think?'

His hands cover his face and he says, through his fingers, 'No. No I don't.' He places his hands on his knees and glares at me. 'I told you I had nothing to do with Harry, and I *certainly* had nothing to do with Alison.'

'You don't think that a man wearing the same clothes at these two incidents is a coincidence?' As I'm saying it, I do wonder if I've jumped the gun a bit. Dan looks destroyed. But his body language is guilt personified. Especially the pinching the bridge of his nose. He did that the night I found him and Penny coming out of his room when I was sixteen, and he'd the audacity to say it wasn't what it looked like.

'I expect there are thousands of men around wearing dark green bloody hoodies! And to be honest, Sam, if you think I'm capable of attempted murder I don't know where we go from here.' Dan gets up and goes back to the kitchen. I hear the fridge door slam and the crack of a ring pull. I follow him in and watch him chug down half a can of lager without coming up for air.

Taking a wine glass from the cupboard, I wonder where to go next with this as I pour myself a generous glug of Merlot. He's rattled. More than is normal for an innocent man, I think. There's the body language, the leaving the room I'm in all the time to avoid eye contact, the indignant anger. But what if I'm wrong? How would I feel if he had accused me of these things on relatively flimsy evidence? Then a thought occurs. 'I can see why you're upset, but the day I told you I knew about you and Alison, you said you were going round there to have it out with her. You were furious, Dan.' I take a sip of wine and turn to face him.

He gives me a withering look and takes another drink, sets the can on the side. 'Yes, I was, because she's a spiteful bitch and said what she said was to deliberately cause trouble. But I wouldn't have bleedin' harmed her – just given her a piece of my mind.'

'Right,' I respond lamely, pick my chair from the floor and sit on it. I honestly don't know what to think. Perhaps it wasn't him in person, did he hire someone? Helena had suggested that when I first saw Hoodie Man that night. A local thug? That would explain why he's guilty. But then that's as good as doing it himself. Could he do something so vile – actually push a woman over a cliff? Also, Helena didn't put two and two together like me yesterday, did she?

But then I don't think I mentioned the colour of Hoodie Man's clothes to her at the time – just said it was a guy in a hoodie.

'What's going through your mind?' Dan asks quietly and finishes his can. 'Do you still think it was me?'

'I don't know. I feel sick, scared, worried, upset that I accused you. I'd never forgive myself if I hadn't asked though. I really hope you wouldn't be capable, but it just seems such a big co–'

'Coincidence. Yes, you said.' Dan stares at the wall behind me for a while, a far-away look in his eye. 'Anyway, while your jury's out I'm going to get dressed.'

I watch him walk away and then close my eyes, try to think straight. My jury, if pushed, would have to say there's reasonable doubt. I know he's lying about something, whether it's harming her himself, or hiring a thug, or something else, I don't know. I love him, but don't trust him though. Not enough. I can't afford to be blinded by love, not again. My sixteen-year-old self won't allow it. I owe it to myself, my family, to get this right. To be sure. But I need more evidence. I know where to look, but getting it will be very tricky. Very bloody tricky indeed.

By the time he's dressed and back in the kitchen with me, I've fleshed out a plan of sorts. This will involve me first and foremost being nice to him, not too nice, or he'll be suspicious, but apologetic and as normal as I can make myself. I get a homemade pizza out of the freezer and say, 'Shall we have this with a salad and a few chips?'

Dan raises his eyebrows. 'Back to normal, just like that?'

I sigh and open my arms for a hug. 'I'm sorry, love. It just seemed very odd – the whole thing. I know you wouldn't go to those lengths… Maybe I'm just stressed with what she told me, your reaction to her, the way the family's behaving and the wedding nearly on us.'

He walks into my arms, nuzzles my neck. 'You hurt me, Sam. I get what you're saying, but to even think for one minute I'd be low enough to–'

'I know, I know.' I kiss him gently on the lips. 'Please, let's leave it now. Do you forgive me?'

His jaw clenches a few times and then I get a fleeting smile. 'I will, but give me time. I'm still smarting a bit. Let's have that pizza and sit in front of some mind-numbing TV. I'm all talked out tonight.'

'Okay.' I follow him into the living room, point the remote, and *EastEnders* comes on.

'Not that mind-numbing.' Dan takes the remote and sits on the sofa, flicking through the channels. He seems very quick to forget it all and get on with his evening. An innocent man would be still fuming, wouldn't he?

I mentally get a few sentences organised in my head and take a deep breath. 'I might go up to Taunton tomorrow to see Auntie Kath. I haven't seen her since Adam's funeral and she keeps asking if she can pop in and see us.'

Dan frowns at me. 'Your mum's sister? Won't you see her at the wedding?'

'Yes, but she's got this new man and I think she's having a few problems with him. We talk on the phone but it's not as good as face-to-face.'

'I don't want you getting mixed up in any bloody domestic. You don't know what he's like.'

'Don't be daft. He's okay, just boring – set in his ways. Anyway, I'll only be gone overnight. I'm her favourite niece and she says I remind her of Mum, bless her.' I feel like I'm asking my dad if I can stay out late, for God's sake. Who does he think he is? I can't say that though, obviously. I so wish my parents were still here. I miss them every day.

'I could drive you. We could have a few days break – go to a nice hotel or spa?'

No we bloody couldn't. 'Honestly, I'd rather go on my own… It might help to have time apart after today. Just to clear the air, you know?'

A sulk sheathes him like a second skin. His mouth turns down at the corners like a sad clown's and he heaves a sigh. 'Whatever you like.'

I slide on the sofa next to him and rest my head on his shoulder. 'Come on, Dan. You know I love you and I'm sorry. We're good – I just want to see Kath.'

'Yeah, okay. How do you know she's free though at such short notice?'

'I was speaking to her yesterday and she's taken a week off to tidy her jungle of a garden, as she calls it. I'll ring her while the pizza's in to confirm.' I get up and he grabs my wrist as I go past.

'Get me another lager will you, love, before you ring her.' Dan stares at a programme about cars, puts his feet up on the coffee table. 'Oh and a few peanuts, I'm starving.'

'Yes, okay.' I smile, but inside I'm seething. He's milking me being the bad guy here. Much as I'd like to, I can't tell him to get it himself, or shove it where the sun don't shine.

***

Switching off the ignition, I stare at a bay windowed 1930s house at the end of the tree-lined cul-de-sac. There's a calico cat in the front garden and neat and tidy shrubs line the path up to the red front door. My phone says two minutes before five and I cross my fingers that I won't have to wait too long. My fingers come up to my mouth and I have to sit on my hands to prevent me from worrying my nails again. No surprise really with the stress of the journey and all the deception.

Auntie Kath was very suspicious and worried when I phoned her from the services on the drive up. I apologised, said I wouldn't be coming after all like I'd arranged last night, but if by any chance – albeit unlikely – Dan contacted her, she must say I was there. If he wanted to speak to me, she must say that I'd get back to him as I was in the shower, at the shop, anywhere. I couldn't tell her why, but she must trust me and not worry. She agreed but didn't like it. Thinking about her reaction now, my heart sinks. I'm using her, drawing her into my world of mistrust and suspicion. And she was so looking forward to seeing me.

Just as I'm wondering whether to call the whole thing off – leave this place and go back to Taunton – a blue Honda comes past me and swings into the drive of the bay windowed house. The driver's door opens, and the calico cat runs to the man getting out. An envelope folder and a wedge of exercise books under his arm, he scoops the cat up and steps to the front door, key in hand. While he's trying to balance the cat, books and the folder and struggling to open the door, I leave my car and hurry along the road, and walk up the drive behind him.

As I do, he turns, the key still poised in his hand. Then his mouth falls open. 'Sam?'

'Hi, Harry, I know me just turning up here must be a shock, but I really need your help.'

Chapter Twenty-Seven

Harry looks like he's going to say something, but then turns back to the door and lets himself in. He sets the cat down and she winds herself around his ankles. 'Shoo, Lulu, before you trip me over!' He claps his hands and Lulu runs upstairs. To me he says, 'You'd better come through, but I have loads of marking to do, and my daughter's coming over in an hour for dinner.'

Relieved that he hasn't just booted me out, I hurry after him down the hallway and into a spacious and minimalist lounge-diner. There are French windows behind the table looking out onto a pretty garden. He walks towards them and I say, 'I won't keep you, Harry, but I really need to get your answers to a few questions.'

Harry drops the folder and books onto the table and shoves his hand through his blond curls. 'The phone might have saved you a journey,' he says, irritation clear in his tone.

I give him a look. 'It would if you'd answer it.'

I get a wry smile, then he pulls out a chair, sweeps his hand towards it. 'That was a while ago. Anyway, no use in going over that now. Have a seat. Do you want tea, coffee?'

He's just being polite, so I decline and sit down. 'I could have tried to phone you again, but face-to-face is best, I feel. Things have happened which I'm hoping you could shed light on. You might not be able to, but...' A look of irritation flits across his eyes again so I get to the point. 'Harry, what happened that night at the pub and why did you leave without a word to me the next day? It's very important that you tell me the absolute truth. My future plans and happiness depend on it.'

Harry frowns and sits down across the table. 'That sounds serious.'

'It could be.'

'Is this to do with Dan?'

A chill of anxiety prickles in my chest. Why would he assume that, if Dan wasn't involved in his decision to leave in such a hurry? 'Yes. And just to get you up to speed, we're supposed to be getting married. Though I'm suspicious about some of the things he's said and done. I think he might have done something awful and lied to me.'

'Shit. I was right about him all along, but stupidly believed his lies!' Harry thumps the table. Then his frown deepens, and he draws his hand down his face. There's sympathy in his expression but also sadness. Then he sighs, leans back in his chair and strokes his chin. 'What I'm about to tell you mustn't be repeated. Not to anyone – especially not to Dan. Do I have your word on this?' He scans my face, his cool blue eyes serious, his lips a thin line.

I swallow a lump of trepidation. Do I really want to hear this? No. No, I don't but I have to. Must. 'I swear on the lives of my children and grandchild. I won't tell a soul.'

A quick nod. 'Right. This is what happened that night. I'll warn you, it does involve your future husband and you won't like it. Still sure you want to know?'

I breathe in and exhale through my nostrils. Why doesn't he just get on with it? 'No, Harry, I don't. But I must.'

He nods again, looks at me then away out the window. 'Okay. As soon as you'd gone to the toilet, Dan comes hurrying over to our table. At first I didn't recognise him in the low light as he had the cords of his hoodie drawn tight around his face...'

My heart rate thumps up the scale and my fingers grip the edges of the chair to force myself to sit and hear the rest. I want to run, scream, but I can't. I'm trapped like a rabbit in the headlights waiting for impact.

'He told me that you were still grieving for your husband and had a breakdown not long after. Therefore, you weren't ready for any other kind of romantic relationship. I said I didn't take kindly to being warned off and perhaps he was a bit jealous.' Harry stops, asks if I'm okay.

My voice has deserted me, but I nod for him to continue.

'Then he says he's not trying to warn me off, just protecting you, and if I saw you come out of the loo I should tell him, as you wouldn't understand and would get overwrought. I said I wouldn't be surprised, and it was obvious that he fancied you himself. That's when his demeanour changed from wheedling to really shirty. He said I couldn't hope to understand, that he didn't just fancy you, he was in love with you, had been for years – tells me your backstory and also what happened to his wife and your part in her death.' Harry stops, leans his elbows on the table, and blows heavily through his nostrils.

What the fuck? My stomach threatens to come up into my throat, but I manage, 'I… I don't understand. What part?'

'Because you were damaged after losing Adam, you weren't to be trusted. You wanted revenge on Penny and had psychotic episodes. He told me Penny took her own life because you'd threatened to steal Dan from her, just because you could. Said you were cruel, played with his affections, leading him on then putting a halt to it. That you might be dangerous if you didn't get your own way. I should leave right then and never contact you again if I knew what was good for me.'

Dear God. I can hardly believe what I'm hearing. 'The absolute shit! How dare he?'

'There's more, unfortunately,' Harry says quietly, touching my hand. 'I said how did I know he wasn't making the whole thing up, so he shows me a newspaper headline on his phone about her suicide in the hot tub at the retreat. I was rattled, I can't pretend otherwise, but it still could have meant that Dan was out to scare me off, so he could have you for himself – I said as much to him.'

I'm impressed that Harry had so much integrity, given I'd only just met him. But I can see he's reluctant to carry on. I'm reluctant to hear it but I press him for the rest.

'This is the worst bit, Sam. I feel ashamed that I cut and ran, but when you hear the last of it you'll understand, I hope.' A sigh. 'Dan said that you'd stop at nothing to get what you want. He said that you knew I had a daughter, but she'd suffer as you had to be number one. If our relationship developed, he'd fear for my daughter's safety and could I risk that? No, I couldn't. Of course I couldn't. I wanted him gone, I told him you'd stepped out of the Ladies and he ran off.' Harry shakes his head and takes my hand. 'I'm so sorry I let him get to me. You must have wondered what the hell was wrong when you sat back down.'

Tears push behind my eyes and I take my hand away – pat his as I do, to show him I appreciate his comfort. I can't have him being nice to me though, or I'll just collapse into a soggy heap. I brush my tears away, stare at the floor and say, 'I totally get why you were off with me after all those lies, Harry. But I just wish you'd asked me about it all at the time. I'd have put your mind at rest.'

A quick nod. 'I was going to the next day. It was a lot to take on, just like that, sprung on me in the middle of dinner – Dan might have been bullshitting, I hoped he was. But I hadn't known you five minutes and the truth is… I wasn't sure I could cope with Dan at every turn if we started a relationship. It was clear already that even if you didn't do what he'd told me you had, and he was just a thuggish ex-boyfriend warning me off, he wouldn't just disappear quietly into the background.'

'And that stopped you talking to me the next day and taking off. I really don't blame you at all, Harry I–'

'No. No it was something else.' Harry sighs and shakes his head again. 'Dan phoned me at midnight just as I'd got into bed. He said that if I was still unsure about sticking around, I'd be sorry. He sounded pissed, to be honest, but I could tell he meant every word. He said you were going to be his at any cost and if I didn't leave before the morning and never contact you again, neither me nor my daughter would be safe.'

My hand flies to my mouth and a chill runs through my body. I can't speak, my whole world's teetering on its axis and about to topple.

Harry continues. 'That was the last straw. I got out of there because my family comes first. I'm sorry, Sam, but the man you're going to marry is a fucking nut job and I'm guessing a very dangerous one at that. I'd put nothing past him.'

Silence grows between us and I wrap my arms around myself, squeeze my chest to stifle a scream. Harry's last few sentences grow and swell, grow and swell – repeat over and over in my head until I'm deafened by his words. I sit motionless and think about what Dan's done. What the man I love has done… my future husband. He's lied to me – lie upon lie, threatened Harry and his daughter with violence, and now there's no doubt. No doubt at all. He also pushed Alison to what he thought must be certain death. And all of a sudden, a lightning bolt of realisation slams between my eyes. If he's done all this – what's to say that he didn't kill Penny too?

Chapter Twenty-Eight

Not accepting Harry's kind offer to stay over might have been a mistake. I didn't want to intrude on his evening with his daughter though. If I were him I would have wanted me gone, pronto. Such a nice guy. Never mind. My hands grip the wheel as I overtake a huge lorry, its tyres spraying my windscreen with muddy water. Torrential rain. Marvellous. It's a long drive back to Cornwall, made worse because of my state of mind. I have to keep stopping at services, as I can barely concentrate on the road.

At the next services, I grab a coffee and phone one of our local hotels – book in for the night. I need to have uninterrupted time to myself. Dan thinks I'm at Auntie Kath's until tomorrow afternoon, so I should have time to decide what to do next by then. My logical brain tells me there's nothing to decide. My gut reaction at Harry's news was right. I should cancel the wedding, ditch Dan and be thankful I had a lucky escape. My heart tells me it's not that simple though and anyway, he won't give up without a fight. I blow across the surface of my coffee and feel a lump form in my throat. It's not simple to just switch off my love for him either, is it?

The bedside clock in the hotel room says 12.03am but I'm not tired despite the driving. I phoned Dan about an hour ago to say I missed him and I'd see him tomorrow. That was tough. I had to focus on what Harry had told me to stop myself from breaking down. Dan said he missed me and couldn't wait to make love to me tomorrow, that the bed was too big. I wonder if we'll ever sleep in it again after this.

The hotel bed isn't the comfiest and I thump the pillow, wish I could confide in someone about it all. There's no one though. I can't burden anyone else with such serious information. This is something I need to do all by myself.

Unable to lay here any longer, I get up and take a sheet of hotel note paper and pen from the desk and sit at it. Adam always swore by writing down the main points or questions and answers for making important decisions. It helps to clear a path through the swamp of emotion and tangled thoughts. At the top of the page I write:

Things I know to be true about Dan – irrefutable evidence.

1) He is Hoodie Man. He threatened Harry, told vile lies about me, all because he was jealous.

2) Dan was furious with Alison because she told me about their one-night stand. He wanted to go to her house and give her a piece of his mind the day I confronted him. He knew she had a new fitness regime walking the paths because I told him – so it was easy for him to find her if he wanted to.

Things I suspect, but can't prove:

1) Dan was Hoodie Man following Alison – he pushed her off the cliff to what he assumed was her death. But was it an accident? Did he just stumble, knock into her? Unlikely, but not impossible.

2) If Dan is guilty of doing the above and the Harry thing, how do I know he didn't drug and kill his wife? He faked a suicide note – is that because it was murder – Penny didn't kill herself at all? Seems likely… and made me think I had something to do with it. Bastard.

The WHY questions:

Q – Why did he do it all?

A – He will stop at nothing to get me, make me his. He's always been in love with me and furious with himself for getting caught out all those years ago. He also hates failing. Does he want to control me – dominate my thoughts, my life, my heart?

Q – If he killed Penny, because he adores me so much, why did he choose a way that implicated me? The character in the novel, the antidepressants, told me I had wet hair etc.?

I bite the end of the pen, puzzle over the answers for a while. Go over the past few months, the way he won me over, the way I've begun to rely on him so much. I write:

A – Because he wanted me to think I could have done it in a drunken stupor. Acting out my plot – oblivious. He wanted my family to suspect me too. He wanted to be the knight in shining armour, writing the suicide note and rescuing me from the police. Drying my hair when he found me "out of it" (he put something in my drinks to make sure I was) in my bedroom – was my hair even wet? Clearly demonstrating he'd do anything for me…

Even though I later realised the tablets in my cabinet were gone – which he must have taken – he still assured me I couldn't have done it. When I was at my most vulnerable, Dan believed in my innocence one hundred percent. Dan had unconditional love for me – very important when my children withdrew, became distant. Dan was my only constant. My lifesaver. He made himself indispensable, easy to love.

The clock says 2.10am as I slip under the duvet once more. My face is wet and my heart empty. What do I do? Where do I go from here? Do I cancel the wedding and write a man whom I still love out of my life, on mere suspicion? Is it my overactive writer's imagination running away with me? Did Dan have nothing to do with Penny – she just killed herself after all, just as I've believed for the last few months? Well, mostly. There was a time when I thought I could have done it – particularly with our past history… I wake up even now from troubled dreams of that night. Penny's screams ringing in my ears, sweat sheathing my skin, sheets tangled – the red glow of that cigarette stark before my eyes in the grey light of dawn.

I turn over, punch my pillow hard, think about Alison. Was her incident just an unfortunate accident? Was Dan hoping to just talk to her and it went horribly wrong and he kept quiet? Then a picture of the irrefutable evidence section concerning Harry floats in my mind, and I ask myself, isn't that reason alone to leave him anyway? Threats of violence and flights of fantasy. It's not normal, is it. Could I ever trust him in future? Would I ever believe another word he said?

Two hours later, I think I've worked out what to do to get at the truth. I've also worked out what I want to do if I get it and he's guilty. It'd be gut wrenching, and unbearably painful to leave this comfortable love-filled nest my life has at last become. But even though my whole world will be torn apart, I'd have to carry on without him. And is my nest really so cosy? What about the controlling nature, the decisions taken behind my back, who knows what else? Lovelorn, I've excused these flashing lights of warning. Jack saw through him, but not me. Stupid idiot that I am. I will *not* turn into Penny – Dan fooled her all his life. He won't fool me again, not like he did all those years ago. Getting my temper under control, I remind myself that a person is innocent until proven guilty. Then, utterly exhausted, at last I drift off to sleep.

***

'What! You have to be kidding me,' Dan says, incredulous, leaning forward and staring up at me from the sofa.

'Nope. That's what I want, and you'll thank me for it.' I smile at him and set the shopping down on the dining room table.

'I'll thank you for enforcing celibacy for the next three weeks – I don't think so.' He flops back and does his pouty face.

'But just think how special it will be on our wedding night.' I pull a bottle of gin out of a carrier and wave it at him. 'Fancy one of these while I'm getting dinner ready?'

'I'll need the whole fucking bottle to get over the shock of no sex we're British!' Dan tries a laugh, but it comes out bitter, humourless.

I do my best earnest expression. 'Please, Dan. It's something I feel strongly about – it will make me happy.' *And the main thing is I can't bring myself to have sex with someone so vile, and a potential murderer to boot*, I'd like to say, but can't.

He follows me to the kitchen and watches me unpack the rest of the shopping. 'If that's what you really want… but sleeping in the same bed is going to be torture.'

'Perhaps we shouldn't then. You could stay at your cottage.' I take two tumblers out of the cupboard. 'Which I've yet to see the inside of, for some inexplicable reason. You hiding a floozy in there?'

Dan turns his bottom lip down. 'Wish I did have a floozy now sex is off the menu.' I give him a withering look. He takes the tumblers and makes us both a G&T. 'And anyway, it's not inexplicable. I told you that the place is a complete mess. It's just a dumping ground 'cos I know I'm going to leave it soon. There's mucky washing about the place, plates unwashed. Can't be bothered to clean – never have time. There's some of Penny's things in there still too – just don't want you to see the state it's in. It might put you off me.'

No. Other things have done that I'm afraid. 'Okay, keep your secret bachelor pad from me, I don't care.'

We talk about nothing in particular for a while – the weather, how my Auntie Kath was, the wedding. Then I make a start on dinner, all the time topping up our gin glasses… except when he's not looking, or out of the room, I pour mine down the sink and fill it with tonic water. Dan's a bit squiffy, drinking so much on an empty stomach, and puts his hand over his glass the next time I go to top up. 'Hey, are you trying to get me rat-arsed? Get the dinner on the table, wench, before I wither away!' He tries to grab me round the waist, but I dodge out of his grasp and drain the rice.

'Sid down, 's ready now…' I laugh and take a swig of my tonic. 'I'm rat-arsed too. It's ages since we had gin – must get it more often.'

Dan gobbles huge mouthfuls of his curry and rice as if he's not been fed for a week. I've made it extra hot and so he downs more of his drink. 'Bloody hell, this is spicy. We need water.'

He gets up but I wave him back down, giggling. 'Here have more gin and tonic – the tonic helps with the heat – I read it in a magazine.' I pour more of both into his glass and he sighs, takes a few sips and then the bubbles make him snort. We both fall about laughing and I decide he's had enough for a bit – I need him drunk, not wasted.

After dinner, we curl up on the sofa in front of the fire and he switches the TV on. Annoyingly, he's poured himself another strong gin, so I hope he's not going to conk out in five seconds. I sip my "gin" and say we should turn the TV off and just talk. It's ages since we had a chat about what really matters. He looks askance, but flicks his finger across the remote and we sit there listening to the crackle of the fire and the wind moaning outside.

Taking his hand, I look adoringly into his eyes and ask, 'Tell me about when you first realised you wanted me back.'

Dan gives his head a little shake. 'Don't have to think about that one. It was as soon as I saw your face the night you caught Penny and me at my house.'

'Really?'

'Really.'

'So why did you give up so easily back then?'

He shuffles the cushions, thinks for a bit. 'I wouldn't say it was easy – I did beg you, numerous times on the phone, but you always slammed it down after a few seconds, then I came round to yours that time, but your dad sent me packing, remember?' I did. Good old Dad. 'But I didn't try hard enough, that's for damned sure. Youthful pride, I suppose. Penny was nice enough – always gave me what I wanted too – and at that age it was very high on the list…' He sighs and takes more gin.

'Then when you realised your mistake a few years later, you tried to find me, but discovered I'd left Sheffield, was married, had Jack?'

Dan gives me a wry smile. 'You know the story, so why are you asking?'

I knock back my tonic and fling my arms out dramatically. 'Because I love hearing how you adored me for years and years – couldn't get me out of your head, yearned to be near me once more!' Then I collapse in a fit of giggles.

'You're pissed, my love,' he says, amused.

'No – just merry. And I do like hearing how you always loved me – it's romantic.' I reach up and stroke the side of his face, drop a kiss on his lips.

A flame of desire lights in his eyes and he tries to kiss me again, but I move away, put a cushion between us, say we can't. The desire flicks to anger. 'Sam, stop messing with my head. You can't kiss me and expect no reaction.'

'I'm sorry. I forgot for a moment that we're being celibate. You're almost just too sexy to resist.'

Dan moves nearer. 'Then don't, it's a stupid idea.'

'Please, Dan. Just think how explosive our wedding night will be if we save ourselves.' I'm cursing myself for kissing him. Stupid of me. He sighs and goes to reply but before he can, I ask, 'When you were with Penny, did you always wish you were with me – I mean, did you ever love her?'

Dan drains his glass. 'What's with the twenty questions?'

'I told you. It's nice to hear about your life since we spilt as kids up to where we are now. These are the important things.'

He shrugs. 'I guess I loved her at first. She couldn't do enough for me, worshipped the proverbial ground et cetera. That kind of thing can boost your ego. When we got married and I was building the business, she was good at dinner parties – networking and so forth. Her career was always secondary to mine. What I wanted, I got.'

'The stuff she told me about all your affairs over the years – was any of that true, or was she just paranoid?'

Dan looks a bit uncomfortable, but says, 'Before I answer – I'd never cheat on you – you know that, right?'

I nod.

'Yes, it's true. I was faithful for about a year but then if an opportunity arose, I took it. Penny wasn't enough for me. Not exciting enough. The main thing is, she wasn't you. She couldn't hold a candle to you. You're the love of my life – it's always been you.' Dan takes my hand, kisses the back of it.

'But you said she was the perfect wife – adored you?'

'But she was too adoring. Too accepting of anything I told her, the lies I spun. She must have been suspicious about the nights I crept in at 3am but never asked.' Dan rubs his chin. 'Until a good few years into the marriage that is. Then she started asking more – said she knew about the flings but hoped I'd grow out of it. Once she asked me why she wasn't enough for me.' He stops, looks at me, a sly smile spreads across his face. 'Guess what I said?'

'Um… that she was enough and was delusional?'

'No. I said because she wasn't you.' The pride in his voice sickens me. How cruel.

'Really? Oh, Dan that's so bad – but I must admit it makes me love you even more,' I say, hoping he believes me.

'It's true. What can I say?' He goes to take a drink but finds the glass empty. 'Time for a refill?'

'Not for me – and should you?'

'No. But it's Saturday tomorrow and at least I'll just crash out when I get to bed – stop me thinking about shagging you.'

I muster a giggle and follow him out to the kitchen. 'Is it true about you having a vasectomy without her knowing?'

Dan pours a drink then opens the fridge, roots around and pulls out cheese and ham. How can he be hungry after a big dinner? Must be the booze. 'Yes. I didn't want kids, I'm too selfish.' He's not wrong there. 'I certainly didn't want them with her.' He cuts cheese and grabs crackers from the cupboard.

My heart goes out to poor Penny. No wonder she was so sad. But then if I had been in her shoes, I would have walked years ago. How could they have been happy? This thought prompts another question. 'Why did you stay with her all those years?'

Dan crunches into a cracker. 'Not sure. Habit, I suppose.' He dangles a piece of ham over the cracker then just chucks it into his mouth instead. 'Like I said – she was a good hostess, great at running the home, gave me respectability with clients. Better than a whoring dirty stop-out that I actually was.' Dan laughs and shows me a mouthful of food. I turn away, sip more tonic water, repulsed more by his words than his manners.

'When you saw me at the reunion, found I was a widow, did you decide right there and then to win me back?'

Dan grins, adds a wink. 'You bet yer sweet ass.'

This needs to be played carefully. He's very merry, but not too far gone to the extent that he doesn't know what he's saying. I go over to him and hop up onto the counter, pinch a bit of his ham from the crackers. He pretends to be shocked but then just laughs.

Through a mouthful of ham, I drop in a casual, 'But Penny would have been a barrier to that. There's no way I'd see you again while she was on the scene.' I swallow the ham and cut a bit of cheese from the block.

'No. But I hoped that once we started seeing more of each other – you know, when we came down here to look for a holiday place, you'd fall in love with me all over again.'

'But even though Penny did the dirty on me back then, I wouldn't have done the same to her, even if I did love you.'

'And did you?'

'Love you?' I ask. He nods. 'Not at first, but I did fancy you. You know damn well I did – remember the night of the dinner party?'

'Oh yes. That was the night that I first had hope we'd be together again – even though your darling Jack warned me off.'

'That didn't stop you, though did it, my hero?' I give him a melodramatic flutter of my eyelashes.

Dan laughs and carries his snack into the living room. Over his shoulder, he shouts, 'Nothing would have stopped me. When I decide on something I get it – no matter what.'

My heart does a somersault. No matter what… including murdering your wife? I go back and sit next to him on the sofa. 'That's one of the things I love about you – your determination not to take shit, and to just go for what you want. I can't help feeling

sorry for Penny though, all those years not loved and cheated on.'
I sigh and down the rest of my water in one.

Dan shakes his head. 'Don't feel sorry. I had no respect for her in the end. She had no respect for herself either. She was like an adoring little dog that still licked its owner's hand even though it had been whipped over and over. Didn't stop her moaning and whingeing all the fucking time though.' Dan's eyes glitter in contempt in the firelight. He seems to really be getting into this.

'You must have had some affection for her though, love? Even when you had decided to get me back, you didn't just dump her.'

'No. Because I wanted her to give me her parents' nest egg. Once she'd done that I was going to. She'd always sponged off me, so why not? Sorry if that sounds cruel, but I'd put up with her whingeing, moaning and accusations for years. Had to put up with her in bed too. She'd got the size of a whale – I can tell you I was nearly sick at the thought of shagging her at times.' Dan links his fingers and stretches his arms above his head and yawns.

Such harsh words to hear, but it's more than I could have hoped for. Dan seems to have dropped his guard completely because of the gin and my sycophantic "drunk" act. I lean my head against his shoulder, put my feet up on the coffee table, say, 'Eww, too much information… and I could tell you were pissed off about the money when you wanted to invest in this place. Penny was refusing it, just to keep you away from me. Of course, I totally get that, she was scared of losing you. God knows what I'd do if you ever left me.'

Dan turns, cups my face in his hands. 'My darling, I would never, *never* leave you. Okay? I've waited too long and gone through so much to get you – there's no way you're ever getting away.' The intensity of his stare chills me.

'Good job. But what do you mean gone through so much?'

He looks shifty, mumbles his words. Then he coughs. 'Just that I waited so long for you. It was hell.'

'Yes, and then once we'd found each other again, Penny stood in our way, didn't she? She'd always be there like a thorn in our side if she'd have lived.' I say in a faraway voice and stare into the fire, watch the flames dancing, hope I'm not overdoing it.

'Um…' he says and shrugs.

'You know that you once said you'd do anything for me.' Dan smiles and closes his eyes. Come on, Dan don't conk out now. I give him a gentle nudge. 'Dan?'

'Huh? Yes, of course. Still would.'

'And you'd stop at nothing to get your own way, like you did to win me back?'

'Yesh, damn right.' He yawns, settles his head on a cushion.

'And… Penny stood in our way, so you got rid?'

'Yeah.' Then his eyes fly open and he looks at me, wide awake now, obviously shocked at what he's let slip. 'Eh? What? Killed her, you mean? No, of course I didn't.'

My heart is thumping so quickly I'm light-headed – think I'm going to pass out. Oh my God he admitted it. Admitted it even though he's now trying to claw back what he said! His eyes are like panicked butterflies skittering about my face, the room, not landing anywhere. Then he closes them and settles back, says, 'Sometimes I do wonder what goes through your head, Sam.'

An attempt at a normal voice fails him. It's strained – higher than usual. I shove my hands under my armpits to stop them trembling and say, 'But if you had, it would be the ultimate show of love, wouldn't it? She was the obstacle in the way of you being happy with the love of your life. Me. Me who you'd waited thirty years to be with again… and as you say, you always get what you want.'

Dan chucks the cushion on the floor, sits up, and frowns at me. 'Are you seriously saying that I'd go that far?'

'To get what you wanted? Perhaps you did.' I look away, back into the flames.

'That's madness.' High pitched and squeaky.

I exhale deeply and go for it. Test the words in my head – the ones I rehearsed last night as I lay awake in the hotel bedroom. 'Look me in the eye and tell me you didn't kill her, my darling.'

Dan's eyes find mine. Through the gin-fog there's fear and mistrust. His fingers come up, pinch the bridge of his nose. Oh God…

'No! I didn't kill her. And I can hardly believe you asked me that, Sam. The drink's gone to your fucking head big time!' Dan pinches his nose again and goes to the bathroom.

I flop back on the sofa, drained, exhausted, shaking with the shock of his revelations. He's lying. Lying, and I can hardly breathe, let alone stand to be in the same house as him. But I must. I must keep up the pretence for what I need to do next.

Chapter Twenty-Nine

How can I carry on as if nothing's happened? Just looking at Dan's face makes me sick to my stomach and when he puts his arm round me, my skin crawls. This man who was my whole world is a murderer. A cold-blooded calculating murderer, and it would have been twice over if Alison hadn't been lucky. It's as if I'm on autopilot today. I'm standing outside myself watching a play about domestic bliss. Dan and I are on stage cooking Sunday lunch, laughing about this and that, talking about the wedding, the weather, the future, and all the time I want to run for the wings, leave the theatre and just keep running.

Last night he'd come back from the loo and sat in stony silence until I'd apologised, said it was the drink talking and please could he forgive me. Dan had shrugged and said he'd have to, he supposed, and then quickly fell asleep in front of the TV. I went to bed in one of the spare rooms and set a chair against the door in case he came to me in the night – he didn't, thank God. He could have, being worse for wear and trying to go back on the celibacy thing. One thing worried me more than fighting off his drunken advances though, and it chilled me to the core. As I'd jammed the chair back under the door handle, it had struck me that I could actually be in real danger. He says he adores me, but how do I really know what he might do when pushed? I remember the chill in my bones when he said he'd been through so much to ever let me get away again.

I chop carrots and relive the look in his eyes when I'd asked him if he killed Penny. An image of his face struggling with the shock of what he'd said in reply. *Yeah*. He'd let it slip, said yeah, then pretended he didn't get what I meant. Pretended to be confused. Then he did the nose pinching, left the room.

Shit! I've nicked my finger with the knife – I need to focus. Dan's seen and he's hovering over me, kissing the little ooze of blood all better, running it under the cold tap and all the while I'm screaming over and over in my head. I want this charade to stop, but it can't – not yet.

After lunch, Dan's outside faffing about at the retreat and examining the new hot tub. It's going to be ready earlier apparently. The thing's still in its packaging and not plumbed in yet, but Dan pushed for it being ready for around the time of the wedding. He's got some romantic notion of us sitting in there, toasting our sunny future with champagne. A humourless bark of laughter escapes me. If I didn't laugh, I'd cry.

He thinks I'm going to write this afternoon, so I stop watching him from the door and go to my study. My Christmas story sits unopened in my documents, and my finger scrolls the screen to a file entitled *Research for Suspense.* Notes I made in there for the suspense novel I had to abandon because of the method of Penny's death aren't forgotten, but I just want to double check on some points. Yes, here we are – *psychopaths/psychopathic tendencies.* Some don't match Dan – so he couldn't be classified as a true psychopath – though experts differ on what that is, or if such a condition exists, but there are many that do match. I read down the list:

Successful.
Good at manipulation.
Charming.
Arrogant.
Controlling.

Yes to all of these, but these traits could apply to many people. I'm looking for something else too… I scroll again… *personality disorders… pride in criminal act/harm/murder…* There's information here about those who commit murder or other terrible acts keeping reminders, trophies or records of what they've done. It's part of their idea that they won't be found out, because they're cleverer than the authorities, than anyone, and sometimes they somehow get off on it. Or perhaps it's a matter of simple pride. This is what I'm counting on. Hopefully Dan's kept some evidence of how he killed Penny, or attempted to kill Alison. I've a good idea of where it might be hidden if he has, and a plan to access it. However, the danger involved makes my fingers on the keyboard tremble as I shut down the computer and leave the room. I need some air, a walk on the beach and a break from being the best actress in the world.

***

'Two weeks today we'll be man and wife,' Dan says, shoving a bit of toast in his mouth and giving me a crumby kiss on the cheek. I'm glad I have a legitimate excuse to wipe it off for a change.

'We will, and I for one can't wait.' I collect our plates and stack them in the dishwasher.

'Me either. I'm not sure how much I can stand of this not living together and no sex either.' He gives me a lascivious look. 'Can't we just do it right now – a quickie? Before the builders get here? It's doing my head in.'

I move away from his searching hands and give him my serious face. 'No. Please, Dan, it won't be long now – and it will so be worth it.'

'It had better bloody be.' Dan sighs and goes outside to wait for the builders. He's here early as they want to discuss the problem with the swimming pool tiles or something. I couldn't concentrate on what he was waffling on about when he arrived an hour ago, and don't really care, because after days of being on tenterhooks, the opportunity I've been waiting for has at last presented itself. On the back of the chair is Dan's jacket, and in that jacket are his keys. Thank you, God.

I saw Dan drop them in his pocket when he took the jacket off to have breakfast. Up until now he's been busy in the day, tying up loose ends before the wedding, and so only arrives here in the evening, or we've gone out. There's no way I could have taken them and done what I had to before he realised they'd gone. Today is the day.

I dry my hands on a tea towel and watch through the window as the builders' van pulls up outside. Dan goes to meet it and three men get out, shake his hand and then from the back door I watch them gather around the hole in the ground which will be the new pool. One of them hands out bits of paper to Dan and they look at them. *Come on, Sam – do it. Do it now!*

Back in the kitchen, I lift the keys from his pocket, feel the cold weight of them in my hand and swallow down panic, but it comes up again bringing nausea with it. I almost put the keys back as the tension of the last week or so nearly gets the better of me, but I have no choice. I owe it to Penny. A dull chink as I toss the keys into my bag, then I'm off out the back door, stomach churning, I feel like I'm watching the scene from the wings.

'Hi there.' I give a quick wave to the builders. To Dan I say, 'Just popping to the shops, love. I won't be long. I'll get a nice cake and some scones, so you can all have them with a cuppa when I get back.'

The men look puzzled and Dan frowns. 'Not sure the guys will be here that long.' He looks at the men quizzically.

''Fraid not, much as we'd like cake and tea,' the oldest of the group says with a smile, 'but we've another job on – half an hour here should sort it.'

'Oh? Okay, never mind perhaps another time,' I say. The men nod and smile, and I hurry away before Dan can ask me anything.

Half an hour. Damn! That's going to be tight, but it'll have to be enough. I jump in my car and set off like a racing driver into town.

Forty-five minutes and Dan looks like a man demented. His normally neat spiked hair is ruffled every which way, his jacket's on the kitchen floor in a heap and he's stalking the living room turning up cushions, tossing throws and panting like an old bull. Upon seeing me, he says, panic in his voice, 'Sam, did you take my keys by mistake when you went out?'

Shit, he looks ready to do murder. Thank God I had a flash of inspiration while I was out. My face assumes a rehearsed hurt expression. I nod and perch on the edge of the sofa arm. 'Yes. I was going to surprise you later with it, just slip them back into your pocket, but I got back too late and you've missed them already.'

Dan scrubs his hair with a fist, looks at me like I'm nuts. 'What the hell are you talking about? You do have my keys?'

'Yep.' I paint on a triumphant smile and pull the keys from my bag, toss them to him.

He catches them, furrows his brow some more and shakes his head at me. 'I don't understand.'

My stretchy smile begins to ache but I keep it up. 'How many keys did you have this morning?'

Dan spreads his hands and the keys clink together, gives me a quizzical stare. 'I don't know, five or six?'

He's not even looked at the keys. 'You had five. Now you have seven. Look at them.'

He sits on the opposite arm of the sofa, lifts the keys, fingers each of the new ones. 'One's just a piece of metal shaped like a heart key – the other's a real key – but to what?' His frown's gone now, and he looks more settled, relieved. The wild look's gone from his eyes. Good.

'The heart key speaks for itself, it's the key to my heart.' My voice wavers on the word 'heart' as emotion threatens. How I wish it could all be different, love can't just be turned off like a tap, can it? Love's dying because of what he is – but not quite dead yet, it seems. 'The other is the key to this house, my darling.'

'Aw, hon.' Dan kisses the heart key and comes over for a hug. 'How sweet of you – and sorry to spoil the surprise.'

'That's okay.' I pat his back and sigh. 'I've been trying to figure a way of taking the bloody things for ages without you knowing and this morning was the only opportunity. Shame I caused you to panic because I was late back.'

'I panicked because I had no clue what the hell I did with them. I knew I had them when I arrived because my car key fob is on there and I drove here. After the builders had gone, I went on the balcony and leaned on the railing for a bit looking at the view. I was just going to fly down to the bloody beach to see if I'd dropped them over somehow, even though I couldn't remember having them in my hand,' Dan says and laughs into my hair.

'That's because I had them in my bag.' I laugh too, move away, stand up and gesture to my shopping bag. 'I got some cake and scones anyway. Fancy some with a coffee?'

'Love some.' As I'm walking to the kitchen, he says, 'I don't get why you needed to take my bunch of keys to the key cutter though. Why couldn't you have the new keys cut while leaving my keys here? Then slipped the new ones on later?'

Took a while for that thought to drop, didn't it, Dan? I'm ready for it though.

Over my shoulder, I say, 'Because I've never been able to undo bloody keys from a fob, or put them on. My nails are like paper. Adam always had to do it for me. So I had to take your keys so the guy in the shop could put the new ones on. Then I was going to present the keys as a big surprise. Never mind. All's well that ends well.'

***

The handful of holiday cottages huddle together on the side of the hill as if they're worried about falling into the surf at Fistral beach. I drive into the scrap of a car park behind the houses and turn off the engine, my heart thumping harder in my chest than the waves against the rocks to my right. It's a wonder I've been able to drive in the state I'm in and have been since I waved Dan off to Sheffield a couple of hours ago.

A week's flown by since the key cutting, and I've waited for this day like a condemned prisoner waits for reprieve. Before yesterday I was worried that there'd be none, and I'd have to come here while Dan was still in Cornwall, wait until he was busy with something and hope for the best. But then there was a call from his partner up north and he decided to go up there in person to sort something out to do with the business. He wasn't going to at first – said he'd manage it from here until I said I had stuff to do – secret wedding stuff, and could do with him out from under my feet. Thankfully he bought it.

Now I'm here though, I can hardly prize my hands from the steering wheel. What if by some crazy chance he's forgotten something and comes back while I'm inside? How will I explain it? I remind myself there's a half-baked idea ready in my arsenal to say I was getting his shirt size as I didn't know it… I wanted to buy him some new ones. Another "surprise". I watch my fingers grow white at the knuckles and force myself to relax their grip. Over and over, I repeat in my head – *Dan's on his way to Sheffield, won't be back until tomorrow. You can do this.*

I pull the cords of my hoodie tight under my chin, jam sunglasses on my face and get out of the car. Then I take a deep breath, fold my fingers round the cool metal of the new key I had cut from his key ring, and make a dash for the front door of Dan's cottage.

Chapter Thirty

I shut the door behind me after sticking my head out and having a quick check in the car park to ensure nobody saw me come in. Then I take off my sunglasses and push back the hood. My God. At least Dan wasn't lying about the unholy mess in here, but I know it's not the main reason he's always put me off when I've asked to see the place. I pull on surgical gloves and start to explore. Clothes strewn on the sofa, his mostly, but some of Penny's in bags. Pizza boxes, some containing the remains of pizza on the floor and coffee table. Empty beer cans crushed and discarded next to the sink, a dishwasher full of clean but unloaded crockery and toast crumbs scattered across a chopping board, the work surface and over the floor under it.

The bathroom is a little better, but the towels could do with a wash, and the toilet is disgusting. I hurry out into the corridor and push open a door which turns out to be a small and neat bedroom. This must be the spare, as the bed's not been slept in by the look of it and there's just a little chest of drawers under the window. I open the drawers – empty. Next door is the master bedroom and there's so much mess in here it's hard to see the floor. Damp towels, dirty socks, pants, shirts. Why is he living like this? He's always neatly presented and clean – I couldn't have coped if he wasn't.

Flinging open the wardrobe, I find clean clothes, mostly suits, shirts and ties hanging in colour order. A few drawers to the left of the hangers have clean towels, socks and pants. Bloody hell. It's as if there's two halves of his living area: one that's a complete mess, one that's clean – functional. A bit like his brain, I imagine. Though I'm not really sure how a murderer's brain looks. I check myself. I have no proof… yet. The mess is going to make my task to find evidence even harder. I turn in a slow circle, taking it all in. I don't know what I'm looking for, or even where to begin.

About to shut the wardrobe door again, my eye is taken to a shoe rack at the back of the wardrobe. The shoes on it are all clean and shiny, but at the end of the rack is a plush red velvet drawstring bag. I reach in and pull it out to get a better look. It's soft and quite light, and it has a gold Harrods logo across it, so I'm betting there's something important in there. I pull open the drawstrings and ease out the folded garment inside. I shake it loose and then drop it to the floor as if it's scalded me.

It's a green hoodie spattered with mud.

I lean my forehead against the cool wall, calm myself. This is what I've been looking for, but it brings me no comfort. There's a tiny illogical part of my brain that's been hoping that I have it all wrong about Dan. But this hoodie says I don't. I don't, and there must be other stuff. Stuff to do with Penny.

Half an hour of picking up mess, searching under it and putting it back carefully where I found it again hasn't turned up anything else. The fridge? No. Nothing apart from cheese, eggs and milk. Freezer – pizza and bread. Think, Sam.

I go back to the bathroom – reluctantly because of the state it was in, but I need to do a thorough search, I won't get this chance again. With my trainer I flick the lid down on the toilet and gingerly open the cistern. Nope, nothing hidden under the water wrapped in plastic like you see on TV dramas. How about the cupboard under the sink? A toilet roll, a bar of soap and some razors.

There's a dressing gown hanging on the back of the door – nothing in the pockets. Nothing in the shower. I look in the bathroom mirror over the sink at my frustrated expression and note that the mirror is gleaming, pristine. Then I note that it isn't just a mirror, it's a very slim cabinet. No handle or knob though, but it definitely has a recess. Carefully, I feel around the edges with my gloved hands, then remember a cabinet I once saw in a showroom when Adam and I were looking for a new bathroom suite. Perhaps this is the same kind. I press the bottom right-hand corner of the mirror and it swings open.

My heart in my mouth, I look past a tube of toothpaste and a toothbrush to an array of tablet packets placed in a precise line on the top ledge. My hand reaches up and I pluck out the first one with trembling fingers. The packet's white with green edging… I turn it over in my hands and read what's written across it in red marker pen – *I will beat you!*

My legs feel like I've borrowed them from a drunk and I slump down on the edge of the bath, the tablets clutched in my hand. I've seen this packet before, this handwriting. I wrote it what seems like a hundred years ago. These antidepressants are mine. The ones that went missing from my cabinet, the ones that I thought I'd somehow used to drug Penny, the ones that were found in her system. The ones that Dan stole and administered… to make it look like I'd something to do with her death.

Forcing myself to focus, I stand up and look on the shelf again. There are some more tablets of the same type. New packets – how did he get them? Easy, he'd just have gone to the doctor's – upset after Penny's "suicide". I read the printed name and address on the front – yes, Dan's. What worries me most is why he's got more. Is he planning on doing the same thing to me if I prove hard to control at some point?

Next and last on the shelf is a different packet. I take it out and see that they're Diazepam… used to be known as Valium. I rack my brains – no, Valium weren't found in Penny's system, but there's some gone out of the packet. The obvious slams into my consciousness like a wrecking ball and nausea rolls. I sit, clutch the side of the bath, try to keep calm but my stomach won't wait, and I lurch for the toilet – vomit. The state of the bowl makes things worse and for some time I'm unable to do anything – helpless, shaking.

Eventually I'm strong enough to stand and splash my face with water. The last time I felt like this was the morning Penny was found. I snatch a length of toilet roll, dab my face and mouth.

Valium. He must have put Diazepam in my drink – I was nauseous, sick in the sink and Helena had to put me to bed at nine. He'd put Diazepam in my drink, why? So I didn't wake and disturb Penny's murder. That's why I felt so rough the morning after… couldn't remember anything. I remember reading an article about Diazepam, some sickos use it as a date rape drug. Too much can put you in a coma when mixed with alcohol.

Fury wells up from my gut and I hurl the packet at the wall. The bastard! Playing with my life like that!

I rush out of the bathroom, fling open the back door and look down the steep incline towards the sea – inhale big gulps of ozone to steady myself.

After a few minutes, I'm feeling stronger. I conclude that my suppositions when I wrote the question and answer section at the hotel a few weeks back had been absolutely right. Dan had wanted everyone to suspect me. Even my family. Even me. That's why he told me my hair was wet that morning, took my tablets to ramp it up – made me vulnerable, frightened – more likely to rely on him. He was the only one who truly cared, would do anything – wrote a suicide note to set me free. My constant, my hero. It would only be a matter of time before I fell for him. Before he won me back – triumphed.

Any trace of guilt I might have harboured in the dark recesses of my heart has now been released, swept away on a breeze out to the blue horizon. Because all this time it had been him. Dan. Dan had attempted to kill Alison and had actually killed his wife. No more ifs or buts, I had his admission on that gin-soaked night – now I have the hard evidence. This is what I came here searching for and I have it. Dan was enough like a psychopath to keep his reminders, his mementos. My hunch has paid off and now I can take it to the police. The hoodie and the tablets.

Back in the bathroom, I check to see everything is as it should be and thump the cabinet shut a bit too hard. There's a shuffling sound and then I see the corner of a little red book sticking out between the cabinet and the wall. I carefully pluck it out – looks like a notebook. I open it. As I read, a prickling sensation runs down both arms and up my back and a weight of gloom settles in my stomach. My legs won't hold me, and I slump to the floor still reading. Just two little entries but their content is massive. Massive and terrifying because they're written in a hand that I recognise. Mine…

I read them again, too numb to do anything else:

Penny, oh God… it's so weird to think you aren't here any more. Just when I thought we were getting back on track… but then you did kind of ask for it. Ever the doormat, you just allowed yourself to slip away – never put up a fight. You never did put up a fight, even when it mattered, I remember…

It's so sad, because when I think about it – you were a bit of a non-person. You pretended to be the life and soul, without much of either really. A sad spineless cow that owed everything to her husband. It was as if you sucked everything of any value from him like a leech. A big, FAT leech. You stayed close, basking in his glory, hoping that some of his personality would seep into you and become yours. Make you interesting to know. Luckily, he had enough charisma and sparkle to share – but it really didn't make an awful lot of difference in the grand scheme of things, did it? You wore his reflected glory like cheap Christmas baubles on a cut-price tree.

And now you're dead and gone. Dead and gone with hardly a mark to show where you've been. No children to carry on your memory, or your line. Just as well. You were a one-off. It could have all been so different if you hadn't opened your legs all those years ago. Your husband would have been with the love of his life, and you wouldn't be dead. But you are, and that's down to you. You brought it on yourself without a thought for your poor husband. What on earth will he do without you? Who will he go to for comfort?

Don't trouble yourself too much though… I expect he has a few ideas about that.

And the next:

Alison's a jammy bitch. Anybody else would have plummeted quietly to their death but no. Not her. She deserved to die almost as much as Penny, but she miraculously survived. How does she get off trying to break up a beautiful and loving relationship? A relationship she could never aspire to because she's a conniving spiteful little troll. The answer is obvious. She was jealous and thought she could take what was rightfully someone else's. When she found she couldn't, she set out to try to destroy it. Alison comes across as a larger-than-life character, a femme fatale gathering men like moths to a flame. But she's just a sad bitch whose husband left her for someone else. Is there any wonder?

God it felt so good, the power-surge coursing through my veins when I pushed her over the edge. I heard her gasp in shock as she tried to suck air and failed. Then I watched her flailing arms, her body bouncing off the side of the cliff and heard the satisfying thud when she hit the ledge way below. Okay, she should have landed on the rocks, but even though she didn't, you'd think the fall would have killed her. She must have the luck of the devil. Seems like she didn't recognise me though, which is a lifesaver. If she had, there'd be some very difficult questions to answer, particularly given it's not so long since Penny's sad demise.

Let's hope Alison doesn't start to remember bits that she shouldn't. Because if she does, I'll have to make sure I finish what I started. Nothing will stand in the way of my happiness now. I've suffered too long, it's time for some smooth waters on this choppy ocean. I think I'll pop along and visit poor Alison soon… see how the land lies.

I stare at the words. Stare and stare. I didn't write this. DID. NOT. But then all the doubts about the vengeful me, the vicious me, the vindictive me, push at my rational thought – rush at it all at once until it's swamped. My hand comes up to my mouth trembles over my lips, stifles a moan that's been building. I look at the words again and slowly my rational thought recovers – pushes back. This isn't my writing. It looks a hell of a lot like it, but my 'fs' and 'ys' are less looped, straighter. The 'ts' are wrong too. But my God it's good. Really good.

The book falls from my hands, falls shut on the tiles. A memory from school thuds into my head. Sick notes from parents written to order, a fiver a time – a nice little earner he'd said. Everyone marvelled at how good a forger he was. Dan, ever the entrepreneur. He'd written another note recently, too hadn't he? That one fooled the police. The implication of these entries is clear. They're insurance for the future. In case I decide I've had enough – want out. I'd be punished – would have to be. A few nights ago, he'd said he'd never let me go. This would stop me leaving because if I did, he'd take the book to the police. If I called his bluff, I'd end up inside.

Tears roll down my face as I look up at the cabinet and it blurs to just a suggestion of square light on the wall as I realise he has more. He's not keeping the tablets as a memento – he's keeping them as proof! Proof that I killed Penny. They were my tablets – my handwriting on them. I wrote the suicide note – tried to kill Alison too. It's here in the book, after all.

I get to my feet and stumble out of the room. Lean against the wall in the kitchen. I have to think about this calmly. Think what to do! I can turn it round on him before he gets back. I have the tablets, the hoodie, the book with my fake writing. An expert could tell it wasn't mine and then he'd be in deep shit. He'd be the one inside. Fury at what he's tried to do builds and I kick a chair across the room, pretending it's his face.

Anger gives me strength, power. But a second later it drains as more thoughts rush in. Some tablets, a hoodie with mud on, my insistence that he confessed, a notebook with my 'so say' fake writing. They're not enough, are they? Would the police arrest him on this? Probably, but is this evidence alone enough to convict him? It will be my word against his about the confession. My writing's on the tablets. If I tell them about the suicide note being fake I'd be implicated in covering up Penny's murder.

My world turns upside down, I stumble into the living room and sit on a high-backed chair – my thoughts in turmoil. I try to unpick a positive strand from the tangled mess in my brain, but I can't. More of the same instead. The antidepressants are mine, I could have planted them on Dan, for all the police knew. But what about his fingerprints? They'd be all over them, wouldn't they? He'd think of something – a way around that. He's better at lying than I am. He's charming too, confident, assured.

Just like me today, Dan probably wore gloves too. He'd get lawyered up – the best money can buy, and he'd get off. Then he'd get revenge no question. My life wouldn't be worth living. I'd end up inside – not him. Hell hath no fury like a murderer scorned. But what can I do? There's only one thing to do. I have to try and bring him to justice – clear my name.

I collect the red bag from the wardrobe, the tablets and book from the bathroom, and put my hand on the front door handle. Then all the arguments flash through my head again and the scenarios of their outcomes. I sigh. There's more than just one thing I can do. Dashing tears from my eyes with the back of my hand, I return the items to their places ensuring everything is as Dan left it. Then, with a heavy heart, I walk out of the cottage and drive away.

Chapter Thirty-One

Early signs of spring are making an appearance along the cliff path. By my feet, there's a shy crocus emerging from slumber, its yellow petals reflecting the weak March sunshine. Below on Mawgan Porth beach, the scene looks like a painting. The obligatory surfers sit astride their boards waiting for a wave, a few seagulls wheel above them screeching at the horizon, and dog walkers hurl balls along the sand from plastic catapults. I wonder how the round red-cheeked lady and her unruly dog Hattie are getting along. I've seen them from time to time, but they aren't here today. My mind's taken back to the day I first met them – me stood in wellies, hoping the tide would carry me away. Today I'm a long way from that sad place – but there's still some dark to come before my dawn.

Despite my situation, the walk has done me good, and adrenalin lifts my spirits as I set out on the last stretch home. It's a week since the wedding. Jack and Felicity didn't come, thankfully. Isn't it funny how life changes? A few months ago, I would have given anything to see my boy's face on the day. The way things have become, I would have given anything to keep him away, if he hadn't done that himself. Helena, Carl and my darling Adam came, so did a few work colleagues and my old boss, Naomi – but not poor Alison of course. No. She's still in recovery, and it's uncertain whether she'll walk again, but Naomi says she's in fine fighting spirit. Determined to get well. She can't remember any more about her attacker though, sadly.

The wedding went as well as could be expected under the circumstances. I put my key in the front door and congratulate myself again on how I avoided the disgust of sleeping with my husband on the wedding night. My husband the murderer. Diazepam in his champagne once we'd got to our bridal suite in the hotel did the trick. A taste of his own medicine – literally. Dan had gone out like a light until morning. When I'd pointed out he'd had the brandy and champagne, plus what he'd had through the evening, he'd accepted that he'd been caning it and didn't seem too suspicious. Why would he? I'd carefully researched how much to add – I didn't want to wake up with a corpse.

The next morning, I unfortunately "found that I had my period" and that it would probably last seven days. I said I was as devastated as him, of course, as we'd both waited so long to consummate our marriage. Never mind.

In the kitchen, I fill the kettle and take two mugs out of the cupboard. I go in search of Dan and find him out by the hot tub, fiddling with the controls. He's like a kid with a new toy since it was declared open this morning. I remember that he wasn't so pleased, in fact he was furious, when I told him that tonight I've treated my daughter and her husband to a rare night out – at a hotel spa and restaurant, and I was babysitting. Tonight was supposed to be our late "wedding night". A romantic evening to celebrate the early completion of the new hot tub with champagne and special canapés. The whole thing had been my idea, but it had just slipped my mind and I'd double-booked. Obviously, I hated to let him down at the last minute and told him I'd see what I could do about it.

The mugs rattle against the plate of biscuits on the tray as I carry it down the path towards the chairs and table on the new raised deck. The view of the coast from this perch is even more panoramic now. Heavenly. Dan looks up from the hot tub and I smile. 'I've made tea and got your favourite biscuits, sweetie.'

'You spoil me, hon.' Dan grins, sits opposite and shoves a whole Hobnob in his mouth at once. Crunching it down, he takes a swig of tea and says, 'Have you had any ideas as to how we can still have our romantic evening?'

I dunk my biscuit and say, 'I have. I'll get Mrs Jacobs, Helena's neighbour, to sit for an hour. She'll jump at it, her being on her own after her husband died last year.' I give Dan a sexy pout. 'God, Dan – it will be so romantic, rushing back here to join you naked in the tub. Get the champagne on ice, but don't start on it until I get back. I'm not having you conking out on me like you did on our wedding night.'

He shakes his head, bewildered. 'I still don't know how that happened. I'd had a drink, yes – but not that much.'

'You know you did. But let's not go over all that now.'

Dan gives me a slow lingering look, his gaze alighting on my breasts and then flicks up to my eyes. 'How about we christen the tub now? We can always do it again later.'

I have to think quickly. 'No. We've waited this long – we can wait until tonight. I want it to be special.' Dan frowns, opens his mouth as if he's going to protest, and I add, 'I have stuff to do, anyway. Stuff to be ready for our special night.' I give him a wink and blow him a kiss.

That seems to have pacified him a little, but he says, 'I wish you weren't staying over at Helena's. If Adam stayed with us, we'd have more time and you'd hear him if he woke because of the baby alarm thing.'

I smile. 'It's called a baby monitor. But I told you, he's going through a funny phase being scared of the dark right now. He'll be better at his own house and settle better in his own surroundings. His parents won't be around to comfort him if we have him here.'

Dan nods grudgingly and kisses my cheek. 'Okay, Sam. Whatever you think best. I love you so much, you know that, right?'

'Of course I do, Dan,' I say, and kiss him back. And I do know. Despite everything he's done and would do in a flash, if he felt threatened, he does love me. Well, whatever love actually means for him. Always has – I never doubted it. That's what makes it all so desperately sad. I'm not sad for long though. Fury drives what I have to do.

***

Bath time with Adam is a delight. He squeals when I blow bubbles at him and he piles a heaped tower of them on his head. With the back of my hand, I add a bubble beard to his chin and show him in a hand mirror. He chuckles so loud and long that I think he'll never stop. It's infectious, so free and joyful, unencumbered by any self-conscious worry about sounding daft or uncool. Toddlers are a tonic. I join in, adding my giggle to his and it feels good. I can't remember the last time I laughed, or even cracked a genuine smile.

Later I lower him into his cot and note that it won't be long before he'll need a real bed. A pang of sorrow touches my heart. Time moves on so quickly, doesn't it? I wish he could stay little for longer. In a few years he'll be at school and not need me as much… but that's just a selfish thought. I need to take each phase as it comes, because each will be different and filled with new adventure. Life is what you make it and I plan to make the rest of mine worth living.

I turn the lamp on by the cot which rotates colourful patterns on the ceiling and Adam watches them, his eyes opening and closing as sleep tries to claim him. 'Story, Andma?'

'Really? I think you're too sleepy for a st–'

Adam's eyes open wide and sets his mouth in a determined line. 'No. Story peese.'

I nod, pick up a storybook and swallow hard. Sometimes I can see his granddad so clearly in his mannerisms. I wish my darling Adam could have seen this little one. He's missed, is missing, so much. Maybe he can see him somehow, see me too. I like to think so, sometimes I feel so close to him, as if he's standing by my side. I'll always love him and keep his memory alive, so perhaps that will be enough until we meet again. I wipe away a tear and begin to read, but when I look up from the first page, I see that Adam's fast asleep.

Breakfast is a messy affair as Adam insists on "helping" me with mine. Helena and Carl walk in to find my face covered in jam, and scrambled egg in my fringe. The two of them look refreshed and happy as if they've been away on holiday, not just overnight, and I'm glad I could give them some time as a couple.

'Thanks again, Mum, for that lovely surprise.' Helena hugs me on the doorstep as I set off for home.

'You're welcome. It will have done you good to have a night away.'

Helena gives me a shy smile and looks over her shoulder at Carl who's boosting Adam into the air. 'Yes. Especially now we're trying for a brother or sister for Adam.' She puts a forefinger to her lips. 'Shh. Our secret for now, yes?'

My heart is bursting with excitement. A new baby, how wonderful! 'That's fantastic,' I whisper and give her a hug.

There are three police cars outside my house as I pull onto the drive. As I get out, DI Nick Brocklehurst and DS Charlotte Jennings come down the side of the house and hurry over. Brocklehurst's face is serious, but there's sympathy in his eyes. 'We've been trying to contact you for the last hour, Mrs Lane – sorry, I mean Mrs Thomas, now isn't it… Is your phone off?'

As I'm scrabbling for an answer and checking my phone, which is off, a private ambulance just like the one that came for Penny pulls up behind my car. I gawp at it open mouthed. I look back to DI Brocklehurst and DS Jennings. 'What's… what's happened?'

DS Jennings takes my arm and says, 'We had a phone call from a Mrs Kellerton – the cleaner of your retreat. She tried to find you, but you weren't here. Have you been out for an early walk?'

'No. No, I've been babysitting my grandson – stayed overnight.'

Brocklehurst and Jennings look at each other, say nothing.

'For God's sake will you please tell me what's happened!' I can't stand this any longer.

Brocklehurst takes my other arm and leads me to the bench outside the kitchen window. I sit down, look up at his grave expression. 'Mrs Thomas… Samantha. I'm sorry to have to tell you that your husband is dead.'

I shake my head open and close my mouth. 'D-dead?'

He nods. 'I'm afraid so. He–'

I stand up. Point my finger at him 'No. No he can't be! There's some mistake…'

As Brocklehurst is struggling for words, a man dressed in a white coverall comes round the side of the house. Then he sees me and quickly turns back. I set off after him, shaking off the attempts of Brocklehurst and Jennings to stop me. The man hurries down the garden path, to where a huddle of police officers and more people in white coveralls are talking, pointing, taking photos. Rachel Kellerton, ashen-faced, is sitting outside the retreat drinking tea, a police officer jotting stuff down on a pad. When she sees me, her cup clatters against the saucer and she half stands. I ignore her and run to the huddle of people and stop.

The babble of voices falls silent and everyone looks at me. Through a gap I can see an arm. It's Dan's arm. I push past to see him naked in the hot tub. Dan's face is white… so white. He's dead. Dead and swimming in a pool of his own blood, and it's Penny all over again. The coppery tang of blood hits the back of my throat, my stomach rolls and my legs give way. I'm only saved from falling by two police officers.

'No. No. No!' I scream and struggle against the officers who are trying to shield my view. Then I let my body go limp and burst into tears, allow myself to be led away from the horror of it all, towards my house.

Epilogue

I can't believe that six weeks have passed since I lost Dan. The calendar says May though, and the scene from my balcony looks like the front cover of a magazine for the Cornish tourist board. Yellow sand, blue sky, fluffy white clouds and hundreds of people on the beach, in the sea, building sandcastles, eating ice cream. It's as if Dan was never here, but life has to go on, doesn't it?

Those people on the beach have no clue what happened in the grounds of this house not very long ago. They have no clue what I had to go through, what I had to endure. But why should they? People's lives are similar, very similar, in the day-to-day. We go shopping, have jobs, need a roof over our heads, have things and people we love, but we are often worlds apart in the wider scheme of things. The way we see the big picture is different for all of us. Some never see all of the picture, some don't want to, and some, if they don't like the one they have, seize a brush and paint a new one with bold new strokes. Like me.

The police found a suicide and a confession note addressed to them folded neatly in the top pocket of Dan's jacket. It said that he couldn't forget what he'd done to Penny – that he'd killed her in cold blood. That he'd sat in the hot tub, taken the same tablets as he'd given Penny which he'd taken from me, and then slashed his wrists with a razor blade. He'd also tried to kill Alison – he'd explained why. The hoodie he wore at the time, and my antidepressants he'd used on Penny and a notebook could be found at his cottage.

The two officers, who stopped me from falling, found another letter addressed to me on my pillow, as they led me to my bedroom to recover from the shock. The police took it as evidence but let me have it back again after they'd closed the case. I can remember it almost word-for-word, but I take it out of my pocket and read it again now.

My darling Sam, I can't live with what I've done. I killed Penny. I let them think it was you who'd killed her at first, because I had to keep them right away from me – it's always the husband who's suspected, isn't it? I didn't think for one minute they'd have strong enough evidence, but I couldn't be sure, so I wrote Penny's fake suicide note to free you. I adore you, my love, and did the worse thing a person can ever do. I killed Penny because I wanted to be with you, to marry you and also because I despised her. Because of one mistake with her when we were teenagers, I lost you for thirty years. We could have been married long ago, had children, maybe grandchildren, by now. I couldn't forgive her for that.

And now I have everything I ever wanted – we are man and wife at last! How ironic – I just can't live with the guilt. Since her murder it's eaten me up. Twisted my heart. Awful dreams of Penny haunt my sleep and guilt stalks my waking hours. Has for weeks. I need to pay. It's fitting that I should go the same way as my poor first wife.

Please try to find it in your heart to forgive me, my darling, and be happy one day...

I fold it back up and wipe a tear. Such a moving letter. Well written. Even one of the female officers who read it at the time had moist eyes, I remember. They had to question me routinely, even though they had the notes, but it was just a formality. I couldn't fault the police in their professionalism, and their compassion overwhelmed me. But then who could fail to be moved by a woman of my age cruelly widowed, not once, but twice in such a short time?

I turn from the beach scene and walk into the kitchen, prepare a gin and tonic. I inhale the sharpness of the lemon, and the ice cubes tinkle as I take a big gulp. That's better. There'll be no more maudlin thoughts of the past for now. I toast Dan, and despite being a widow again, I know for certain that my life will get better as each day passes. Goodness knows I've had enough misery.

I decide a few crisps will go well with the drink and I grab a packet before going along to the study. I'll get a couple hours of writing in before it's time to pop to Helena's for dinner. Our relationship is back as it should be, thank heavens. And she's pregnant! I can't stop thinking about it. Early days, but we're all overjoyed.

I fire up the laptop and think of Jack. Poor love was so upset for me, when he'd found out about Dan's suicide and what he'd done. He'd kept apologising that he'd been too pig-headed and washed his hands of me. He said he should have tried harder to keep me from marrying Dan. But I told him that it really didn't matter. And it really didn't; how was Jack to know the extent of Dan's evil? I'm just glad that Jack and I are big friends again. I think he and Felicity will pop up this weekend. They often do, now Dan's not around. So, all's well that ends well.

I look at the blank screen and take a sip of my drink. I've a fantastic idea for a new suspense novel. A woman goes skinny-dipping in their new hot tub with her new husband, but drugs him because he's done some despicable things. He has to pay for what he's done. Besides, he's dangerous and unpredictable – she has to protect herself and her family from him. Who knows what he might do in the future? Champagne and antidepressants don't mix, and as soon as he's unconscious, she slits his wrists. The woman has an alibi, however, because she was babysitting her grandson at her daughter's house at the time. The grandson that sleeps through, who's never scared of the dark, or wakes until morning. But how is this possible? She can't be in two places at once, can she?

No. Because she isn't. She leaves her sleeping grandson and dashes back up the road to her house and husband, does the deed, and rushes back to the daughter's house. She then pops round to the daughter's neighbour, Mrs Jacobs, to make sure she's seen around the time the husband died to borrow an iron to help her daughter out with her laundry. She couldn't find her daughter's iron anywhere. Mrs Jacobs, if questioned by the police would say what a lovely mum the woman was to Helena and how thoughtful. Mrs Jacobs has seen how busy poor Helena the daughter is, and so to come back to a freshly ironed pile of clothes would be such a help. She'd say that the woman would have loved to have stopped for a chat, but she had to go back next door as the grandson might wake at any moment. He's going through a bit of a phase you see.

Even though the woman had written a fake suicide note for her husband in a scrawly shaky hand, just like Penny's, she had to be sure her alibi was watertight. Wouldn't her hair be wet, or at least damp if she'd been in a steamy hot tub? Wouldn't Mrs Jacobs ask about that when she went round to borrow an iron? The woman could say she'd just washed her hair – or better still, she could have worn a bathing cap in the hot tub, told the husband she didn't want to get her hair wet because she'd have to dry it back at her daughter's and the hairdryer noise would disturb the child. Yes, no point in having wet hair to cause the police to be suspicious. Hmm, that would work… And it bloody well did.

I swirl the ice cubes round my drink with my finger, drink and smile. A good idea for a story, certainly – but a shame I can never write something like that. People might get a bit suspicious.

For the first few days after I killed Dan I felt terribly guilty, but it had to be done. I was able to rationalise the guilt away fairly quickly. It was me or him, and the way he'd killed Penny, attempted to kill Alison, and constructed evidence to frame me if necessary – well, it had to be him. He was an egotistical controlling maniac who wouldn't hesitate to have me put away. And he'd a temper – he used to hit Penny, how could I be sure he wouldn't do the same to me, or worse if I told the police what I knew?

I was a bit guilty too about how I'd fooled the police – but only a bit. I'm mainly proud of my response on that fateful morning. If anyone deserves a bloody Oscar, it's me. The way I'd collapsed in a heap between two coppers when I'd seen my "poor darling Dan" dead in the tub. The way I'd sobbed as if my heart would break. That bit wasn't too hard – I was crying because I was shitting myself about being caught out somehow.

I drain my glass and pick the lemon out, enjoy the bitter-sweet taste as I suck it dry. That's what Dan was doing to me. If I'd not killed him I'd have been sucked dry, chewed up, spat out. And if I'm honest, the guilt I felt wasn't really about killing him. It was about doing something so wrong, so calculating – the worst thing you could ever do in life to another person. He turned me into a murderer and I'll never forgive him for it. I'm a bit ashamed now of the power surge I felt on that night. It was intoxicating – liberating, necessary. The shame will fade though, I'm sure.

I think back to that night when he was slipping into unconsciousness, slumped to one side his head back looking at the stars. I was able to relive the scene in my novel – the one I never got to write because of Dan's antics. He looked so beautiful, so accepting of where he was going – the next step on his journey. Then he'd closed his eyes and I'd got out of the tub, taken his wrist, held it under the water and drawn the razor blade swiftly across the vein. A spurting fountain of crimson tried to break the surface of the water and just for a second, Dan had opened his eyes and looked at me. I think I might have seen surprise, but I couldn't be sure. I slashed his wrist again and let the blade sink to the bottom. His eyes closed, and he peacefully slipped away.

I stare at the screen some more and decide I don't want to write a suspense novel for a while. I can take my time over choosing the next book now, thanks to Dan. Because of becoming Mrs Thomas, I never have to worry about money again, not with all his property and savings. Marrying him was a necessary evil, just like his murder, but the path ahead is full of sweetness and light. I'm so looking forward to reopening the retreat in a few months. It's been closed since Dan's "suicide" to show respect. But that venture was one of Dan's better ideas. Over the past week since it's been re-advertised, there's been a flurry of bookings. I'm convinced that some of them have only booked because they've heard of Dan's macabre passing. According to their forms, a good few are attempting to write murder and mayhem – some suspense writers must be sick in the head.

For now, I won't start anything new. I think I'll just do a bit on finishing that bloody Christmas story I started ages ago. A nice gentle Christmas romance with a happy ending is what's needed. If I get it done in time, my publisher might put it out this year. I need to get my work out there again. It's been too long, and I don't want to be forgotten. Thinking of happy endings, in a few weeks I might contact Harry, see how he's doing. He'd sent me a sympathy card with his new phone number in it last week. He'd said how sorry he was to learn of Dan's passing, Lydia had told him apparently.

I'd emailed Lydia recently to say the retreat was closed and why – and I was sorry, but I'd had to cancel her rebooking for this year for now. Harry had also said in the card that anytime, day or night, if I wanted a chat he'd be there for me. I picture his handsome face in my mind's eye and remember how well we got along. I smile at the thought of getting to know him better in the very near future.

Come on, Sam. All this pondering isn't going to get this damned Christmas story finished, is it?

I flex my fingers over the keyboard and begin to type.

Acknowledgements

To my family for your continued love and support. A special thank you to my editor Morgen Bailey and the rest of the fantastic Bloodhound team. You're all wonderful! And, of course, a huge thanks to all the bloggers and readers who have left fantastic reviews for my books over the years. I couldn't do it without you.

40519481R00141

Printed in Poland
by Amazon Fulfillment
Poland Sp. z o.o., Wrocław